« A Sporting Chance »

based on the television stories

A SPORTING CHANCE
and
PULSE

Andy Lane

First published in Great Britain in 1996 by
Virgin Books
an imprint of Virgin Publishing Ltd
332 Ladbroke Grove
London W10 5AH

BUGS the television series is produced by
Carnival Films Ltd and broadcast in the UK by BBC1

Text copyright © Andy Lane 1996
adapted from screenplays by Colin Brake and
Stephen Gallagher

Cover photographs © Carnival (Film & Theatre) Ltd,
1995

ISBN 0 753 50036 1

Typeset by Galleon Typesetting, Ipswich
Printed and bound in Great Britain by
BPC Paperbacks Ltd, Aylesbury

Acknowledgements:

Steve Gallagher and Colin Brake, for being friends,
and Stuart Doughty, for taking risks.

« Prologue »

There were two of them in the room: Patrick Marcel and Death.

Patrick Marcel stood by the office window, staring greedily out at the carefully landscaped industrial park.

Death was in a packing crate by the wall.

Ignoring its baleful presence, Patrick let his gaze wander from detail to detail. The buildings were prefabricated units encased in metal exoskeletons of blue and red pipes. The wide expanses of grey car park surrounding them were too new to be marred by weeds or cracks, and the grass verges separating the car parks were so green, the flowers so bright, that Patrick half-suspected they were artificial. The access roads leading into and out of each car park had been topologically designed to link every building on the industrial park to the highway using the smallest amount of tarmac. It was mathematically perfect.

Sometimes he let his imagination run riot, picturing it not as a mosaic of research laboratories, analysis consultancies and games designers but as a living creature whose blood was information and whose body was painted metal and glass. The car parks were the cells: the buildings their nuclei. The grass verges were the cell walls, and the roads were the blood vessels. The highway was the artery, pumping life from the heart of the beast – the mirrored glass towers of the city.

It was a strong, healthy beast, but like all living creatures it had a weakness. Cut off the blood supply, and it died.

And that was what Patrick Marcel intended to do, along with his monstrous brother.

A movement distracted his thoughts: an executive car, buffed to a glossy black finish, crawling like a beetle along the highway. As he watched, it turned off onto the road and into the nearest car park. Steadily it made its way to the front of the building and coasted to a halt. His brother was driving: he recognised Jean-Daniel's style. Unflustered. Unhurried. Uninterested.

The driver's door opened and his brother stepped out: a shaved gorilla in a chauffeur's uniform that was two sizes too small for him. Thick rolls of flesh spilled over his immaculately laundered collar, his cap was perched on his shaved head like a toy and, even from the window, Patrick could see his cuff-links tearing through the material of his sleeves. His face was one that not even their mother could love, although his eyes were surprisingly brown and placid, like a cow's.

Carrying an attaché case, Jean-Daniel walked in that curiously precise way of his around the car to the left-hand passenger's side and opened the door. Nobody emerged for a moment. Without any change in expression, Jean-Daniel reached into the car with a hairy hand and yanked a man out by the collar. The man was dishevelled and scared: his hair was stuck up at the back and one of the lenses of his glasses was broken. His suit had the unmistakable cut of Savile Row, although its tailor would have wept at seeing the

2

way the sleeve had been almost pulled off. His name was Dominic Neville, and he was the managing director of a firm whose success was causing heads to turn all over the city.

It had caused Patrick's head to turn too, but for a rather different reason.

Neville gazed up into Jean-Daniel's impassive face. Jean-Daniel handed the attaché case to him and Neville flinched, like a dog expecting to be hit. After a few moments he hesitantly reached out to take it. Jean-Daniel glanced towards the foyer of the building and nodded slightly. Neville opened his mouth as if to ask a question, but some flicker of expression in Jean-Daniel's eyes made him slowly close it again. Cowed, he scurried towards the building and the waiting Patrick. Jean-Daniel carefully brushed a speck of dust from his uniform and followed.

While he was waiting for the two of them to arrive, Patrick glanced around the room, trying to gauge the effect it would have on Neville. The partition walls were crudely finished and the entire office space was minimally lit, but the office furniture – top-of-the-range computers, walnut-panelled desks, pastel-coloured filing cabinets, chairs that were more like sculptures than furniture – was the best that money could buy. Patrick hadn't actually bought any of it, of course – the Marcels never bought anything they couldn't just take – but he hoped that Neville would appreciate the thought. Neville's opinion was important to him. Neville's *attitude* was important to him: a mixture of fear and respect was very conducive to discussion. The packing crates and bubble-wrap spoilt the effect slightly, but perhaps if Patrick explained that they were in the process of moving into their new offices Neville would understand.

Not that Neville had a choice.

How best to be discovered? He wanted Neville to be

3

simultaneously impressed and put at ease. The hulking presence of Jean-Daniel behind him would add the ever-present hint of threat to their discussion without anything crude or unpleasant being said. Perhaps if Patrick were to be typing something into one of the computers ... No, none of them were set up or switched on, and besides, it would be obvious that Patrick didn't know how to operate one. On the telephone perhaps, discussing large sums of money? Neville wouldn't know that the phones were dead.

The *chunk-hiss* of a lift coming to a halt and the doors opening panicked Patrick slightly. He walked rapidly across the room to a crate of assorted paintings he had acquired to brighten up the offices – instinctively avoiding the crate that contained Death – and pulled the top one off the pile. As footsteps approached the office door – one set almost stumbling, the other shaking the floor – he held the canvas at arm's length and pretended to examine it critically. The geometric shapes and bright colours did nothing for him, but he pursed his lips knowingly and nodded when the footsteps entered the room.

'Oh,' he said brightly, looking over to where Neville was dwarfed by Jean-Daniel's bulk, 'Mr Neville. Welcome. Thank you so much for coming.'

'I wasn't given much of a choice,' Neville stammered, reflexively raising a hand to his glasses. Close up, Patrick could see that the wire frame was bent on the same side as the broken lens.

'What?' Patrick feigned indignation. He was getting pretty good at it by now, even if he said so himself. 'Jean-Daniel, this is inexcusable.' He adopted his best apologetic expression, and tossed the painting to one side. 'What can I say? He's an oaf, and he misunderstands even the simplest instructions, but he's family and so I can't fire him. I apologise. From the bottom of my heart, I apologise.' Holding out a

4

hand, he approached the puzzled Neville. 'My name, by the way, is Patrick Marcel.'

Automatically, Neville reached out a hand in response, then drew it back as if he'd been about to absent-mindedly pet an alligator. 'Please,' he said, trying to command but succeeding only in begging, 'let me go.'

Patrick gestured towards Neville's torn suit and ripped collar. 'In such a state?' He shrugged. 'I couldn't possibly.'

'I'm late for an extremely urgent meeting!'

'The one with the people you're hoping will refinance your company, no?' Patrick watched the stunned expression creep across Neville's face. 'Yes.'

'How do *you* know about *that*?' Neville snapped, the shock making him momentarily bold.

Jean-Daniel didn't move or make a noise, but somehow his presence must have communicated itself to Neville, and the businessman quailed.

'Oh,' Patrick said with a casual smile, 'big secret. I'm in the business of knowing big secrets, believe me. Knowledge is power, Mr Neville, and the more I know, the more powerful I become. I know, for instance, how your company expanded too quickly into a market that hasn't produced the results you so glowingly wrote up in your prospectus. I also know that you desperately need a large injection of capital before your financial bubble bursts, and that you have a meeting arranged for' – he glanced at his watch – 'five minutes ago to discuss the possibility of obtaining a loan. I simply had you brought here so I could make you a better offer.'

Patrick reached into his jacket and Neville flinched. Slowly, Patrick withdrew a slip of paper and handed it to Neville with a reproving shake of his head. The businessman scanned its contents quickly, and for a moment Patrick could see that he had forgotten about the state of his suit, forgotten about Jean-Daniel looming behind him like the Massif Central, and was thinking only of abstractions and the unreal numbers of high finance.

Neville frowned, and glanced up at Patrick. 'But this would give *you* overall control of the company,' he said accusingly.

'But the company would be saved from extinction, and you would still be running it. On a day-to-day basis. At double the salary.'

Neville swallowed. 'And what happens if I say no?' he asked in a quiet voice.

'It's a serious offer, Mr Neville,' Patrick replied, shrugging slightly. 'I'm a serious player. But if you don't want to take it . . .' He spun the moment out, enjoying the dawning look of horror on Neville's face. 'Then you can go.'

Patrick could tell from the sudden twist of Neville's lips what his decision was going to be. A pity. He would have preferred to avoid unnecessary bloodshed, but still . . .

'I wouldn't touch this deal if you were the last person on earth willing to talk to me,' Neville said quietly, but firmly. He turned towards the corridor and found Jean-Daniel standing in his way. He stepped to one side, and seemed surprised when Jean-Daniel didn't move to block him. 'Will he come after me?' he said over his shoulder to Patrick.

Patrick shook his head. 'No,' he said. 'Nobody will come after you.'

'Then you'll be hearing from my solicitors about your methods.' Neville squared his shoulders and, trying to regain some sort of dignity, walked rapidly towards the corridor. It obviously hadn't occurred to him that Jean-Daniel still had the keys to the car.

Such a pity.

Jean-Daniel glanced across at Patrick. There was, as usual, no expression on his face. He wasn't seeking

6

agreement – he was going to kill Neville whatever happened – but Patrick nodded wearily. It would have been so much simpler had Neville agreed. Why did they all have to struggle so much?

Moving without any haste, Jean-Daniel moved to one of the packing crates – a long, thin box with a nailed-down lid – and pulled the lid off as if it were damp cardboard.

Reaching inside, he pulled out Death.

Death was a grey metal tube that was as tall as he was, and as thick as his arm. A bulge in its centre section made it look like a python that had suffered rigor mortis halfway through digesting a rabbit.

It had a pistol-grip. And buttons. Lots of buttons.

The manuals that had come with the stolen box described it as a guided rocket-launcher with ammunition that could be programmed with the target's general dimensions or description. Jean-Daniel called it a big bazooka. Patrick just thought of it as Death, pure and simple.

Jean-Daniel grasped Death by its pistol-grip and slung it over his shoulder. Without any change of expression, he walked towards the doorway leading into the corridor.

Patrick walked over to the crate and retrieved a set of industrial-strength ear-defenders. Carrying them loosely in one hand, he moved to a position behind his brother. He was careful to ensure that he was a few feet to one side.

He didn't want to be scalded by the exhaust gases, after all.

Neville was halfway down the corridor, and striding as if he wanted to break into a run but didn't dare. The corridor turned through ninety degrees ahead of him. The lifts were just around the bend.

Any second now, Patrick thought, he'll remember the car keys.

7

Jean-Daniel swung Death around until it was pointing at Neville's Savile-Row-suited back.

Neville glanced at his watch and speeded up, breaking into a half-run.

Jean-Daniel casually tapped range (*30 feet*), target description (*human*) and warhead selection (*heat-seeking*) into Death. *Heat-seeking* was his favourite type of warhead. No, Patrick corrected himself, it was his second favourite. He preferred *incendiary* above everything else, but even Jean-Daniel wouldn't dare use an incendiary warhead in their own offices.

'Oh, Lord,' Patrick heard Neville moan, 'if I don't get to that meeting –'

Patrick slipped the ear-defenders over his head. Everything was suddenly hushed, as if creation itself were waiting for something momentous to happen.

And Neville suddenly remembered the car keys.

He turned, a frown of indecision on his face, and saw Jean-Daniel with Death aimed squarely at the centre of his forehead, and beyond Jean-Daniel's bulky form, Patrick Marcel's smiling face.

Neville turned to run, his feet tangling together as panic flooded his body.

Jean-Daniel squeezed the trigger with the same casual aplomb as a man opening a can of fizzy drink.

Death jerked in Jean-Daniel's hands, and scorching, bitter smoke sprayed past Patrick's face. For a moment, the back of Neville's head was invisible behind a white-hot point of light, and Patrick could have sworn that the missile's force had picked him right off his feet and was boosting him down the corridor; then the light expanded to fill the space from wall to wall and floor to ceiling, and the building shook for a long moment.

Even through the ear-defenders, Patrick could hear the explosion.

Smoke roiled towards them down the corridor, and

8

for a moment Patrick could see the licking red tongues of fire before the nozzles of the sprinkler system sprayed halon vapour across everything, replacing one set of billowing clouds with another.

Of Dominic Neville there was no sign.

Jean-Daniel nodded very slightly, then walked across the office and replaced Death in its packing crate. Straightening, he met Patrick's reproving gaze, and shrugged slightly.

'You will have your little games,' Patrick sighed.

« One »

The restaurant had been Beckett's idea, and Ros had gone along with it. It was expensive, it floated above the city suspended from a helium-filled airship and it served the best *sashimi* outside Japan.

And it impressed potential clients no end.

This one's name was Frances De Freitas. Doctor Frances De Freitas. She wore a black silk suit as if she had been born in it, her hair was cut into a bell and she moved with the self-conscious poise and tightly controlled power of a dancer. Or a fighter.

Beckett was distinctly impressed. He liked women who could take care of themselves, and De Freitas looked like someone who could break his back if she wanted. With one hand.

They had met her at the airship's landing pad on top of the tallest building in the city and made their introductions as they entered the luxuriously appointed gondola and were shown to their table. Ed's eyes gleamed as he shook De Freitas's hand, and Beckett had to elbow him discreetly in the ribs before he would let go.

The waiter didn't give out any menus. The restaurant was so exclusive that there *wasn't* a menu.

Whatever you wanted, they would prepare. Beckett had yet to find any food, no matter how obscure, that wasn't stored in their capacious freezers.

This should really impress Doctor De Freitas, he thought as he glanced out of the windows. The mighty turbines attached to the rear of the gondola were just spinning up into a blur of bright ceramic material. If she had any reservations at all about trusting them with her problems, they should evaporate completely by the end of the meal.

'So, what can we do for you?' Ros asked as the electrostatic couplings were released outside the gondola and the airship began, almost imperceptibly, to rise from its moorings.

'I run the International Sports Academy,' De Freitas said. 'We train people in various disciplines using scientific techniques – biofeedback, virtual reality simulation, neuro-reinforcement and so on, as well as marketing sports-related products. You may have seen the ISA Isotonic Sports Drink on sale in exclusive sports shops – it's an electrolytically balanced vitamin and nutrient drink for people taking part in high-performance sports. Our aim is to help people achieve whatever they are physically capable of – taking them to the limits of their performance. The trouble is, I'm losing students.'

A pigeon floated past the window. Beckett watched it go, then turned his attention back to the table.

'When you say you're losing students,' he said, 'you mean they're just not coming back? Surely that's an occupational hazard?'

De Freitas shook her head. Her hair swung, obscuring her face. 'No, not like this. Some of them vanished while they were on the equipment. One minute they were there, the next minute they were gone.' She saw the glance that went between Beckett and Ed. 'Look, I'm not imagining this. Doctor Hunter will back me up.'

'Doctor −?' Ros started to ask, but the waiter appeared and asked for their order. 'I'll just have a salad,' she said. 'And a glass of water.'

Beckett was taken aback. 'You realise you could have anything you wanted, Ros?' he asked. 'Anything at all?'

She nodded. 'I know. I want a salad. And a glass of water.'

Beckett shrugged, and turned to De Freitas. 'How about you?'

'Still deciding,' she said calmly. 'You go ahead and order.'

He smiled. Time to make an impression. 'I'll have the *chirashi zushi*, *gyuniku teriyaki*, *saba nitsuke*, *yuzen ae* and *chawan mushi*.'

'And sir?' the waiter asked, turning to Ed.

Ed cast a disbelieving glance at Beckett. 'Anything?'

'Anything your little Antipodean heart desires, Ed.'

Ed's face took on that sceptical look Beckett knew all too well. 'All right,' he challenged the waiter, 'any chance of the Australian national dish − a crocodile steak?'

'And how would you like it cooked, sir?'

Ed shrugged, unfazed. 'Rare,' he said, then grinned suddenly. 'And make it snappy!'

Beckett cringed inside. Trust Ed to lower the tone of the meal. He just couldn't pass up the chance to make a cheap crack.

The waiter didn't react. Turning to Doctor De Freitas, he said, 'And for madam?'

'Oh, I'll just have the usual,' she replied.

That took the wind out of Beckett's sails.

The waiter nodded. 'Of course,' he said, and glided away so smoothly that he might have been on wheels.

'You've been here before, then?' Beckett added casually.

'Once or twice.' She smiled. 'Sales of the ISA Isotonic

Sports Drink are very healthy at the moment.'

Ros coughed to gain their attention. 'You were telling us about Doctor Hunter.'

'Peter's our head of sports medicine,' De Freitas said, shrugging slightly. 'He developed the Isotonic Sports Drink for us, and he's working on the next generation of performance enhancers.'

There was something she wasn't saying – something implicit in her choice of words. 'You mean there's some kind of sports drug abuse going on?' Beckett asked, trying to force the issue.

De Freitas paused before answering. It looked to Beckett as if she didn't want to make an outright accusation, but she wanted to leave them in no doubt as to what she really thought. 'Hunter claims what he's doing is all above board. Using natural substances that can help athletes achieve their best possible results . . .'

'But you don't believe him?' Beckett was determined to pin her down.

'I'm not sure. He's highly motivated. He'd do anything in the interests of sport.'

Ros, sensing Beckett's tactics, attacked from the other side. 'Even something illegal?'

De Freitas hesitated again. 'I need *you* to tell me that,' she said finally. 'What he's been developing is a performance-enhancer called tri-meserone; it's a tree-bark derivative that's similar to methylene-dioxi-methyl-amphetamine but without the side effects. Peter swears it's harmless but I can't help feeling that the missing students might have been involved in testing it for him . . .' She tailed off. There was a faintly guilty look on her face, as if she'd already said more than she had intended.

The waiter arrived with Beckett's food and Ros's glass of water. By the time he had finished setting them out, the thread of the conversation had been disrupted. De Freitas wasn't going to come out and accuse Hunter of anything. Not openly. Not now. Beckett glanced out of the window at the towers and skyscrapers, reaching like bony fingers for the airship. 'Why come to us?' he asked.

'You were recommended,' she said. 'Roland Blatty is one of our members.'

Beckett and Ros swapped glances. Beckett remembered Roland Blatty: he was something powerful in a secret branch of the government. And he had been to university with Ros.

'With your agreement,' Ros said, 'I think our first move should be to test some of your students close up for signs of drug-enhanced performance.'

De Freitas nodded. 'That sounds like a good first move. How do you intend going about it?'

'Ed here is our resident limb-risker – we could introduce him as a visiting expert in –' Ros hesitated and turned to Ed. 'What do you think, Ed? It's got to be convincing. What's your speciality?'

'Freestyle irritation?' Beckett suggested.

Ed shrugged, ignoring the jibe. 'How about tae kwon do?' he said. 'I used to be pretty good.'

'Pretty good isn't good enough,' De Freitas warned. 'Some of my students fight in international competitions. What level did you reach?'

'D'you think a gold medal's good enough?' Ed replied with honest concern.

'A gold *what*?' Ros and Beckett chorused.

Ed blushed. 'Hey guys – I did have a life before Gizmos, you know?'

Gillian Cooper picked the telephone receiver off her desk and hit the redial button for the third time that morning. As the handset burr-burred in her ear, she took a covert glance over her shoulder. The high-level team from the World Bank were visible through the boardroom doorway. Their suits were all double-breasted, their ties were all striped in the same direction

14

and they didn't look happy. They didn't look happy at *all*.

She'd offer them coffee, but they'd already drunk enough to keep their kidneys afloat for weeks.

Cook, the deputy CEO, hovered in the doorway. Gillian caught the reassuring tone of his voice as he said something to the visitors and turned towards her. The smile slid off his face like an egg off a frying pan the moment they couldn't see his expression any more. 'Where the *hell* is Neville?' he mouthed.

Gillian made shushing gestures with her free hand as a woman answered the telephone.

'Hello?' the woman said with just a hint of worry.

'Mrs Neville? It's Gillian again. I'm afraid your husband's still not arrived for his meeting, and his mobile's off the air. Could you tell me what time he left?'

'About an hour ago,' Mrs Neville said. The worry in her voice was clear now. 'Your car picked him up from the front door. I waved him off.'

Gillian tried to inject as much reassurance into her voice as she could. After ten years of dealing with boards of directors she could have reassured for Europe. 'I'm sure he's just caught in traffic.'

'Could you ring me when he arrives? I don't want to be a worry-wart, but –'

'I'll call you the moment he walks in, don't worry. Goodbye.'

As she put the handset back, she glanced into the boardroom again. The executive in charge of the bank team – a man in his mid-fifties with hair in its mid-thirties – pulled a gold watch on a chain from a waistcoat pocket.

'Well?' Cook was by her elbow. A small tic had started in the corner of his mouth.

'She says a car picked him up to bring him here an hour ago.'

Cook frowned. 'I didn't send any car. Neville always prefers to drive himself in – you know that.' He took a deep breath, and Gillian could hear his nervous shudder. 'Check the medical centres – in case there's been an accident.'

'Isn't that a bit desperate?' she asked.

'Absolutely.' Stretching his mouth into an unconvincing grin, he moved off to join the gathering in the boardroom.

As Gillian dialled the number of the local medical centre, she heard the executive in charge of the bank team saying, 'For a man in serious need of a major refinancing package, your chief executive's playing this very strangely.'

'I'm sorry,' Cook apologised. 'He'll be here.'

The executive wasn't taking any prisoners. 'I hope so. Because we either close this by noon or we forget the whole thing.'

There were certain places that Ed came alive in.

Helicopters were one, preferably flying at speed, ultra-preferably doing something crazy like flying beneath a bridge or looping-the-loop.

Cliff faces were another, although the sheer sides of buildings were an acceptable substitute, with his fingers feeling for narrow ledges that might or might not support his weight.

A high-performance sports car, travelling at a hundred miles an hour around a bend.

A rolling tunnel of translucent green surf at Bondai Beach.

Not spread-eagled inside the suspended ceiling of an auditorium with his neck bent up at an angle against a stanchion while balancing a miniature CCD camera rig and microphone on his head and trying to prise one of the pegboard ceiling tiles up with numbed fingers. This wasn't his scene. This wasn't his scene at all.

It wasn't even as if he'd had to break in against impossible odds, and might have to make a daring last-minute escape with crazed Dobermanns nipping at his hamstrings. Doctor De Freitas had given him the keys, for God's sake!

The tile came up in a puff of dust, and Ed choked back a sneeze. He stashed the tile to one side and glanced through the gap into the auditorium below. Moonlight stippled the floor, dimly illuminating piles of crash-mats and rolled-up badminton nets. Horizontal bars lined the walls, and geometric patterns of overlaid tape on the floor marked off badminton courts, volleyball courts and martial-arts *dojos*. Two banners hung from the ceiling: just black geometric patterns against the shadows.

'Are you sure this transmitter is powerful enough to send a decent picture?' he murmured.

'It's fine,' Ros's voice said in his earphone, as clear as if she'd been standing behind him. 'We've got a good angle on the area where they'll be carrying out the competition.'

'Looking good,' confirmed Beckett, slightly fainter. Ed could imagine him, leaning over Ros's shoulder and watching the pictures on the monitor. Why was it always Ed who ended up fitting the kit, and Ros and Beckett who ended up watching it? Oh yeah. Because he always volunteered, that's why.

'Is there anything you can fix the camera to?' Ros asked.

He glanced around. 'Looks like I can use one of the stanchions supporting the ceiling tiles. I'll have to cut a hole in the tile to poke the lens through, though.'

'Go for it,' Ros confirmed.

Ed reached back to the toolkit clipped to his belt and removed a tiny battery-operated drill. It took him only a few moments to create a hole large enough for the lens. He was careful not to let any of the dust settle through the gap and drift down onto the floor of the auditorium – although they had permission to be there, the idea was to disguise all trace of the camera. With the tile back in place, Ed removed the camera from his headband and clamped it onto the nearest stanchion so that it was pointed at an angle through the hole and at the area beneath.

'Spot on,' Ros said in his ear. 'We'll be able to see everything.'

'Now get out of there,' Beckett added. 'You've got to practise for the fight.'

'Oh great,' Ed muttered. 'Whatever happened to a fair division of labour? Can't one of you take my place in the competition?'

There was a moment's silence. Ed imagined Ros and Beckett glancing at each other.

'You're irreplaceable, Ed,' Ros said finally. 'That's what we love about you.'

The auditorium in daylight was almost unrecognisable. Blue metal air-conditioning ducts. Yellow rubber mats. Black metal bars like designer ladders fixed to the dazzlingly white walls. Like a big child's puzzle, thought Beckett as he watched the images on the computer monitor, transmitted in real time from the camera that Ed had placed the night before. Or like some abstract painting of geometrical shapes in primary colours.

The banners hanging from the ceiling were legible in the bright sunlight that streamed in through the high windows. THE INTERNATIONAL SPORTS ACADEMY MASTERCLASSES, they read in an unfussy black typeface. The resolution of the camera was so good that Beckett could make out the inch-high words beneath that read, DIRECTOR – DOCTOR FRANCES DE FREITAS.

Ed's positioning had been perfect: the camera's field of view was not only centred exactly on the large competition area but wide enough to take in the audience of tae kwon do exponents squatting on their haunches around it as well. It looked to Beckett like the most uncomfortable position in the world, but they seemed to be enduring it well. They'd been squatting there for half an hour. They looked like they could go on squatting for the rest of the day if they had to.

Ros walked up to the monitor, a cup of coffee in her hand. She was wearing a loose blue trouser suit. It looked good on her. Then again, so did most things. Behind her, the Gizmos workroom resembled a high-tech building site, what with the various PCs and stand-alone workstations, as well as the various printers, scanners, modems, high-capacity memory units and, for all Beckett knew, coffee machines, all sitting on racks and desks and all linked by a cat's cradle of ethernet cabling. Every time he came in, there was a new machine sitting on a cabinet or a desk, lights flashing merrily, doing God knew what.

'How's it going?' she asked brightly.

'If that's what tae kwon do enables you to do,' Beckett said, indicating the audience, 'then I'd rather have an armchair any day.'

'I'm sure there's more to it than that,' she replied, smiling. She pointed to two chairs that had been set up behind the squatting audience. One was empty, but the other was occupied by the only person who wasn't wearing martial arts costume, a pear-shaped man who looked as if he had woken up that morning fully dressed and rushed straight to the academy without combing his hair. 'Who's that?' she asked.

'That's probably Hunter,' Beckett said. 'Doctor Peter Hunter – head of sports medicine at the International Academy of Sport. He works for Doctor De Freitas. She told us about him, remember?'

Heads turned in a ripple on the monitor as Ed and De Freitas entered the auditorium from a door that was outside the camera's field of view. De Freitas wore a yellow hooded tracksuit top over a black singlet and tracksuit bottom. Like the audience, Ed was dressed in the standard baggy martial arts jacket and trousers. A black band cinched his waist. It suddenly occurred to Beckett that everyone in the audience was wearing a black belt as well. A high-powered masterclass indeed.

Together they walked out into the centre of the yellow mat. The audience applauded, bobbing slightly to keep their balance as they did so. It looked rather absurd to Beckett, and he stifled a chuckle.

'Come on,' Ros murmured, 'the least we can do is take this seriously. That's what we're being paid for.'

On the monitor, Ed bowed to the audience and to De Freitas. 'Thank you,' he said, his voice carrying clearly to the microphone attached to the camera. 'It's a great pleasure for me to be here leading this masterclass.'

De Freitas bowed back. 'I'm sure all our students will gain enormously from watching someone with your . . . world-class experience.'

'What world-class experience?' Beckett scoffed.

'Now, now,' chided Ros, 'just because you'd never heard of him before you met him.'

On the monitor, De Freitas nodded to a man in the audience. 'Now, your first opponent – Jason Rupta.'

Rupta stood and approached Ed. He was a small, muscular man with hair cropped so close that Beckett could see the bumps of his skull. He moved as if he knew what he was doing, but Beckett had seen Ed in action before. Ed was good. Ed was better than good: Ed was the most talented fighter that Beckett had ever seen. Rupta didn't have a hope, no matter *how* good he was.

While Rupta was still walking, De Freitas muttered something to Ed. Beckett couldn't tell what she had said, but Ed glanced up towards the camera. She followed his gaze, and nodded.

'She's checking that we're watching,' Ros guessed.

'What's the matter? Doesn't she trust us?'

As Rupta walked out onto the mat, De Freitas backed out into the audience and sat on the empty chair next to Hunter. He smiled at her. She smiled back, but even on the monitor Beckett could tell that there was something false about the expression. She didn't like him. Perhaps she didn't like anybody who didn't have a black belt in squatting on their haunches.

Rupta bowed to Ed. Ed bowed back so deeply that he could have kissed his knees. When he came up, there was a smirk on his face.

'He does love being the centre of attention,' Beckett said.

Ros laughed. 'You could have done it. He offered you the chance.'

'You don't catch me wearing my pyjamas in public,' Beckett said under his breath.

Ed and Rupta began to circle each other warily, hands held away from their bodies, eyes fixed on each other's face. They reminded Beckett of two cats fighting over territory.

The audience were yelling encouragement to Rupta, punching their fists in the air. It was hard to reconcile their passion with the fact that they were all still squatting around the mat like devotees around a shrine.

Rupta was just a blur on the screen as he stepped forward and shoved Ed hard in the chest. Ed stumbled backwards, his face an exaggerated Greek mask of surprise. For a moment Beckett thought he was going to trip over his own feet, but he kept his balance. Just.

Rupta twisted, his foot lashing out like a striking cobra to take Ed hard on the inside of his thigh. Ed backed away fast, but it looked to Beckett like he was limping. Rupta followed, pressing his advantage. His eyes were narrow slits of anger. Tendons stood out in his neck like guy ropes under canvas.

21

Someone stood up in the audience, a tall man with his blond hair tied back in a ponytail. 'Go on Jason!' he shouted, 'knock him flat on his ego!' Hunter leaned forward and said something to him. The man sat down. Even on the monitor, Beckett could see him blush.

Out on the mat Ed made a grab for Rupta, but the smaller man stepped inside Ed's reach. Pulling Ed's shoulder down he kneed him hard in the chest. Twice. Ed's face puffed out like a trumpet-player's and his eyes went wide.

'Is that legal?' Beckett cried.

'Apparently,' Ros said calmly. Beckett shot her a glance. She was frowning, and her coffee was going cold in her hand.

Ed shoved Jason Rupta away and backed off to catch his breath, but Rupta followed: remorseless, relentless, he hooked a foot behind Ed's left leg. Still backing away, Ed went sprawling onto the yellow mat. Rupta pounced on him and delivered two swift punches to his heart. *This is a competition*, Beckett kept telling himself, *he's pulling those punches*, but the expression of shocked pain on Ed's face was real enough.

'I don't believe it,' Beckett whispered.

Ros shook her head. 'Doctor De Freitas said this might happen, remember? That's why we're watching.'

'I know.' Beckett clenched his fist impotently. 'But I still don't believe it. It's getting a bit out of hand. I thought *Ed* was supposed to be the gold medallist.'

On the monitor Rupta had backed away to allow Ed to climb painfully to his feet. They began to circle around each other again. Ed's face was pulled into a scowl. The noise from the audience was swamping the microphone. Ed leaned back and aimed a kick at Rupta's head, but the smaller man ducked and Ed's foot sliced through the air above him. Rupta kicked back at Ed's chest, but Ed blocked with both arms. The

22

impact drove Ed back a pace.

De Freitas leaned towards Hunter. Ros, her gaze fixed on the monitor, leaned forward and twiddled with a dial.

'What are you doing?' Beckett asked as the roar of the audience became muffled, distant, like waves on shingle.

'Fine-tuning the directional mike,' Ros replied. 'I want to hear what they're saying.'

De Freitas's voice came through clearly on the speakers, riding the sound of the audience like a surfer. 'Is Jason Rupta on your *special treatment* too, Doctor Hunter?' she said. Beckett could hear the emphasis she put on 'special treatment'.

Hunter just smiled shyly, and turned his attention back to the battle.

Ed's foot flicked up in another high kick as his body leaned back at an impossible angle. Rupta stepped away, and Ed's foot pistoned an inch from his nose. Even Beckett could see the opening that Ed was inadvertently leaving as he recovered his balance, but Rupta seemed curiously reluctant to take advantage of it. He stood watching Ed, a frown on his face.

Ed moved in close and grabbed Rupta's shoulder. Pulling the man down, he rammed his knee into Rupta's ribs once, twice, three times. The impact shook the camera.

The audience fell silent.

Rupta stayed in place as Ed backed away. The little man looked puzzled. Puzzled and scared. His hand crept up to his chest, feeling beneath his disarranged jacket. A strangled cry filled the stillness of the auditorium.

And Rupta slumped to his knees. His other hand came up imploringly, reaching for Ed, and then he fell, face forward, onto the yellow mat.

The audience of students were suddenly on their

feet, crowding around their friend. Ed was backing away, an expression of consternation on his face. He glanced momentarily up at the camera and raised his hands in ... In what? Supplication? Apology? Beckett couldn't tell.

De Freitas pushed her way through the crowd towards the fallen Rupta. Hunter had pulled a mobile phone from his pocket. His voice came through clearly as he shouted, 'I want the paramedics *now*!'

Ed's hand came down on De Freitas's shoulder as she passed him. 'Is this what happened before?' he asked in anguish, his voice on the fringes of the microphone's range.

'Yes,' De Freitas replied, obviously distracted. 'Almost exactly ... a sudden collapse ...'

'Will he be all right?'

De Freitas opened her mouth to answer, but couldn't find the words. Ed's face crumpled.

Two paramedics in white uniforms had entered the auditorium. They carried a stretcher. The crowd parted for them as they approached Rupta's prone body.

'The ambulance got here quickly,' Ed said in relief.

Hunter, following the paramedics, caught Ed's words. 'Yes,' he said. 'Don't worry, I'll go with him ...'

The two paramedics – burly men with hard faces – rolled Rupta carelessly onto the stretcher and carried him away. It was like a conjuring trick, Beckett reflected. One moment Rupta was there, the centre of attention, the next moment he was gone as if he had never existed.

The tall student with the ponytail followed the stretcher for a few moments like a puppy, then trailed to a halt. He looked lost. Lost and alone. Seeing Ed, his expression changed, anger washing over it and disfiguring his face. 'What have you done?' he yelled, grabbing Ed's jacket and shaking him. 'You've killed him! You've *killed* him!'

Ed just shook his head.

Beckett looked away from the screen, his fist clenched so tight that it hurt.

'Let's watch it again,' Ros suggested. 'There might be something we missed.'

Ros slipped into the chair beside Beckett and started accessing the networked computer memory, isolating the past five minutes, putting them on a continual-loop playback and directing the result to her monitor. Beckett, meanwhile, made sure that the network was continuing to archive to memory whatever picture the camera was still transmitting. You never knew what you might miss otherwise.

The crowd was splitting up in the auditorium. Students were drifting away, leaving a hard core discussing the fight and Jason's probable condition. The microphone picked up snatches of their conversation. The tone was part anger, part disbelief and part concern.

Ed and Doctor De Freitas had disappeared.

'OK,' Ros murmured, 'let's see it all again. I've cleaned up the sound a bit.'

'It might help,' Beckett pointed out, 'if we knew more about tae kwon do. I can't even name the moves, let alone analyse whether anything odd is going on. I don't even like watching violent movies. Ed's the expert.'

'And with any luck he'll be on his way here to interpret for us.'

Ros clicked on a virtual button, and the screen sprang to life. Time had rolled back. The mat was empty. The audience were waiting.

They watched the playback.

Then they watched it again.

And again.

They were watching it for the fourth time when Ed and Doctor De Freitas walked into the Gizmos workroom. Ed had changed into a loose-weave orange top and orange trousers. De Freitas was still wearing the black tracksuit bottom and yellow top. She looked more like a sailor than a martial-arts expert.

Ed walked over to stand at Beckett's shoulder. He gazed at the monitor, eyes narrowed, a grimace twisting his mouth.

On the monitor, his recorded image brought its knee savagely up into Jason Rupta's chest.

Ros froze the picture with a click of the mouse. Rupta's face was contorted in agony.

'Oh man, this is awful,' Ed whispered. 'I didn't want to put someone in hospital.'

Ros started the playback again and let it run forward in slow motion, frame by painful frame. Ed's knee dropping, then hammering up again. Dropping, then hammering up. Rupta contorting each time, his body almost leaving the ground with the impact. Ed backing away, wary, poised. Rupta not moving, a surprised frown darkening his face. His hand moving up experimentally to his chest. Checking for broken ribs? Checking for a heartbeat? And then that slow collapse, as if every muscle in his body had suddenly let go at the same moment.

And the raised hand. The pathetic appeal.

And the final slump.

'Don't blame yourself,' De Freitas said to Ed, 'I'm sure Jason will be all right.' She didn't sound convinced.

Looking at the expression on Rupta's face as he fell, Beckett didn't blame her. He'd seen men die before, and they all had that slightly startled expression on their faces. *This can't be it*, the expression said. *I'm not ready to go.*

But everybody did, in the end.

One of the computers beeped. Ros clicked her mouse at various points on the screen. 'Incoming fax,' she said. Another click and the printer nearest her whirred into life and disgorged a sheet of paper.

'So where is Jason now?' Beckett asked, still watching the screen. 'A local hospital?'

'I'm afraid I don't know.' De Freitas looked blank. 'I would presume so.'

Ros waved the sheet of paper. 'I've just checked,' she said grimly. 'No ambulance was called to the Sports Academy. Not from anywhere.'

Beckett frowned. On the monitor, the two paramedics were rolling Jason Rupta onto their stretcher and picking him up. Within a few seconds they had vanished from the screen. 'So who the heck were those guys?' he asked. He glanced at De Freitas, at Ros and finally at Ed. 'And where did they take Jason?'

Nobody answered.

Beep.

Apart from the shallow rise and fall of his chest, the man in the bed didn't move.

Beep.

Beneath his closed eyelids there was no flicker to indicate that he might be dreaming.

Beep.

A silver thermal blanket covered him up to his chest. His arms lay on top of the blanket. A strap ran across his chest, fastened to the bed on both sides. His bed was surrounded by plastic sheets, forming a tentlike room.

Beep.

His chest had been shaved in a circular patch above his heart. Eight small sensors covered in blue plastic had been attached to the skin. Wires ran from them to a box on a rack behind the bed. On the box, a small monitor registered the activity of his heart.

Beep.

A transparent tube ran from a bag of saline solution on a rack to a vein beneath a dressing on the back of his left hand. A similar tube containing glucose solution ran from another bag into a vein beneath a dressing on the back of his right hand.

Beep.

A small rubber thimble covered the tip of the index finger of his left hand. Wires led from the thimble to a box built into the rack. LED lights flickered on the box. A small LCD screen on top of the rack displayed the amount of oxygen in his blood.

Beep.

A flaccid black rubber ring encircled his left arm, just above the elbow. A black tube connected the ring to another box on the rack.

Whirr.

The ring began to inflate. Within a few seconds its surface was taut, and the skin of his arm beneath was crimped by the pressure. Blood-pressure readings scrolled across the LCD screen on the rack.

Hisssssss.

The ring deflated again. A red flush spread down the man's arm as the blood crept back in.

Beep.

A lift door opened nearby. Footsteps sounded, echoing back and forth as if an entire battalion had arrived in the building. The walls of the plastic tent that surrounded the bed waved, disturbed by currents of air.

Beep.

Two men marched into the room. One of them stood by the door and brought his heels together smartly. He wore nondescript casual clothing of an unnoticeable colour, but he still made it look like a uniform. His hair was short and black. His eyes were a clear, undiluted blue. His face bore the marks of old fights. His hand hovered close to his open jacket, and the sleek machine-pistol beneath. The other man stopped by the bed. He wore a brown leather jacket over heavy cotton trousers and a faded turquoise polo-neck shirt.

His hair was red turning to grey, and his eyes were greyer still.

Beep.

'Keep him sedated, Hex,' the man by the bed said. 'Doctor Hunter will need to do some tests. And I need to talk to Doctor Hunter.'

'Yes, Colonel,' replied the man by the door. The words came easily to his lips, as if he had said them many times before.

The two men left. The sound of their footsteps retreated down the corridor, accompanied by the echoes of a phantom army.

Beep.

Jason Rupta kept on breathing.

« Two »

Ed's motorbike swept so smoothly up to the doors of the International Sports Academy that it might almost have been on rails. He squeezed the brakes at the last moment and came to a perfect stop, killing the engine as he did so. Kicking the stand down, he climbed off and removed his helmet. The breeze on his face felt good, and he ran a hand through his hair.

His heart was racing as fast as his engine had been.

He could smell the hot metal of the engine and the lingering bitterness of the exhaust. With the engine quiet, the sound of birdsong and distant traffic infiltrated back across the industrial landscape of tarmac, brick and metal.

He hadn't wanted to come back. The sight of the academy – a warehouse-sized building with the auditorium occupying one half and various offices and laboratories the other – made him feel nauseous. It wasn't that he was squeamish – he'd seen people injured before, and even caused a few injuries himself – but there was something about Jason Rupta's collapse that bothered him. Something about the suddenness of it. Downing a man in a fight was one thing, but seeing him fall down for no apparent reason . . .

It could happen to anyone.

Ed took a deep breath. That was what was bothering him. It could happen to anyone. A stroke, a heart attack, a sudden collapse. The body showing its age. You couldn't stop time. Everything decayed.

It could happen to him.

It *would* happen to him. One day.

But not today.

He reached into his jacket and pulled out the tiny radio that Ros had given him earlier. Turning to interpose his body between the radio and the building, he pressed the transmit button. 'Beckett, can you hear me?'

'This isn't a tin can and a bit of string, Ed,' Beckett snapped. 'This is cutting-edge communications technology. Of course I can hear you.'

'Just going in now.'

'OK. I'll start with Hunter's office. Try and delay him if you can. Ros, how about you?'

'I'm already at the laboratory,' her voice responded. 'Keep Hunter talking, Ed.'

'Will do,' Ed replied, and pushed the radio back into his jacket. Slinging his helmet on the back of the bike, he dashed up the steps and walked so fast towards the automatic doors that they almost didn't react to his approach in time.

He checked the auditorium half of the building first, but it was empty. He gazed for a moment at the spot where Jason Rupta had collapsed, then sighed and retraced his steps back to the entrance hall. He checked the signboard. ASSESSMENT CENTRE. If Doctor Hunter was anywhere, he'd be there.

The office and laboratory half of the building was erected around a central atrium. White pillars supported the tinted-glass ceiling. Vines climbed the pillars. Two glass lifts glided between the seven balcony levels around which the various administrative and research functions of the International Sports

31

Academy were carried out. Fountains plashed discreetly out of sight.

The assessment centre was a series of brightly lit rooms on the ground floor. Each room had a different set of exercise equipment in – exercise bikes, rowing machines, steppers, treadmills and weightlifting benches so complicated that they looked like explosions in aluminium factories. About half of them were occupied by intense, focused men and women who were sweating freely as they worked. People in yellow tracksuits over black T-shirts walked between the various pieces of equipment, timing the exercises and taking notes on palmtop computers. Every open doorway had a chin bar fixed a few inches below the lintel.

Doctor Hunter was in the fifth room. He was standing next to a man on an exercise bike and keying information into his palmtop. His flabby bulk was in stark contrast to the athletic looks of the people working the exercise machines. The man was hunched over the handlebars, his face screwed up in what was either concentration or agony. Or both. Sweat was dripping off his chin and into a pool on the floor. It looked to Ed as if the only thing left keeping his legs moving was sheer willpower.

'Doctor Hunter?' Ed said.

Hunter glanced up. He frowned for a moment, trying to remember where he had seen Ed before, then nodded and turned back to the man on the bike.

'Doctor Hunter, how's Jason? I feel terrible about that accident. Is he all right?'

'Jason's doing fine,' Hunter said reassuringly. He pushed past Ed and walked over to the next bike in the row. The woman pounding away at the pedals was flushed, but she looked in better shape than the previous man.

'I wanted to visit him, but no one seems to know what hospital he's in.'

32

Hunter's eyes flickered towards Ed, although his head didn't move. 'His father arranged for him to be flown home to –' he paused, as if trying to remember. 'To Miami. He thinks Jason will get over it quicker in the sun.'

'I didn't know he was American,' Ed said.

'No?' Hunter shrugged. 'Well, excuse me.' He looked across the room, and caught the eye of a tall man with a ponytail. Ed recognised him as one of Rupta's friends from the fight. 'Kane! If you're ready.'

Kane walked over, glaring at Ed all the while. Hunter waddled across to join him, and together they walked away.

Ed checked his watch. Not enough time. He had to delay them for longer.

'I'm surprised that Jason was well enough to travel,' he called.

Without turning, or even slowing down, Hunter waved a dismissive hand. 'You know how fit the academy students are – they just bounce back.'

Damn. Try again.

'And does anyone know what it was that made him collapse?'

It was Kane who stopped and glared back at Ed. '*You* ought to,' he snarled.

Hunter had walked on a few paces, oblivious of the fact that Kane was no longer with him. Suddenly realising, he turned and waddled back. 'We don't know it was Mr . . . ah, Ed's fault for certain,' he said, patting Kane's arm. 'Now come on, we have a schedule to keep.'

One more try.

'Perhaps it was the tri-meserone,' Ed said.

Hunter turned to gaze at Ed, his expression guarded. 'I don't know who you've been talking to, but you've clearly been misinformed. There's nothing sinister

33

about tri-meserone. It's nothing more than a new kind of vitamin pill.'

'It works better than any vitamin,' Kane agreed with the zeal of the newly converted.

'Students are all keen to get on the tri-meserone test programme,' Hunter said. 'It's a genuinely natural performance enhancer. I suggest you keep quiet about something you don't understand.'

The words were a threat, but the fact that Hunter looked something like a large hamster ruined the effect as far as Ed was concerned. He watched as Hunter and Kane walked over to a nearby doorway and turned out of sight. His hand stole inside his jacket. 'Beckett,' he murmured, 'I delayed him for as long as I could, but he's coming your way. You've got about twenty seconds.'

'OK,' Beckett whispered into his radio. He glanced towards the open door of Hunter's office. No sign of anyone. No sounds of anyone approaching. Perhaps they weren't coming this way after all.

Still, best to assume the worst and finish fast. He stowed the radio into a pocket of his bright yellow coveralls and glanced around the room, looking for the best place to fit the second bug. The first bug was already superglued beneath the desk, but he wanted some insurance. He spotted an access point in the carpet, and knelt down beside it. A small square of floor hinged up, revealing a recessed metal port containing a telephone point and two electrical sockets. Working quickly he began to unscrew the telephone jack. The open door at his back made him nervous, and his fingers fumbled the screwdriver. *Calm down* he thought to himself. *More haste, less speed, or somesuch bollocks.*

The open door made him nervous, but it was standard operational procedure in undercover infiltration missions. If anyone passed by an open door and

34

saw him working openly they would be more likely to accept him than if they had opened a closed door and found him working secretively behind it. Same with the yellow coveralls: someone skulking in camouflage is automatically suspicious, but someone wearing bright colours is so obvious that they can be overlooked.

The jack cover came away, and he slipped a lozenge-shaped bug inside.

A door opened nearby, and he could hear two pairs of footsteps walking along a corridor. They were getting louder.

He slipped the telephone jack cover back and tried to insert the screws, but the cover was misaligned and the screws wouldn't fit.

The footsteps suddenly increased in volume, as if their owners had turned a corner.

He pushed hard on the cover, and felt it click into place. Half-pushing the screws, he pumped them flush to the cover with quick, jerky motions.

The footsteps stopped in the doorway.

'What do you think you're doing?' a voice snapped peevishly.

Beckett stood up slowly and turned around. Doctor Hunter was standing in the corridor gazing at him, the corners of his mouth turned down in disapproval. Another man stood behind Hunter. Beckett recognised him: he'd been at the fight. The guy with the ponytail. A friend of Jason Rupta's.

Beckett raised his eyebrows at Hunter. Reaching into his pocket he retrieved a roll of sticky labels. He peeled one off and held it out for Hunter to inspect. 'This appliance was checked and passed on . . .', it read. 'Health and Safety,' said Beckett. 'We have to check all your electrical equipment annually.'

Hunter pursed his lips, like a child refusing food. 'Why wasn't I informed?'

'Don't ask me,' Beckett said. 'I just work here.' He knelt down and stuck the label on the telephone jack, deliberately ensuring that it covered the seam around the cover. The glue was specially formulated to be a bastard to remove. If Hunter was suspicious enough to check what Beckett had been doing to the jack, it would take him a good five minutes to peel it off enough to remove the cover. By that time Beckett would be halfway to Gizmos.

Hunter was still watching him. Beckett very deliberately reached into his coveralls and removed a pen. With great care and precision he dated the sticker, then replaced the pen in his pocket with a flourish, slid the cover back across the access point and stood up. 'Now,' he said cheerfully, 'I've got to check your light fittings.'

Hunter sighed theatrically and rolled his eyes. 'Oh *really*! I was just about to give an injection . . .'

'Nearly done.' Beckett smiled, and moved across to the desk lamp. He made a show of checking the fitting and the bulb while still watching Hunter from the corner of his eye.

Hunter slipped a black case out of a pocket. Opening it, he removed a device that looked like a cross between an asthma inhaler and an executive fountain pen. 'Up with your sleeve, Kane.' Kane complied expectantly. Hunter pressed the device to the flesh of Kane's arm and pressed a hidden button. A sudden sharp hiss, like the noise of a startled viper, made Beckett flinch.

'There you go,' Hunter murmured reassuringly as he stowed the high-tech syringe away. 'That should improve your times.'

Kane rubbed his arm, where a red weal was developing. 'Thank you, Doctor.' He sounded genuinely grateful.

Beckett couldn't resist asking. 'Go-faster juice?'

'None of your business,' Hunter snapped without looking at him.

A brief military rap at the door made them all turn. A man stood in the doorway. There was nothing obviously impressive about him. He was forty and dressed as if he was thirty, in a worn brown leather jacket over faded casual clothes. His hair was red peppered with grey. At first glance Beckett took him for a businessman looking to improve his squash scores with a little pharmaceutical help, but then he glanced at the man's eyes. They were flat and grey, like polished slate. And he held himself like a man who was expecting trouble: balanced on the balls of his feet.

'Doctor, we need to talk,' he said. It wasn't a request.

Kane glanced at Hunter, then quickly sidled out of the room, past the newcomer. Kane had a weightlifter's build, and the man was shorter than he was, but somehow Kane came off worse in the momentary comparison.

Hunter looked at Beckett in frustration. 'Can you come back and do this later?'

'Sure,' Beckett said. 'I'm finished.' Gathering up his implements, he headed towards the door. The man shifted slightly to let him pass. Their eyes locked for a long second. Beckett felt the intense force of the man's dispassionate scrutiny and tried to look away, but it was as if he had surrendered control. He couldn't break the lock.

And then the man looked away from him and towards Hunter, and Beckett was free to walk away. As the door closed behind him he became aware of the sweat prickling in his scalp and down his back. Who *was* that man?

As he walked away he pulled his radio out. 'Ed? Where are you?'

'In your car, outside the building.' Ed sounded concerned. 'What's wrong? You sound awful.'

'It's nothing.' Beckett shook his head firmly. 'There's a bug under the desk and a tap on the phone. Start recording.'

'You don't appear to be producing the results I need,' the colonel growled.

Hunter shrugged, feeling a ripple run through his flabby frame. 'Just give me more time,' he said. 'I'm a doctor, not a magician.'

Colonel Easterhaus stared at Hunter without saying anything. Hunter felt the coolness of perspiration across his upper lip. He didn't like the colonel. He didn't like him at all. The colonel reminded him of all those boys in the showers at school who used to make fun of him and flick him with wet towels. The colonel was a bully. Older. Bigger. More powerful. But still a bully. Hunter wished that there was some other way of getting what he wanted, but he couldn't think of one. The colonel was involved, like it or not.

'What went wrong last night?' the colonel said finally.

'It was an adverse allergic reaction,' Hunter replied, 'just like the others. It won't happen again.'

More silence.

'It's just a minor flaw,' Hunter added desperately. 'We'll eliminate it during the final testing.'

'For which there is only a limited time.'

Hunter felt a sudden fluttering sensation in the pit of his stomach. Surely the colonel couldn't be serious. 'But . . . but if I don't complete the tests, the flaw will just keep occurring.'

'It had better not,' the colonel said quietly. 'Otherwise tri-meserone is worse than useless.'

'I'll sort it out. Give me another forty-eight hours.' Hunter hated the way he tried to make it sound like an instruction, only for it to come out like a plea.

'You're already behind schedule.' The colonel paused,

and Hunter knew that he was enjoying watching Hunter squirm. 'You can have twenty-four hours. Not a moment longer.'

Hunter opened his mouth to argue, but by the time he had worked up the courage to speak, the colonel had left the room.

'Bastard,' he whispered to the empty air.

The sign on the door said LABORATORY. Just that. Nothing to tell what sort of laboratory it was. Or whose. Just LABORATORY.

Still, it was the only laboratory Ros had found. Chances were, it belonged to Doctor Hunter.

Ros glanced down the corridor towards where it opened out onto the atrium. She was on the fourth floor, and she felt as obvious as a fly on a sheet of paper. It could have been worse – Hunter's laboratory could actually have been *on* the balcony, rather than just off it – but anybody glancing across the atrium from the offices opposite would have a clear view down the corridor. Fortunately the windows of the offices were covered by venetian blinds. Nobody was visible. Even the glass-sided lifts were empty. The International Sports Academy seemed to Ros like a very understaffed organisation.

The laboratory itself had a long window running up to the door, looking out onto the corridor. As with the ones across the atrium, the blinds were closed. She couldn't even tell if there was anybody inside or not. Hunter was in his office, according to the brief conversation between Ed and Beckett, but that didn't mean it was empty.

Still . . .

She entered the room and closed the door rapidly behind her. She quickly glanced around the room. Two benches running down the centre. A computer. Test tubes in racks. Test tubes rotating in centrifuges, looking like toy roundabouts. Bunsen burners. Coils of glass tubing in wraparound glass jackets. An industrial microwave oven. A walk-in fume cupboard in a corner. A safe with a combination lock.

No people.

Ros breathed out slowly. She hadn't quite realised how tense she had been. Turning, she teased up one of the venetian-blind slats with a finger and peered out across the atrium. There was still nobody about.

Time to get to work.

She walked up and down both benches, hoping that there might be a few sheets of paper labelled 'tri-meserone formula', but it looked like Hunter was a careful man. The important stuff was probably in the safe. At a pinch she could take a sample from one of the tubes and pull some favours to get it analysed by a friend, but knowing her luck it would be Hunter's own-brand hooch rather than anything sinister. No, her best chance was the computer.

She sat in the chair – especially wide, to accommodate Hunter's large rear end – in front of the computer and turned the machine on. It was a year or so old, and a brand she was familiar with. She shouldn't have any problems getting the information from it.

The computer booted up into an unfamiliar menu system. Probably a bespoke job written specially for the academy. Ros's eyes flickered down the list of options until she found *Retrieve File*. Moving the cursor down to that line, she pressed the return key.

Filename? the computer asked. Ros thought for a moment. She didn't know what any of the files were called, and there appeared to be no way of calling a list up on screen. It was a crude security measure – if you didn't know what the file you wanted was called, you had no right to be looking for it. On the face of it she was stymied, but if she was lucky then whoever designed the system would have built in a series of hot

40

keys or macros – short cuts to save time. That was what programmers did most of – trying to save themselves a few seconds whenever they wanted to do something.

One at a time, she pressed the function keys along the top of the keyboard.

<F1> gave her nothing.

<F2> gave her nothing.

<F3> put a message up on the screen asking her if she wanted to abort the session. She pressed <Esc> and the message vanished.

<F4> gave her nothing.

<F5> made the machine hum for a moment as the hard disk was accessed. A box appeared on screen with a list of filenames inside. Bingo! As she had suspected, whoever designed the menu system had known that one day someone using it would forget the name of the file they wanted. She glanced down the list. *Letter.001* to *letter.435*. Not only did Hunter write a lot of letters, he was obviously the sort of man who never threw anything away. Not even electronically. Probably a trainspotter in his spare time. A handful of reports. Various files with vaguely chemical names.

Including *trimeser.001*, *trimeser.002* and *trimeser.003*.

Trimeser. Tri-meserone?

Ros would have put money on it.

Thanking God that Hunter was such an obsessively organised man, she moved the cursor down to *trimeser.003* and pressed the return key.

The hard disk hummed for a few moments, and the menu screen vanished. In its place was a mass of letters and numbers jumbled into no discernible order.

Ros didn't know much about chemistry, but even she could tell that this wasn't a chemical formula. The file was encrypted.

It wasn't an insurmountable problem. Ros had software back in the Gizmos office that could break –

had in fact broken – the best encryption algorithms the Hive had ever constructed. Unfortunately she wasn't back at the office. She was in someone's lab. Illegally.

Ros reached into her pocket and took out a disk. She slipped it into the machine and hit the <Esc> key until she got back to the original menu. One of the options was *Copy file(s) to disk?* Knowing the name of the files she wanted, it took her only a few seconds to move them across. When she got back to the office it would take only as many seconds to decrypt them.

'What are you doing?'

Ros's shoulders tensed so fast that a pain shot through her neck. She hadn't even heard anyone enter the lab.

She turned her head slowly, feigning nonchalance. The young martial artist with the ponytail was standing behind her. Close behind her. There was something about his eyes that bothered Ros. The pupils were just pinpricks, even though the laboratory wasn't brightly lit.

'Who are you?' Ros asked, doing her best to look innocently impatient.

'Kane. Who are you?'

'I'm the new research assistant,' Ros said calmly, even though her heart was beating fast and she was having difficulty catching her breath. 'I'm working with Doctor Hunter on tri-meserone.'

Kane frowned. 'Doctor Hunter never mentioned an assistant.'

'I'm monitoring students taking part in the trials,' Ros said, pressing home her advantage over Kane's confusion.

'Then why weren't you in his office just now when he gave me a shot?' Kane challenged.

Ros reached out casually, as if it was the most obvious thing in the world to do, and removed the floppy disk from the slot in the computer casing. 'He should've told me,' she sighed. 'I'll have to have words with him. Still in his office, is he?'

To get to the door she had to step around the young martial-arts student. He stepped with her, blocking her path.

'I think the colonel will want to see you,' he said, and reached out for her shoulder.

No way, she thought.

Ros sidestepped and caught Kane's elbow, jerking him forward and off balance. He went sprawling into one of Hunter's benches, sending a wave of glassware crashing to the ground. Multi-coloured liquid spilled across the tiled floor. A sharp smell, like nail polish remover, made Ros's eyes water. She ran towards the door, knocking one of the spinning centrifuges off the other bench. It went flying across the room like a tiny propeller. Kane picked himself off the ground and shook his head. As Ros ran through the door and turned right, away from the atrium and towards the nearest stairwell, she caught sight of the expression on his face. Angry? He could have fried eggs at fifty paces with one glance.

Halfway towards the stairwell was one of the automatic fire doors. It was made of some heavy-duty transparent glass – unscuffable, unscratchable and completely fireproof. Ros was heading towards it at full tilt. The infra-red sensor above the door didn't pick her up until she was a few feet away, and she had to slow to let it operate. She glanced over her shoulder. Kane was pelting down the corridor towards her, his pumping legs rucking the carpet tiles up behind him. His face was contorted in feral rage.

The door hissed open and Ros sprang through. Her hand fished in her coat pocket and closed on a small remote-control unit.

The door hissed closed.

Ros pulled the remote out, turning the pocket almost

inside out, and pointed it at the infra-red sensor. It was a general-purpose device, keyed to several different functions. Buggering up sensors was one of them.

Her pursuer was racing full pelt at the door. His fingers were hooked into claws. His lips were pulled back from his teeth, and spittle was flying from his mouth.

Ros backed away as fast as she could, unable to tear her eyes away from Kane's unstoppable approach. Convulsively her finger jabbed one of the buttons on the remote. The remote beeped as it burned the sensor's innards to slag.

The man seemed to have grown to fill the entire corridor. His arms were swinging so wide as he ran that his knuckles were brushing the wall. Ros kept on waiting for him to slow down to let the fire door operate, but he didn't even seem to register its presence.

The sensor didn't react to his approach.

Even if he'd decided to stop, his momentum was going to carry him straight into the door. Ros slowed, waiting for him to hit it and bounce. The shock would knock him unconscious long enough for her to make her escape.

But it didn't.

Kane ran straight through the fire door. Razor-edged slices of glass exploded around him. He burst through them like something nasty coming out of a cocoon.

Heading straight for Ros.

« Three »

Kane had one arm up shielding his eyes from the flying glass. Ros turned and ran towards the stairwell while he couldn't see her.

She could hear his feet pounding the carpet tiles behind her. Pounding as fast as her heart. She felt sick. Her lungs burned, crying out for more oxygen. Tears blurred her eyes. Any moment she expected to feel Kane's hand clawing at her neck.

The door to the stairwell loomed out before her. She closed her hand around the doorknob and fell through into the plain concrete landing. Up or down? Up and Kane would catch her for sure. Down and she might just have a chance to outrun him.

She took the stairs three at a time. Thank God she'd worn flat shoes. She misjudged the turn at the second landing and almost twisted her ankle, but caught the rail just in time. Spikes of pain shot up her leg, but she still managed to make it to the next landing down. A door led out onto the third floor. Take it, or keep going down?

The door above her burst off its hinges as Kane smashed through into the stairwell. His face was a mask of blood from the cuts he'd received. He glanced

45

up, then down. Seeing Ros below him, he jumped halfway down the stairs and vaulted over the rail, bypassing the middle landing altogether and plummeting towards where Ros was standing.

The decision taken for her, Ros pulled the door open and hobbled out into the corridor.

It was a mirror image of the one she'd just left. The only difference was that the fire door was intact. Ros ran past it, slowing again to let it operate then speeding up again when she was on the other side. She aimed the remote control over her shoulder as she ran and destroyed the infra-red sensor. It might slow Kane down for a few more seconds. She didn't hold out much hope, though.

A detonation of glass behind her proved she was right.

She ran past the point where the laboratory was, one floor up, and out onto the balcony running around the atrium. Faces were beginning to appear at windows around the open space, wondering what the noise was. Ros didn't hesitate, but turned left and ran towards the nearest lift. If she could just get into it and shut the door before Kane got to it then she could gain a few vital seconds on him.

She heard a growl behind her as he emerged onto the balcony.

The lift was on her level. *Please God don't let anybody call it while I'm still running.*

Doors and windows blurred past her as she ran.

The lift was fifteen feet away.

For the first time she could hear the grunting of Kane's breath as he ran.

Ten feet.

Maybe it was just the way the air whipped past her head, but Ros could have sworn that she could feel Kane's hot breath on the back of her neck.

Five feet.

Fingers scrabbled at the back of her raincoat.

Ros drew on her last reserves of strength and accelerated towards the finish line. The crowd were on their feet now, their faces just blurs of pink and brown. The ribbon was fluttering just ahead of her. She coasted on a wave of cheering. The baton was cool in her hand as she breasted the ribbon and –

– collapsed into the lift, her fingers scrabbling for a button, any button. Up, down, it didn't matter as long as she got away from him.

Turning, she watched with horror as the man approached her like an avenging angel. His body seemed to be growing as she watched, but Ros realised with relief that it was the gap getting smaller as the metal doors closed.

The view along the balcony closed down to the last few inches as he thundered towards the lift. He was close enough for Ros to see the burst blood vessels in his eyes.

The doors clamped shut.

Ros slumped back against the glass wall of the lift.

And the metal dented in five places as Kane's forehead, elbows and knees hit it.

Ros found she couldn't breathe. Every muscle in her body was locked solid, waiting for him to prise the doors open.

The lift juddered upward.

Ros could hear Kane's frustrated cry. She turned and gazed out across the atrium space. One or two people had come out of their offices, but they were looking down at Kane rather than at her. Bit by bit she felt her muscles relax. She was heading in the wrong direction, but she could find a way down again. All she had to do was keep track of where Kane was, and stay away. He didn't seem to be thinking straight, otherwise he would have raised the alarm much earlier. He almost seemed to be acting like an animal. Instinctive. Aggressive. Immensely resilient.

Just like Jason Rupta.

Before she could follow that thought to its logical conclusion, Ros noticed that the heads of the people standing on the various balconies were moving. They were raising their gazes, almost as if –

Oh no.

She pressed her face against the glass wall of the lift and looked downwards.

Her pursuer was climbing one of the pillars that supported the tinted-glass roof of the atrium. His arms were spread wide to encompass it, his fingers and toes finding impossibly small cracks to support his weight. And it wasn't as if he was straining to climb the pillar. He was shooting up it like a monkey up a pole.

Ros sighed. It was like being trapped inside a nightmare – except that her nightmares usually revolved around power spikes and unsaved data. Someone else's nightmare perhaps.

The lift stopped on the top level of the academy. Ros knew that her choices were limited. She could go back down again, or she could try and get out onto the roof. If she went back down, all Kane had to do was drop to the ground and he'd have her. Given the look in his eyes, he'd probably rip her apart with his bare hands. If she went out onto the roof, she might be able to find a fire escape. Or something.

Or she might just sprout wings and fly away.

What other option did she have?

Ros stepped out of the lift and ran down the nearest corridor towards the stairwell. For a moment she was alone. No noise. No superhuman pursuer powering after her. She reached the door and grasped the handle. With a terrible sense of déjà vu, she turned around.

Kane's muscular form was blocking the light from the corridor.

48

She yanked the door open and pelted out into the stairwell. The broad concrete steps led downwards, but a smaller set of metal steps led upwards. Without hesitation, she went up.

The steps terminated at a door covered in signs saying THIS DOOR MUST BE KEPT LOCKED AT ALL TIMES. Ros took a deep breath, and twisted the handle. It opened. Mentally blessing all surreptitious smokers who crept out onto the flat roof for a quick cigarette, Ros emerged there herself.

The wind whipped her hair into her face and made her eyes water. All she could see was blue sky.

The building was effectively a square with a hole in the middle. The roof was covered with tarmac. The hole was covered with the tinted-glass dome that she'd seen from the atrium. Spars and struts braced it from above, and a rail ran around it to stop maintenance men or smokers from stumbling into it.

Ros gazed desperately around the roof-space. A clutch of antennas. The caged ends of air-conditioning vents, from which sounded the lazy throb of fans. Brackets for a window-cleaning cradle. The small building housing the top of the stairwell.

No fire escape.

No escape at all.

The door in the stairwell building opened. Kane stepped out. His face was covered in dried blood. Ros saw with disbelief that small shards of glass still projected from some of the cuts.

He didn't smile. He didn't snarl. He didn't say anything. He just walked forward, muscles rippling beneath his tracksuit, hands reaching out to either side of her face.

Ros backed away until she could feel the cold metal rail guarding the tinted-glass dome behind her. If she could just sucker him into making a grab for her, and duck out of the way in time . . . She'd only wanted to escape, but if harming him was the only way to get away, then that was what she'd do.

She tried to duck beneath his outstretched arms, but he was too quick for her. His hands closed on her shoulders, pushing her back against the rail.

She twisted round, fighting to escape his grasp, but his hands were like metal clamps.

Through the glass she could see the mosaic tiles of the floor, seven storeys below, and the fountains, and the vines.

Kane's grip tightened, pushing her forward.

She kicked backwards, but there was nothing there to kick.

And then he let go.

With the resistance gone, Ros almost fell forwards into the glass dome. Catching the rail just in time, she pushed herself away. She moved across the tarmac to the building housing the top of the stairwell. Only then did she turn to see why Kane had let her go.

He hadn't moved. He looked puzzled, as if he was hearing something unexpected. Or as if he *wasn't* hearing something he expected to hear. His hand was clutching at the material above his chest. There was something familiar about the plaintive gesture, but it took Ros a moment to work out what it was. Then she remembered – Jason Rupta had looked like that just before –

Just before he collapsed.

Kane's eyes met Ros's, and it seemed to her that he was trying to apologise; but then his face contorted and he leaned forward, bending over the rail. The weight of his upper body pulled him forward. His feet left the ground and, for a moment, he hung there like washing left out to dry. Then gravity took over, and he slowly toppled forward, slipping off the rail and crashing into the glass dome.

And straight through it.

After that: silence.

Ros waited for a while, but there was no sound of impact, no screams, no shouting. She waited until she could breathe properly again, and her heart had slowed down to normal. When the cold wind began to bite, she walked across to the railing and the glass dome.

Through the hole left by the man's falling body, she could see all the way down to the ground. Kane was spread-eagled in one of the fountains. The water was scarlet, fading to pink as it drained and fresh water fell like rain onto his body. People were just beginning to gather around. They stood in small groups, uncertain what to do.

Ros took a deep, shuddering breath and reached for her radio. When she walked out of that building, she wanted Beckett and Ed to be waiting for her.

With the engine running.

Stephen Ingless leaned gingerly back in the leather swivel chair. It gave beneath his weight, and he allowed himself to stretch out and luxuriate in the comfort. He hadn't got used to it yet. He hadn't got used to the office, either – all minimalist Swedish furniture and stripped-pine panels. That would all have to change – when he got his feet under the table. When he felt comfortable in his new position of responsibility. Redesign the office – redesign the company as well. There were going to be some big changes to Stross Security Systems, not the least of which was that he would make the company profitable for once. Assuming, of course, that he could pay off its debts.

The intercom box on his desk buzzed. 'Mr Ingless? Two . . . gentlemen to see you.'

Ingless twisted his chair towards the computer on the desk, fiddled with the mouse the way his secretary had shown him and called up his desk diary on the screen. Most of the appointments were holdovers from his predecessor – Ingless himself hadn't had enough time to arrange many meetings of his own, although he had assiduously gone through and added in his dental checkups and doctors' visits. Ah yes, there they were. *Computer Recall – 14:00* it said. Trust bloody Stross not to put in any details of what they wanted.

'Show the gentlemen in, Miss Shaw,' he said to the intercom.

The door to his office opened and a man in a very expensive suit walked in so confidently that Ingless almost felt like scooting out from behind the desk and letting him have the swivel chair. Behind him, filling the doorway, entered a uniformed flunky with a shaven head and bored, listless eyes. The flunky was carrying a package in one hamlike fist.

'Mr Ingless,' the first man said, extending his hand, 'so good to finally meet you. My name is Marcel – Patrick Marcel.'

'Pleased to meet you,' Ingless said, standing up and shaking hands. As he sat down, he noticed that the uniformed flunky was turning the knob that locked the door.

Patrick Marcel noticed Ingless's preoccupation. 'We don't want to be disturbed, do we?' he said, smiling broadly. 'After all, we have matters of import to discuss.'

Ingless felt a pang of alarm. 'Is that really –?'

'Necessary?' Patrick Marcel nodded. 'Absolutely. Your predecessor understood how important secrecy was. At least, he did before his untimely disappearance.'

'Ah.' Now the conversation had moved onto firmer ground – ground that Ingless was familiar with. 'As you know, Mr Stross vanished some weeks ago. I've only recently been promoted into the chairman's position, and I'm still a little uncertain as to exactly –'

'Finance, Mr Ingless.' Patrick Marcel nodded sagely. 'Stross Security Systems could be a successful little company in the executive protection field, but aggressive marketing by your competitors has left you in a parlous state.' Ingless detected a hint of an accent on the word 'parlous', and wondered briefly if Patrick Marcel was foreign. 'We are offering a large cash injection, enough to pay off your creditors and leave a significant bonus for yourself.'

'In return for what?' Ingless asked nervously. There was something about the man's oily charm he didn't trust.

'We can discuss that later. Are you willing to entertain my offer?'

Ingless shook his head. He had his own plans for the company, and he didn't want to be beholden to anybody. Maybe he would succeed, maybe he would fail, but he wanted to do it by himself. 'No,' he said, getting to his feet. 'I'm sorry that you've wasted your time, Mr Marcel, but the company is in a very healthy situation and we don't need any –'

'Your previous director took much the same attitude,' Patrick Marcel said, still sitting. 'In fact, he became quite irate at our offer of help.'

Ingless glanced pointedly at his watch. 'Mr Marcel, I –'

'When I pressed him to reconsider our offer he lost his temper with us and threatened to have us thrown out of this very office.'

'I really don't have –'

Patrick Marcel waved a hand at the huge, bald-headed man by the door. The arrogance conveyed in that one little gesture silenced Ingless as the man crossed the room, still carrying the package, and placed it in front of him. The package was big enough to hold a football, and it was wrapped in brown paper. The bottom was marred by a treacly stain. A faint, sharp odour made Ingless think briefly of his biology classes at school, many years ago. What the hell was in it?

'I would almost go so far as to say,' Patrick Marcel continued, 'that Mr Stross completely lost his head.' He smiled, and gestured to the package. 'But I'm forgetting my manners – we bought a little present for you.' His eyes hardened. 'Please feel free to open it in front of us. We won't be . . . shocked.'

'It was like being chased by a robot,' Ros said. 'He wouldn't stop – just ran through things as if they weren't there. Nothing fazed him. He didn't seem to feel any pain.'

The three of them were sitting in the Gizmos office, comparing stories. Ros looked as calm and collected as usual, but Beckett could see the strain beneath the surface. Her knuckles were white as they gripped the mug of coffee, and she wouldn't meet anyone's gaze. 'I haven't run so fast since school,' she added with a shudder.

'Kiss chase?' Ed said with what he probably believed was a winning smile.

'Fifteen-hundred-metres champion actually,' Ros replied.

Beckett opened his mouth to say something comforting and meaningless, but a noise from one of the computers distracted him. For a moment he wasn't sure which one it was. All of the many networked PCs and workstations were humming, clicking, beeping, whirring or just silently working on their various projects in the background. The combined low-level racket was like some post-modernist symphony composed by a demented musician. His gaze flicked around the screens until he found one that was showing a query message. To his embarrassment, it was the one that he'd set working earlier.

'Hey, look at this,' he said, reaching across and pressing a key. 'I've been running an ID check on the guy who turned up in Hunter's office – skipping through the various databases we're plugged into, looking for a match. Looks like we've found something.'

'How did you manage that?' Ros asked. 'I didn't think we knew his name.'

Beckett nodded. 'That's true, but Ed took a photo of him as he left the academy. I digitised the image and fed it into the computer, then asked it to look for matching faces.'

'Neat' was Ros's only comment.

The screen blanked, then filled with words and a photograph. The modem next to it blinked rapidly as the data was transferred down the telephone lines.

Beckett studied the photograph. 'That's the same man.'

'What database is this coming from?' Ros asked.

'Defence Department,' Beckett replied, checking the legend at the top of the screen. 'Hey, I didn't know we even had a link to them.'

'We didn't,' Ros said, straight-faced. 'I cracked their firewall last week.'

Beckett scanned the information as it appeared on the screen:

DEPARTMENT OF DEFENCE

Personnel Files

TOP SECRET – Access Level 8+

Name: EASTERHAUS, Conrad

PoB: Unknown

Nationality: Unknown

Comments: Claims rank of Colonel, although no
              record of posting to this rank.

Profession: International mercenary/soldier of
              fortune. Implicated in many *coups d'etat*.

History: Attended Land Defence Forces College –
              Commissioned 1970, 2nd Lieutenant.
              Promoted Lieutenant 1974. Resigned
              commission 1974.

              Served Royal Dutch Marines as Captain,
              1975–1978.

              Mercenary soldier in Angola, Somalia,
              Nigeria, Laos, Afghanistan. Strategic
              adviser: Haiti, 1980-1988; Montenegro
              1992–1993.

              Deported, 1994.

WANTED FOR QUESTIONING IN LESOTHO,
NIGERIA, MOZAMBIQUE. APPROACH WITH
EXTREME CAUTION.

'Look at his record,' Ed breathed. 'He must be some
kind of warfare junkie.'

'Ex-marine,' Beckett murmured, still reading. 'Skilled
strategist as well. If you added together all the wars this
guy's been involved in, you'd cover half the world.'

'Yeah,' Ros said with a bitter smile, 'he's probably
from the same unit as the man who chased me around
the academy: Kane.'

Beckett terminated the connection with the Defence
Department database and leaned back in his chair.
He ran a hand through his hair, smoothing it back.
Something was bothering him. A question without
an answer. Facts that collided but didn't provide a
solution. There was still something missing. 'If this

Easterhaus wants tri-meserone,' he said, 'I don't think it's just to win a few sports cups.'

Predictable as ever, Ed asked the obvious question. 'So why *does* he want it, then?'

'To create super-soldiers? Make an invincible army?' Beckett was just free-associating, but the ideas that his subconscious was throwing up had the horrible ring of authenticity about them.

Ed's tanned face was screwed up into almost comic bafflement. 'But it doesn't work yet, does it?' he said, painfully thinking his way through the chain of logic that Beckett had already completed. 'Something's wrong with the drug.'

Ros held up a floppy disk. 'And the reason for that may be on here. This is Hunter's research log – I think. I nicked it from the lab before Action Man chased me out. It's encrypted, of course, but –'

'But that won't delay you for long, will it?' Ed said with a sunny smile.

Ros slipped the disk into the nearest computer. 'I think I still have my Secret Squirrel Decoding Ring around somewhere,' she said. Her hands wandered over the keyboard with the precision of a concert pianist.

Something else beeped. Beckett looked around wildly for the source. A third computer was flashing a message. It took him a moment to remember what it had been doing. 'Hang on,' he said, 'that's the bug on Hunter's phone. He must be getting a call.'

'Let's hope it's not his mum calling to find out how he is,' Ed murmured, grinning.

'Trace it,' Ros called without looking away from her own screen.

'Already on it,' Beckett said, reaching forward and keying codes into the computer. The hard disk whirred into life, recording the conversation. Another few commands and the computer's speakers crackled with the distinctive sound of a satellite telephone link. The screen flashed up a map of the entire country. A large area was blocked in red.

'Hello?' said a cautious voice.

'That's Hunter,' Beckett confirmed.

'Another failure, Doctor?' A cold voice. Cold and harsh. There would be no arguing with that voice.

'Colonel Easterhaus?' Beckett speculated as the blocked red area on the screen shrank to an area centred on the city.

Ed grinned. 'Well it's not his mum.'

Beckett shot him a dirty look.

'I'm beginning to get seriously concerned,' the voice continued. 'If you are unable to produce a reliable strain of tri-meserone, I may have to withdraw your funding.'

'It's just a matter of correlating the data from the students who have collapsed,' Hunter pleaded.

The screen changed to show a street map. The red area covered several portable telephone network cells.

'And with that you will be able to correct the problem?' Easterhaus asked.

'Yes, of course.' Hunter didn't sound sure. 'I'm very nearly there. It's just a matter of time. Give me another forty-eight hours . . .'

'You're already behind schedule,' Easterhaus snapped. 'You can have the twenty-four hours we agreed. No more.'

'It's only a performance enhancer,' Hunter protested. 'What's the hurry?'

'I depart tomorrow. My flight is booked. I'll be on that plane, Doctor – with or without the tri-meserone.'

The red area shrank to cover three streets.

The line went dead.

'Got it!' Beckett shouted, punching the air.

'Snap,' Ros said, leaning back from her screen. Hunter's file was sitting there in all its unencrypted glory. 'My God – tri-meserone's a mess!'

Beckett leapt up. 'Tell us on the way.' Snatching up an electronic route-finder, he sprinted towards the door. 'Come on!' he called back over his shoulder, 'Easterhaus isn't going to wait around for ever!'

The sun was hidden behind the built-up horizon, backlighting the jagged skyline of apartment blocks and skyscrapers with strands of glowing orange light. As Beckett steered his four-wheel-drive vehicle down the canyon-like gaps between the glittering buildings of the city, Ros gave Ed and him a quick briefing on what she had picked up from Hunter's files.

'Tri-meserone works by affecting serotonin levels in the brain,' she said. 'It gives you a feeling of confidence in your own abilities, and reduces pain and stress. It doesn't make you physically stronger, but it works because you *feel* stronger.' She grimaced. 'Your mind has its own built-in limits to stop you pulling your muscles away from your bones when you exert yourself, or snapping your tendons. It's a bit like a speed governor on a car. Tri-meserone removes those limits and allows you to use your full strength. No matter what the cost.'

There was silence in the jeep for a moment as they all considered the implications of that thought.

The jeep vibrated as it zoomed across a skeletal metal bridge. Water glittered to both sides of them. They were passing through a sector of faceless corporate buildings that sprouted from lush gardens. Canals began nowhere and meandered through the gardens for a while before stopping dead. The road system had been designed to look as little like a grid as possible, and curved as meaninglessly as the canals.

'So why have people been collapsing?' Beckett asked finally.

'Hunter's notes say it's a side-effect in certain subjects only. It seems to cut in when some athletes' heart rates reach one hundred and eighty beats per minute.

He thinks it might be due to an interaction between the tri-meserone and the increasing levels of stress hormone causing a toxin to be produced.'

'He *thinks*?' Ed said scornfully from the back seat.

Ros shrugged. 'Hunter's not the most meticulous researcher I've ever seen. His notes are skimpy and his basic research is perfunctory, to put it kindly.'

Beckett consulted the electronic route-finder. They were getting close to where Easterhaus had made his call from. 'So this stuff is too risky for Easterhaus to use in its present state ...' he said, thinking the problem through on one level while navigating on another.

'But if Hunter solves the glitch ...' Ed ventured, 'what then?'

Beckett pulled over to one side of the road and stopped the jeep. According to the route-finder, they had arrived. But arrived where?

And then he saw it.

'Well,' he said, 'that's where Easterhaus was calling from. Maybe we'll find out in there.'

Ed and Ros followed his gaze. And gawped.

A massive skyscraper of some thirty or forty floors loomed over the nearby buildings. The upper floors were still under construction, and Beckett could see stars through the gaps. No lights shone in its empty window frames. Its girders and pillars were an ominous, skeletal shadow against the pink glow of the sky.

Ed scanned the building through a pair of hi-tech night-sight binoculars he'd retrieved from Beckett's back seat. 'Beckett, are you sure? The building's completely empty. It doesn't even look quite finished yet.'

'That's where he phoned from,' Beckett confirmed.

Ed got out of the car and walked across to the building's dark base. There was no sign of any entrance on their side.

'Maybe he's got a day job as a construction worker,' Ros said. She smiled at Beckett, then left the car and walked over to join Ed. Together they looked up at the lowering building, still not believing they'd come to the right place. After a moment, Ed started off in one direction and Ros in another. Within a minute, they had both vanished around their respective corners.

Beckett glanced at his watch. If they weren't back in three minutes, he'd have to go in and rescue them.

They were back in two, having crossed somewhere on the other side of the building. Ed was shaking his head. 'This is weird,' he said. 'There's no sign of any doors. Only thing we found was a chute for waste building materials coming down from the second floor into a skip, but I wouldn't fancy climbing up it.'

Beckett looked to Ros for confirmation. She nodded. 'He's right, Beckett. There's no way in.'

'Perhaps they haven't built it yet,' Ed said brightly.

Ros glanced scornfully at him. 'You don't put up a tower block and forget to build an entrance.'

'I was only joking,' Ed muttered, crestfallen.

'There must be *some* way in,' Beckett said, gazing up the sheer side of the building towards the distant gridwork at the top.

Before anyone could reply, a deep rumble shook the air. Beckett glanced wildly around, trying to locate its source, but he couldn't see anyone or anything moving.

'Look,' Ed said, pointing. Beckett followed the direction of his arm. A section of the building's wall was sliding upward, then pivoting on some hidden hinge. Belatedly, Beckett noticed that a section of road led from that area of wall to a point near where they were parked.

The moving wall vanished, leaving a square of darkness.

The rumble stopped.

Faintly, but getting louder, they heard a car approach from within. Twin searchlights suddenly blinded them, cutting swathes through the air, then the lights dipped as the car breasted the underground ramp and levelled out on the short spur of road. It was a sleek, smooth, executive limousine. Obviously expensive. Obviously fast.

Two men sat in the front seats.

One had a face that was all hard angles and flat planes – the sort of face that always needed a shave.

The other was Colonel Easterhaus.

As the car purred past, Easterhaus turned to look at the three of them. Beckett turned his head away. He was the only one that the colonel would recognise.

'I don't like to say I told you so,' he murmured as the car sped into the distance, 'but . . .'

« Four »

'Quick,' Beckett said, 'get down there before the entrance closes up again.'

Leaving the jeep, the three of them sprinted together down the ramp. They emerged into a cavernous underground parking area. Sunlight streaming in through the entrance cast their shadows across rank upon rank of empty parking bays. The white markings on the floor, unmarked by the passage of tyre treads, reminded Beckett eerily of a circuit-board diagram.

With a deep rumble, the entrance shut behind them.

The shadows closed in.

'No lights,' Ed said. 'There aren't any lights down here.'

'Well spotted,' Beckett murmured. The only illumination was the red sunlight that filtered in through narrow ventilation grilles and cast crosshatched shadows over the floor. Motes of dust danced in the beams of light. When the sun set, they would be in darkness.

Spotting a thick pillar in the centre of the cavern, Beckett walked briskly towards it. The other two followed. As he got closer, Beckett realised that the pillar was the base of a lift-shaft. The walls of the shaft were made of concrete. No signs saying where they were.

No signs saying where they should go. All very bare.

Beckett walked around the lift-shaft until he found the lift doors. They were recessed several feet into the concrete. A single button sat in a dimple. It wasn't labelled. A thin strip of metal ran around the concrete doorway and across the floor. It was impossible to get to the doors, or even press the button, without crossing the metal strip.

'What do you reckon, Ros?' he said, indicating the strip. 'Alarm system?'

Ros removed a small box from a poacher's pocket in her raincoat and waved it near the strip. 'No power. If it *is* an alarm, it's not switched on.'

Ed reached out and pressed the lift button. Nothing happened. No motor whirred into life. No lights came on.

Ros waved her box across the button and the area surrounding the lift doors. 'The power's completely off,' she said. 'Or not connected yet. Either way, we're stuck.'

'There must be some kind of power,' Beckett pointed out. 'That door at the top of the ramp was automatic, remember?'

'Probably on a different circuit.'

'You know what's weird?' Ed said suddenly.

'No, Ed,' Beckett replied patiently, 'what?'

'No stairs. Anywhere.'

Beckett glanced around. It hadn't occurred to him, but Ed was right. The only thing built into the pillar was the lift-shaft. From where he stood he could see the majority of the walls around the edges of the car park, and apart from the ramp they'd all come down, there was no break.

'Isn't that against fire regulations?' he asked.

'Depends how much you pay for your fire regulations,' Ros replied grimly.

'You know what else is weird?' Ed asked.

'No, Ed,' Beckett and Ros chorused. 'What?'

'That.' He nodded towards the top of the lift doors, where a small, black, metal object sprouted from the concrete lintel. It was only a few inches across, and looked like an upside-down mushroom.

'Part of the security system?' Ros ventured, waving her box of tricks at it. 'Radar sensor, maybe? Well, it's no more alive than anything else in this place.'

'Except us,' Beckett pointed out. He looked closer at the mushroom – or, rather, at the area of the lift doors just behind it. There was a small hole in the centre of the metal jamb. Reaching into his pocket, he removed a metal tool.

'What's that?' Ed asked.

'It's a widget,' he replied, inserting it into the hole.

'Silly of me to ask,' Ed muttered.

With a bit of wiggling, Beckett felt the widget engage with the lift's door-locking mechanism. 'All lift engineers carry them, just in case the doors get stuck or –'

'– or the power goes off,' Ros finished. 'So what are you doing with one? Scared you might get trapped in a lift with a beautiful woman?'

Beckett twisted the widget. The doors slid open half an inch, revealing nothing but a slice of blackness.

'Scared I might not be,' he muttered as he strained at the widget. The doors groaned, and the gap widened a few inches more.

Ed closed his hands over Beckett's, and together the two of them heaved at the locking mechanism. The doors held for a moment, then slid all the way open. The shaft was empty, apart from a loop of metal cable that hung just above their heads, parallel tracks attached to the walls on either side of the door and a set of rungs like large staples that led upward on the far side.

Ed fished a penlight out of his pocket and shone it

up into the darkness. He leaned into the lift-shaft and looked up. 'Goes up for ever,' he said, his voice echoing back to them. He looked down. 'And there's another two levels below us.'

'The lift's probably at the top,' Beckett said.

'Something's got power.' Ros was frowning as she waved her box inside the lift-shaft. Beckett could see a red light flashing on it.

'Yeah, there's a light up there,' Ed said. He clamped his hand onto the metal door surround and leaned further into the shaft.

'But,' Beckett pointed out, 'we can't check it out if the lift isn't working.'

'Yes we can,' Ed said, smiling. He pulled himself back into the car park. 'There's a service ladder in the shaft.' Taking two steps back, he suddenly ran at the shaft.

'Ed, no!' Ros shouted. Her voice reverberated around the cavernous space.

Ed reached the lip of the shaft and jumped, sailing across the gap and landing neatly on the rungs. His knees flexed, absorbing the impact. One hand closed on a rung. The other was still holding the penlight.

Ros glared at him. 'Ed, it's a thirty-storey building!'

'Shouldn't be a problem for a school sports champion,' he taunted.

'No way, guys,' Ros said, shaking her head. 'I'm not climbing up there just on the off-chance that someone's at home. No *way*.'

'Come on, Ros, where's your sense of adventure?' Beckett said.

'That's not adventure, that's sheer stupidity.'

'OK, where's your sense of stupidity?' he responded quickly.

'Come on,' Ed said, grinning back at them. 'Last one to the top's a drongo!'

He clamped the penlight between his teeth and

began to climb. Within a few moments he had vanished up into the shaft. The illumination from the penlight flickered as his head moved.

Ros and Beckett exchanged glances. Beckett gestured towards the shaft. 'After you, champ,' he said.

Ros leapt lithely across the shaft. Her raincoat billowed out behind her like a superhero's cloak. She quickly shinned out of Beckett's way. After a last look around the car park, he too made the leap into the unknown.

Beckett tried to count the rungs as his hands closed around them, but after a few minutes he gave up. Ros's heels moved with metronomic precision a few inches from his face. Looking past the flapping hem of her raincoat, he could see the shaft receding to infinity above them. The only illumination came from the penlight that Ed was holding between his teeth.

By the time Beckett had passed ten floors his calf muscles were burning and his breath was hissing in his ears. The metal of the rungs was cold and hard, cutting into the palms of his hands. He looked down, and a small shudder ran through him as he realised he couldn't see the bottom of the shaft. The rails, the rungs and the dangling lift cable all dwindled into the distance and met at a point that seemed infinitely far away.

'I'm sure Easterhaus didn't go up and down this way,' he called in an effort to distract his mind.

Ros's voice floated down from above. 'Perhaps he was never in the building.'

'You mean he was just sitting in the car park?' Beckett yelled back. 'I don't think so, somehow.'

By the time he passed the fifteenth floor, Beckett could feel the thudding of his pulse in his temples and neck. His hands were throbbing and slicked with sweat. He didn't dare think about what would happen if he lost his grip.

'How's your fear of heights, Beckett?' Ros called.

'I do not have a fear of heights,' he shouted back. His voice reverberated back and forth inside the concrete throat of the shaft. He paused, and rested his forehead against the cool metal of the next rung. 'Just of falling,' he said to himself.

Ros must have heard him. 'You know what they say: it's not the fall that kills you –'

'It's the sudden stop when you hit the ground,' he finished. Beckett smiled, despite himself, and started to climb again.

Time and consciousness seemed to fade away for a long while. Beckett's body kept on climbing, but his mind drifted somewhere else. Somewhere warm and quiet. With a sudden shock, he realised that they were passing the twentieth floor. The last time he had looked, they were at the sixteenth. Had he been asleep?

His muscles were screaming with fire, but he forced himself to keep moving. He desperately wanted to rest for a moment and catch his breath, but he knew that if he stopped he would probably never get moving again. He would remain frozen on the side of the shaft until his fingers slipped and he plummeted to his death, or until the power was switched back on and the lift started its descent, scraping him off the rungs.

Occupied with his morbid thoughts, Beckett didn't notice that Ros had stopped until her heel poked into his eye.

'Ow!'

'Ssh!' Ros whispered. 'Listen . . . sounds like electrical equipment.'

Looking up, Beckett saw that Ros's body was outlined by sterile white light. Ed appeared to have paused by an opening in the shaft. He'd switched his penlight off and slipped it back into a pocket.

Ros was resting just below him, her elbow hooked through one of the rungs.

Beckett did the same. 'What's going on?' he hissed.

'Lift doors have been opened on this floor and the next one up,' Ed replied. 'There are lights on both floors, but I can't hear anybody. You two check this floor – I'll go up to the next one.'

'Ed,' Ros called, 'keep your radio with you just in case we need to talk to you.'

Ed waved a dismissive hand, then climbed on up to the next level.

Ros followed as far as the opening, then leapt across the shaft and into the square of light. Beckett heard her hit the floor and slide on her stomach.

'Very graceful,' he called.

'Let's see you do better, Nijinsky,' she snapped back, winded.

There was a scramble from above. When Beckett looked to see what it was, Ed had vanished.

He forced his muscles to pull him the last few feet. When he was on a level with the entrance he turned and manoeuvred himself so that he was facing it. Ros was just a dark silhouette against the light. There was a large '22' stencilled in white paint on the wall by the door. 'Better move out of the way,' he called across. 'I'm coming through!'

Beckett crouched as well as he could on the rungs, then sprang across the gap, hands outstretched. As soon as they passed across the threshold of the floor, he tucked himself in to execute a perfect forward roll and spring to his feet before an astonished Ros.

At least, that was the theory.

In reality, he mistimed his leap and managed to catch his heel on the rung as he went. Visions of him cartwheeling into the side of the doorway and bouncing off down the shaft filled his mind, but he somehow managed to fly through the gap sideways and sprawl backwards across the floor.

Ros stared down at him, a tight little smirk on her

face. 'Nine point nine for style, nought point nine for content,' she said, extending a hand to pull Beckett to his feet.

Beckett gazed around the twenty-second floor as he brushed himself off. It seemed to be the same size as the car park beneath the building, and just as unused. Pillars blocked most of his view across the floor, but what he could see looked like a building site. Glowing light fittings hung from the skeleton of a suspended ceiling. Carpet tiles were interrupted every few yards by cable-run trenches. A cold breeze suggested that the windows hadn't yet been glazed.

'Look.' Ros indicated a CCD camera suspended by a bracket from a pillar. Beckett recognised the torchlike affair attached to it as an infra-red searchlight.

Ros moved closer, taking care to remain outside the camera's line of sight, and pointed her power indicator at it. The little red light failed to illuminate. 'It's all right,' she said, turning to Beckett. 'It's dead.'

Beckett frowned. 'Strange thing to put into a half-finished building, isn't it?'

Ros nodded. 'That's not all that's weird.' She pointed across the room. A pillar was in the way, and Beckett shifted position.

'Interesting,' was all he could think of to say.

An area of floor had been set aside as a small gymnasium. Beckett spotted a weightlifting bench, a running machine, a rowing machine and a multi-gym. Beyond them, sheets of translucent plastic hung from the incomplete ceiling. They linked four pillars, forming a tentlike space. Pearly light spilled out from inside.

Beckett swapped glances with Ros. He nodded towards the tent. She shrugged. He took the lead walking towards a gap where two of the plastic sheets met.

A noise began to intrude at the edges of Beckett's

attention: a hoarse, regular wheeze, like a pump that was badly in need of repair.

And as he got closer still he could hear another noise.

Beep.

Beep.

Beep.

Ed gazed around the twenty-third floor. It was, if anything, even more unfinished than what little he'd seen of the floor below through the open doorway. Most of the carpet tiles were missing, and only half the lights had been fitted. He guessed it would take most of a week of full-time work to get it to a habitable state.

Except . . .

Except that a tower computer unit sat beside a desk in the centre of the floor. A cable connected it to a recessed power socket in the floor. Humming optical disk units clustered around it. The computer monitor and keyboard sat on the desk itself. The monitor looked, to Ed's untutored eye, to be a high-resolution job, of the type they used in architects' offices.

An executive leather chair in front of the desk looked tempting, especially after the climb. Ed walked closer and fell backwards into it.

Bliss. Sheer bliss.

A fax machine and a modem sat on the desk next to the monitor and a pile of floppy disks. A telephone was almost buried beneath a pile of photographs. He reached out to sort through them. They seemed to be photographs of towns taken from an aeroplane. Or a satellite. Routes had been marked on them in Chinagraph pencil, as if someone was planning an expedition. He leafed through the pile to see whether any of the photographs had any keys or legends on them, but apart from the marked roads and paths they were annoyingly blank.

That left the computer.

If Ros could pull data from Hunter's system then Ed could do the same with this one. They'd be proud of him.

He reached down and switched the tower unit on. The hard disk hummed into life. The monitor flickered with rainbow colours, then settled down into a set of self-test instructions. Ed leaned back in the chair, enjoying the rest.

A red light was flashing on the modem. Was there some sort of call coming in? Or going out?

The red light went out. Ed relaxed. Probably some kind of automatic back-up procedure that he'd started by accident. Nothing to worry about. No alarms were going off.

The monitor flashed through the usual operating-system prompt and began to load a program. A screenful of text flashed up, too quickly for Ed to follow, and then the screen flashed twice and displayed a computer-generated landscape. An urban landscape. Textured geometrical solids for buildings, a flat blue sky, green spheres on brown sticks for trees.

Ed smiled. He couldn't help himself. It was like one of those computer games in which you have to move around a complicated location of some sort, blasting anything that moved – monsters or aliens or guys with guns. He loved those games. He particularly liked getting up close to the monsters with a rocket-launcher and watching them splatter across the floor when they got hit, or machine-gunning them until the tops of their heads blew off. Ros said that the games were a prostitution of what computers should be used for, but Ed didn't care. It wasn't like it was real. Just fun.

Experimentally he pressed one of the cursor keys. The point of view on the screen moved forward. He rotated, and found he could see down a grey tarmac road. No sign of any weapons or ammunition or power-ups. Obviously a bit of exploration was called for. Rotating his point of view in the other direction he found an imposing building. Plenty of monsters in there, he guessed. Looked like this Easterhaus enjoyed a bit of relaxation whenever he took a break from the mercenary business. Good on him.

Ed pulled the radio out of his jacket. 'Guys, I think I've found the games room,' he whispered. 'This Easterhaus has got what looks like a shoot-'em-up game on his system. I wouldn't mind a copy myself.'

'Ed,' Ros said, her voice sounding stressed, 'I'm sure you think what you've found is important, but you aren't looking at what *we've* found. This is spooky . . .'

'I'll finish up up here and come down,' Ed said, and stashed the radio away. He was just about to get up from the chair when he noticed the pile of floppy disks. If he was lucky, there'd be a copy of whatever game Easterhaus was running. If not, there might be something that Ros and Beckett could use to tell them more about what was going on.

He stashed the disks in a convenient pocket and began to look for the command to switch the game off.

Down in the car park, the door across the entrance ramp suddenly rumbled into life. A knife-edged beam of late-afternoon sunlight cut across the pristine floor and opened into a wedge as the gap widened.

A car purred down the ramp and across to the lifts. The door shut behind it. The car's headlights came to life, illuminating the open door and the empty lift-shaft.

In the car, Colonel Easterhaus held a small electronic device. A red light was flashing on it.

'Still think it's a false alarm, Hex?' he asked.

The man beside him shook his head. 'I'm sorry, Colonel. I assumed –'

'Never assume anything,' Easterhaus said. 'You'll end up dead one day.'

He opened the passenger-side door and climbed out. Hex switched the ignition off and joined him. They stood together in front of the open lift doors. Easterhaus aimed his device at the mushroom-shaped sensor and pressed a recessed button. The device made no noise, but a flicker of light ran around the roof of the car park as the neon tubes sprang to life one after another. Somewhere below their feet, a deep rumble started up as generators awoke.

And, inside the shaft, the lift started to descend.

Beckett held one plastic sheet back while Ros held the other. Together they looked through the gap.

Four hospital beds were arranged in a cross between the four pillars. Each had a rack of monitoring equipment beside it. The equipment on the racks hummed gently to itself as it took blood pressures, monitored oxygen levels and pumped various solutions through tubes. The beeping that Beckett had heard came from the four monitors as they displayed the glowing peaks and troughs of cardiac activity.

And each bed was occupied by an unmoving body, wrapped in silver thermal blankets.

Beckett ducked through the gap between the sheets. Ros followed. They approached the nearest bed from opposite sides.

They both recognised the body at the same time.

'This is the kid Ed fought with – the one who collapsed,' Ros said, her voice low. 'Jason Rupta.'

Beckett nodded. 'Still alive, at least.'

'Yeah, but he should be in a hospital.' Ros turned to the bed behind her.

Beckett walked around Rupta's bed to join her. He only had time to register the battered, bloodied face on the pillow before Ros took an involuntary step backwards.

'And this is the man who chased me,' she said bitterly. 'Kane. I thought he was *dead*!'

Beckett patted her shoulder reassuringly. 'Maybe not, but he's not in a position to do any chasing for a while.' He walked around to a position between the other two beds. 'I don't recognise these two. Must be previous victims of tri-meserone – Doctor De Freitas's missing students. All hidden away from the authorities. Very convenient.'

Ros moved closer to Kane's equipment rack and read the label on one of the bags of solution hanging from it. 'They're being sedated,' she said. 'And it's a powerful sedative as well. Presumably they're being kept here for Hunter to experiment on.'

'Looks like it.' Beckett repressed a shudder. He didn't like hospitals and he didn't like heights, and this place combined both his fears into one.

The lights flickered. From the direction of the lift-shaft, Beckett heard the sound of the doors slamming shut and the lift motor whirring into life.

His radio squawked, and he pulled it out of his jacket. 'Ed?'

'Beckett. Ros, was that you two jokers?'

Beckett had a bad feeling, but he had to ask. 'Why, what happened?'

'I think someone paid the electricity bill. Everything's come to life up here – lights, motors, cameras – and the lift doors closed.'

Beckett walked over to the gap in the plastic sheeting and peered across at the video camera by the closed lift doors. A little light was glowing on it, and it was slowly turning to scan the room. He ducked back before it saw him. 'Nothing to do with us, Ed. I think the mysterious tenant has come back.' He looked at Ros. She nodded. 'Let's get out fast.'

Beckett stowed the radio away and headed towards the lift-shaft. Ros ran after him and caught his shoulder. He paused, glancing at her questioningly.

'Not that way. Someone's already using it,' she pointed out.

She was right. An LED display above the door indicated that the lift was in the basement.

And, as Beckett watched, it started to rise.

Not a lot of choices left.

'Come on,' Ros snapped, pulling Beckett away from the lift-shaft and towards the edge of the building. The forest of pillars meant that the windows were invisible. There might be another lift-shaft over there. Or a stairwell. Or something. At a pinch they could wait until whoever was using the lift emerged, then nip around the other side of the shaft and get in. Just so long as Ros didn't suggest climbing down the outside of the building.

'Hey, guys – the lift's stopped at my floor,' Ed's voice crackled from the radio. 'Someone's got out.'

'I hope you're not hanging around to find out who it is,' Beckett said as he and Ros made their way across the floor, hopping over cable-run trenches.

'No way. I'm trying to find another way out of here. There must be one.'

'Yeah,' Beckett muttered, 'but where?'

A cold breeze cooled Beckett's face, and through a gap between two pillars he caught sight of a bruised purple glow. The windows? It was a fair bet. 'Over there!' he cried, pulling Ros in that direction.

From behind, he heard the whine of the lift coming to a halt. He paused, and looked back. There was a direct path between two lines of pillars, leading right back to the lift doors.

Beckett moved out of sight behind the nearest pillar. Ros did the same.

Nothing happened for a moment.

The lift doors opened and a man stepped out. He was wearing a black leather jacket. He didn't look worried; he didn't look angry; he didn't look scared. He didn't even look tense. He just looked very, very professional.

And he was holding a gun with silencer and a laser sight attached.

« Five »

'Beckett – look!'

Following Ros's urgently pointing finger, Beckett could see scarlet streamers of cloud against a darkening sky. 'Very pretty, Ros,' he whispered, 'but can we get away from the goon with the gun before appreciating the beauties of nature?'

'No, Beckett – *look*!'

He looked closer. His view was chopped into strips by the pillars, but to one side of the glassless windows he could just make out a stretch of wall. It was difficult to be sure, but it looked like there might be a darker door set into the wall.

'Fire escape?' he hazarded.

'It's either that or the restrooms.'

Beckett glanced back at the man standing outside the lift-shaft. He was looking towards the plastic-sheeted hospital beds, his head cocked in a listening position. 'Go!' Beckett hissed, and Ros sprinted towards the windows and the possible door. Halfway there she turned and gave him a quick thumbs-up. He launched himself into action, trying to plan his path to keep as many pillars between him and the man with the gun as possible. It wasn't Easterhaus, so Beckett reckoned it was the driver from the car. That meant Easterhaus was probably on the floor above, looking for Ed.

He arrived at the door, panting. There was nothing on it to say whether it was a fire escape or not. Perhaps the builders hadn't got around to putting the signs on yet. Or perhaps it wasn't a fire escape.

Ros pushed it open and slipped through. Beckett joined her on a bare concrete balcony that projected out into a square shaft. A railing ran around the edge, following the line of a stairway that led upwards and downwards. Beckett leaned against the railing and followed the stairway as it spiralled dizzyingly away from him. 'Why couldn't we find these stairs on the way up?' he complained.

'Because that would have been too easy,' Ros replied.

Beckett led the way down to the next landing. Rescuing his radio from his pocket, he said, 'Ed, there's a staircase in the –'

'Southwest,' Ros said.

'– Southwest corner of the building. Follow the wall until –'

'I found it too,' a voice said from behind them. Beckett whirled, his heart pounding. Ed was standing on the landing they'd just left, grinning. Didn't he ever worry?

Ros's hands and teeth were clenched. 'Ed, if you ever do that again I'll throw you off the edge and let you take the quick way down.'

'Fair dos,' Ed protested, 'I was only trying to cheer you up. Come on – let's get going.' He took the steps two at a time, overtaking Ros and Beckett and vanishing towards the floor below.

'One day –' Ros murmured.

'Let's get out of here first,' Beckett said. 'Then we can argue over who gets a crack at him first.'

Together they raced after Ed, past level after level. Twenty . . . nineteen . . . eighteen . . . seventeen . . .

Beckett's feet throbbed with the repeated impact against the concrete, and his head spun with the constant turns.

Sixteen . . . fifteen . . . fourteen . . .

A sound, above them. A door banging open. Feet scuffling on concrete. A voice – 'Hex, they've found the stairs. We can pick them off at our leisure.'

Thirteen . . . twelve . . . eleven . . .

Pain shot up Beckett's arm every time he clamped his fingers on the railing. His muscles were spasming because of the repeated exercise. It was only a matter of time before he got a cramp in his calf muscles, and then he'd be reduced to a hobble.

Ten . . . nine . . . eight . . .

Beckett's vision was misting over with a red haze. 'What we need,' he hissed, 'is some tri-meserone.'

Ros barked a short, agonised laugh. 'Don't even joke about it,' she said.

Sudden hysteria bubbled up like lava within him. 'Who's joking?' he muttered to himself.

Seven . . . six . . . five . . .

A quiet thud, like someone punching their hand through wet cardboard, made him flinch. The railing next to his hand suddenly exploded into sparks. There was a *spang* sound and a bullet buried itself into a concrete wall.

'Keep away from the side,' he gasped. 'They're firing on us.'

Four . . . three . . . two . . .

Beckett's mind suddenly went blank. What came after two? He couldn't think through the pounding of blood in his skull. For heaven's sake, what came after two?

It didn't matter. There wasn't a next floor. The stairwell ended in a blank concrete wall.

'That's why we couldn't find it in the car park,' Ros hissed. She was bending over, her hands on her thighs. Even Ed was sweating. Although they had stopped,

80

Beckett could feel the entire stairwell rotating steadily around him like the world's biggest merry-go-round ride.

'Up!' Ed shouted, and began to sprint back up the stairs.

'What?' Beckett was lost.

'We have to get out on the second floor before whoever's chasing us gets down to it!' Ed called back.

Beckett and Ros scrambled back up the stairs, clutching their hands around the railing to pull themselves up. By the time they got up to the door Ed was holding it open. Footsteps were rattling like machine-gun fire on the concrete a few levels above. Beckett's heart was pumping so hard that he could feel the throb of blood in his fingers as he closed them around the cold metal rail.

'Quick,' Ed urged. The three of them tumbled through the doorway –

– and into what looked like an impromptu security control centre. Row upon row of television monitors displayed empty floors, empty stairwells, empty lifts. Five of them showed the car park from various angles. Some of the screens seemed to be showing their scenes in infra-red, others as a microwave radar picture. Cables snaked off in all directions across the floor. The whole thing looked as though it had been recently installed by someone who was concerned with functionality rather than permanence.

Ed sprinted between the rows, looking for an exit. Beckett and Ros followed, but Beckett paused for a moment, looking back at the door.

'What is it?' Ros asked breathlessly.

'Delaying tactics,' Beckett said. Grabbing one of the monitors, he picked it up bodily and threw it towards the door. The equipment shattered as it hit the floor, scattering sparks and circuit boards across the carpet. 'Right, let's go.'

As they ran after Ed, Ros panted, 'That was a Sol Graphics Twenty-Nine Fifty, Beckett. Even *I* can't afford one of those, and you destroyed it!'

'Rather it than me,' he snapped.

On cue, the door from the stairwell was wrenched open behind them. Beckett turned to see Easterhaus and his thuggish colleague rush through. Easterhaus's gun was aimed straight at Beckett. He knew that he was imagining it, but he could feel the warmth of the laser-aiming spot centred between his eyes.

Easterhaus's foot caught the wreckage of the monitor and he pitched forward as the gun went off. The shot went wild, shattering a nearby monitor with an explosive crash. Easterhaus's colleague tried to backpedal, but succeeded only in falling across Easterhaus as the colonel was trying to get up. Beckett grinned, and ran on.

He found Ed and Ros across the other side of the second floor. Ed was standing by the windows. They were glazed on this floor, but one of them had been removed and replaced with one end of a blue plastic chute. God knew where the other end was.

Ros was scrambling into the chute.

'It's our only chance, Beckett,' Ed said. 'Go for it.'

As Ros disappeared from sight, Beckett speeded up and aimed himself at the opening. He heard a shout behind him. A red laser dot skidded across a nearby window for a split second, then the window burst outward as a bullet hit the centre of the dot.

Beckett dived into the chute.

For a few seconds Beckett felt like he'd taken refuge in a blue tumble-drier, then he shot out of the chute and into the open air. A confused morass of buildings, road and purple sky spun in his vision, then he landed in a skip full of bricks. Agony shot through from a hundred sharp edges.

Hands pulled him to the side of the skip.

'Out of the way!' Ros yelled. 'Ed's coming through!'

Beckett pitched out of the skip like a diver falling out of a boat. The tarmac hurt, but not as much as the bricks.

Ed clattered into the skip with a curse. The breath rushed out of him with an audible *whooomph!*

Catching his breath, Beckett tried to orientate himself. They were outside the building, and on the opposite side from the jeep. The sun was a red circle, just touching the horizon. The sky was the colour of an old bruise.

Two shadows appeared in the window by the waste-material chute.

'I think,' Beckett said, 'we should get to the jeep sharpish.'

They got.

Easterhaus stood by the window, watching the three intruders vanish around the corner. Hex stood by his shoulder. Easterhaus's finger tightened on the trigger of his gun, but he knew it would be worthless. He couldn't have hit all three of them before they vanished, and killing just one would have been pointless.

Options sorted themselves out in his mind. He could send Hex after them, but they would be long gone by the time he got down there. He could move the subjects to one of the subsidiary bases, but they were so near completion of the mission that he was reluctant to do that. Besides, he wasn't going to take precipitate action until he knew who or what he was fighting.

'Should I go after them, sir?' Hex asked.

Easterhaus shook his head. 'Who are they?' he snapped.

'Freelancers,' Hex said. 'Surveillance experts brought in by Doctor De Freitas. I found a camera in the auditorium, and two bugs in Doctor Hunter's office.'

83

'Well-meaning amateurs who want to keep sport clean and gentlemanly,' Easterhaus sneered. 'They're not allied to any official organisation. We can ignore them. Did you remove the bugs?'

Hex shook his head. 'I thought it best to leave them in place until I talked to you, sir.' He hesitated. 'They may be working for the academy,' he cautioned, 'but I don't think we should underestimate them.'

The faint noise of a revved engine drifted around the edge of the building. It faded, and was gone.

'Tri-meserone is going to make us a breed apart,' Easterhaus said quietly. 'An utterly invincible army. Our enemies will be crushed under foot like insects. We have no need to worry about amateurs.'

'If they're amateurs, how did they find us here so quickly?' Hex asked.

Easterhaus tried to find a confident comeback, but he couldn't.

When she woke up, Jessica Belhampstead found herself strapped to a table in a darkened room.

She tried to remember how she had come to be there, but the details were blurry. She had been working late, sitting at her desk and going over the accounts again, trying to get the bottom line out of the red. She had packed up around sunset and walked out through empty corridors to her car. Empty because her staff had gone home, and empty because she'd had to lay so many of them off. She had deactivated the alarm, opened the door and slipped behind the wheel. The last thing she remembered doing was deciding to get a takeaway chicken tikka masala on the way home rather than defrost something in the microwave. After that, nothing.

But the back of her neck hurt like hell.

Had someone hit her from behind? Had she passed out and hit her head? Where the hell was she?

She glanced around, trying to keep her neck as still as possible, but the room she was in was as blurry as her recent memories. Her first thought was that she was strapped to a hospital bed, but it didn't smell like a hospital. And besides, why would they strap her down unless she was insane?

Cold terror washed over her and left her weak and shaking. Had she gone mad? Had they locked her up and strapped her down for her own safety? Was she in an asylum?

No. She could still taste the coffee she had bolted down before leaving the office. She was still wearing the same trouser suit. Whatever else had happened, she had been unconscious only a short time. Relief made her feel slightly sick.

As her eyes adjusted to the darkness of the room, Jessica began to make out the sketchy outline of something hanging over her head. Something bulky and cylindrical that reflected what scant light there was. And details of the room itself were coming into focus now: the suspended ceiling and the outline of a glass window high in one wall. It was familiar, so terribly familiar, but she couldn't place it. It was a little like catching sight of herself by accident reflected in a shop window and knowing she knew the face from somewhere.

It was only when she tried to picture the view from the room behind the glass window that she realised where she was. The room was in her own building: it was the cleanroom housing the high-power, focusing, electron-beam generator.

She hadn't recognised it straight away because she wasn't used to the view from where she was, strapped to the bench of the electron-beam generator, directly beneath its sharp end. Normally it was used for micro-etching circuit boards under conditions of extreme cleanliness. If she was there, wearing her everyday clothes, without a facemask, then something was seriously wrong.

Of course, a little part of her mind replied, if she was strapped to the bench beneath a device that focused electrons to a point that achieved temperatures approaching that of the sun's outer layers, there was something seriously wrong anyway.

'Ms Belhampstead,' a voice purred in the darkness. A vaguely familiar voice with the trace of a foreign accent. 'So pleased you're awake.'

'Who are you and what the *hell* is going on?' she shouted, her fear manifesting itself as a corrosive anger. It had got her into trouble before, but she'd never expected it would get her into *this* much trouble.

The voice chuckled. 'My name is Patrick Marcel. You may remember we spoke on the telephone. I made an offer for your company. You were rude to me. *Very* rude.'

Was that what this was – revenge? Her heart sank further with every word he spoke. If he was willing to tell her who he was then he didn't expect her to be in a position to tell anyone else. She felt like screaming, but instead she spat, 'That wasn't an offer, it was an insult. If I'd accepted it I'd have had to sign control of my company over to you. That's not what I spent years of my life working to achieve.'

'Neither is bankruptcy, Ms Belhampstead. Circuit-board production is such a perilous business, and the burning down of a resin factory in Hong Kong can bring a company on the other side of the world to the brink of collapse. We offer protection. We offer security.' The voice paused. 'More to the point, we offer you your life. Think carefully, but don't think for too long. My brother's finger is on the controls of this little electron-beam device, and he's just aching to try it out.'

She remembered seeing the beam at work: a searing light too bright to look at except through heavily polarised goggles. 'You wouldn't dare. *He* wouldn't dare.'

'I assure you, Ms Belhampstead, he would. He could quite happily spend hours on this machine, tracing patterns on your skin.'

'But why?' she asked. 'I've tried everything to make this company viable. I've worked as hard as it's possible to work, and it didn't make any difference. It's still going to fail. The competition's too intense: the big boys have got the market sewn up and the little people like me just can't find a way to break their monopoly. What makes you think you can do any better?'

'Inside knowledge,' the voice said. 'I foresee some changes ahead, and I want to be in the best position to take advantage of them. That means I need your firm.'

She thought for a while. She shoved her anger and her fear down deep inside, and she considered her options, one by one. Not that there were many options to consider. Eventually she said, in a weary tone, 'OK, unstrap me and give me a pen. I assume you have something for me to sign.'

'A simple form,' Patrick Marcel said happily. 'Simple and *quite* comprehensive.'

Back at the Gizmos offices, Ros loaded the floppy disks – the ones Ed had stolen – into a computer disk drive while Beckett and Ed went to fetch Doctor De Freitas. Beckett had argued against De Freitas's involvement, but Ros had pointed out that she was their customer after all, and deserved some sort of explanation of what was going on.

While they were gone, Ros played around with the software on the disk. It was crude landscape simulation, but there was something about it that bothered her. The sense that she was missing something flitted around her mind as she worked, disturbing her concentration and making her irritable. If either of the boys had been there, she would have snapped at him. As it was, all she could do was grumble at her own slowness under her breath.

She made herself a cup of coffee, and thought around the problem while the software sat and ran through a programmed loop on her screen. The point of view swooped along a boulevard, across a square and up to an impressive building, then flicked back to its starting point and repeated the sequence. By pressing a few keys Ros could break out of the pre-set sequence and go down any road, or move up into the air and hover over the city.

Pretty, but hardly cutting-edge stuff. Not worth killing someone for.

And how did it connect with tri-meserone?

She made herself another cup of coffee.

The software wasn't a game. Ros knew that because of the obvious lack of anything to play against. It looked more like a schematic someone had put together to plan out a new shopping centre or an inner-city regeneration scheme. But that wasn't it either. Ros had done her share of landscape simulation for customers in her time, and there was something wrong with this one. Not with the software itself, but with the size of the files.

She realised her second coffee had gone cold, so she made a third one.

Nobody built cities from scratch. Not using computer simulations. And besides, the landscape in the simulation wasn't changeable. What was the point of planning a city on computer if you couldn't change the size and placement of the buildings? And the files were too large. It had taken almost half an hour to load the simulation. That was twenty-eight minutes too long. The key to successful landscape simulation was to use a small set of bitmapped textures and repeated map elements to save space and speed up run-time.

So . . .

So the city was real. The files were so large because they were representing a real location, street by street, building by building. It wasn't a game, or an urban planning aid. It was a map. A fully interactive computer map.

Hadn't Ed said that there were satellite photographs on the desk where he'd found the disks? Easterhaus must have digitised the images and used them to build the city in the computer's memory.

But still the question: why?

Ros slipped a CD containing maps of all the world's cities into a separate but networked computer and set it running in parallel, trying to match the place in Easterhaus's simulation with a real location. The maps she had on the CD weren't anywhere near the same level of detail, of course, but all she needed was a coincidence of rivers, or shapes of major roads.

The computer found a match just as Beckett and Ed returned with Doctor De Freitas.

'At first, Ed thought this was a computer game,' Ros explained once they had all settled down, 'but it's actually a three-dimensional map of a city. I've scanned through our geographical database and matched it up.'

She gestured to the two screens, side by side. The computer running Ros's map CD showed a street plan. Ros could see, from the expressions on Beckett's and De Freitas's faces, that they recognised it. The computer running Easterhaus's software showed what was obviously the same city – the same roads, the same overall shape – but as if it were real and observed from above.

'Easterhaus must have had this modelled using satellite photography and some local knowledge,' Ros continued. 'Interestingly, look at the prominence given to government and military buildings.'

'It's a plan for a military coup,' Beckett said, frowning.

'Must be. The arrows that Ed saw on the satellite photographs indicate possible routes of advance.'

Ros nodded. 'And with this software he can try out those routes, checking for cover and possible obstructions. He can rehearse his attack time after time, until he's got the optimal route straight to the government building.'

'I did a little trawling through our databases,' Beckett said. 'The office block was financed by a big multinational bank. Construction started about a year ago. They got most of the superstructure in place and half the electrics fitted, but the bank got taken over, the new owners decided they wanted their headquarters somewhere else and the project got halted midway through the final stages of fitting the carpets and the furniture.'

'I remember something about that,' Ros interrupted. 'Didn't the new owners want to sell the building?'

'Yeah,' Beckett agreed, 'but apparently the whole thing's tied up in litigation at the moment – the contractors claim they're owed money, the new owners claim the project's way over budget, and nobody's entirely sure who owns it or who should pay the bills.'

Ed smiled. 'So Easterhaus moved in,' he said. 'A high-tech squatter.'

'He must have decided that it would make a good base of operations,' Beckett agreed. 'It's nice and central, and he's unlikely to be bothered or even noticed. He moved in and set up his various bits and pieces of equipment around the stuff that was already there, installed by the contractors before the money ran out. I guess from the outside that the building's meant to look unoccupied. That's why, when Hex and Easterhaus went out they left an alarm on but turned all the power off, to maintain the illusion that the place is empty. With the thing shut down, the only power is to the life-support systems for the injured athletes and the alarm. When we went in, we must have tripped that alarm.'

De Freitas obviously felt out of her depth. 'But . . . but what's this got to do with my sporting academy?' she asked, bewildered.

Ros opened her mouth to answer, but Ed beat her to it. 'It's the drug he's interested in, isn't it?' Ros nodded, and he continued, 'He's just using your students as guinea pigs.'

'Optimum soldiers,' Beckett said grimly, 'advancing along optimum routes. How can it fail?'

'What about Hunter?' Ed asked. 'Does he know what the drug is for?'

'I doubt it,' Ros said. 'He's a fool, but I don't think he's a criminal. And remember that telephone conversation we intercepted between him and Colonel Easterhaus? He didn't seem to know why Easterhaus wanted the drug perfected so quickly.'

De Freitas was shaking her head in disbelief. 'This is outrageous. It stops right now. I'm going straight to Hunter to tell him.'

'I'm coming with you,' Ros said.

De Freitas didn't say anything during the short drive to the International Sports Academy. Her jaw was clenched, and her knuckles were white against the steering wheel. Ros watched her in silence, impressed by the force of the woman's energy.

Ros felt a chill as she entered the building again. They'd replaced the glass in the roof and mopped Kane's blood off the floor, but she couldn't forget the terror she'd felt. The sheer gut-watering terror of being chased by an unstoppable force.

They found Hunter in his laboratory, slaving over a hot test-tube. Ros glanced around. There was no trace of her fight with Kane. It was as if it had never happened.

Hunter glanced up at them, grunted, then went back to his work.

'Hunter, I'm closing down the tri-meserone research programme,' De Freitas snapped.

Well, Ros thought, *full marks for bluntness.*

Hunter's eyebrows rose in comical astonishment. 'But . . . but you *can't*. Not now. Not when I'm on the verge of perfecting it.'

'But for what purpose?' Ros said.

Hunter swivelled to look at her and frowned, as if he had suddenly realised he didn't know who she was. 'What do you mean? It's designed to revive this country's sporting fortunes. To give us back the competitive edge we've lost.'

'By cheating?' Ros asked. 'You know how tight drug-testing is in sporting events.'

Hunter smiled, obviously proud of his baby. 'That's the beauty of tri-meserone: it's completely undetectable. We'll win everything there is!'

De Freitas shook her head in exasperation. 'Peter, it's *illegal*. And besides, it's dangerous. Look at the damage steroids can do.'

'But tri-meserone isn't like that.' Hunter's face was as innocent as a baby's. 'It's harmless.'

'Not for Jason Rupta,' Ros pointed out. 'Or Kane. Or the others.'

'I don't know what you're talking about.' Hunter turned away, folding his arms as if to block her words.

'Doctor Hunter, I've seen them: Jason and the other three. All unconscious.'

Hunter's face collapsed like a souffle. 'You've seen them? How?'

'You know that Colonel Easterhaus wants to use tri-meserone for military purposes, don't you?' Ros said provocatively.

Hunter's face travelled through surprise, concern, outrage and worry before battening down into an expression of exaggerated innocence. 'No, no, you've got that completely wrong. I have no idea what you're talking about.' He swivelled away as if the mere motion could dismiss them and allow him to return to his research. 'Easterhaus runs a peace foundation. They finance the tri-meserone testing programme for altruistic purposes. They believe that by promoting sport they can encourage peace in the world.'

Ros swivelled Hunter's chair back and planted her hands on the desk to either side of him. Her face was inches away from his. 'Believe me – Easterhaus has no interest in sport, or in peace come to that. He's planning a military takeover in his own country.'

Hunter's face flickered with uncertainty. Before he could respond, a voice from the doorway cut through the air. 'That's quite enough.'

Ros spun round. Colonel Easterhaus stood in the doorway, hands clasped behind his back as if he was on parade. The man he'd previously called Hex was at his shoulder.

'You really shouldn't give lectures on subjects you don't understand,' Easterhaus continued. His face was expressionless. 'Doctor Hunter, are you ready to begin the final testing?'

Hunter frowned. He didn't seem to want to meet the colonel's gaze. 'Yes . . .' he said uncertainly.

Doctor De Freitas scowled at Easterhaus. 'I've already told Doctor Hunter that the test programme is finished.'

Easterhaus shook his head slightly. 'It's not. And I've found a perfect guinea pig to test the new batch of tri-meserone on.' He brought his hand out from behind his back. There was a gun held in it. Without any dramatic flourishes or macho posturing, he pointed the gun at Doctor De Freitas's head.

'You're going to test the tri-meserone on Doctor De Freitas?' Hunter said. Ros couldn't tell whether he was shocked or intrigued by the idea.

'No.' Easterhaus jerked his head towards Ros. A shiver ran up her back, and she felt her heart thud heavily. 'On her.' His eyes met Ros's, and there was no compassion in them. No acknowledgement of her as a human being. Just a means to an end. 'Do as you're told,' he ordered, 'or I'll kill Doctor De Freitas.'

Ros shrugged. 'Doesn't look like I have much choice, does it?'

Easterhaus nodded at her sensible reaction. 'Good.' Turning slightly, he spoke over his shoulder to Hex. Ros tensed, ready to make a leap for his gun, but it didn't waver as he said, 'I'll take these ladies and Doctor Hunter to HQ. We can carry out the tests there without interruption.'

'But sir,' Hex said, 'the other two know about HQ. Won't they alert someone?'

'Your job is to stop them. You know what to do. Bait the trap and eliminate them both.'

Ros shuddered. It wasn't his orders that bothered her so much. It was the emotionless way he gave them.

Easterhaus noticed her reaction, and smiled for the first time. 'Don't get any clever ideas. I won't hesitate to kill you if I have to.'

And she believed him.

Ed tapped hesitantly at the keyboard. He didn't like computers. Not unless they were encased in large, garish boxes and running flight simulators or shoot-'em-ups. He could use them. Sure, Ros had bored him rigid with ROMs, RAMs, EPROMs and WORMs. He could trace a hardware interrupt in his sleep, and strip a PC down to its circuit boards almost as fast as he could disassemble a Harley. But he didn't *like* them. They weren't sexy. You couldn't feel the wind whipping past your ears when you used them.

The screen showed the city Easterhaus was planning to take over. Beckett had told Ed to 'walk' down all the streets and check whether there was anything unusual. Like Easterhaus's headquarters, or some hint of how he was going to pull off his plans. Ed had told Beckett how pointless it was, but Beckett had insisted, putting his jacket on, tossing his car keys up and catching them again, and grinning that infuriating grin of his. 'I'm going out,' he'd said. 'Have fun.'

The door slamming caught Ed's attention. 'Beckett?'

'Yeah.' Beckett strode into the workroom. He didn't look happy. 'I've been trying to warn the embassy.'

'And did they listen?' Ed asked, already knowing the answer from the look on Beckett's face.

'I only got as far as a junior trade attaché, which is what they call the guy who makes the coffee I think. He wouldn't listen to me. What he *did* tell me was that they've got a bit of a flap on at the moment. Their president's due here tomorrow on a state visit.'

'That explains the urgency then,' Ed said. 'Easterhaus must be planning the coup for while the guy's out of the country.'

Beckett nodded. 'And it's up to us to stop him,' he said, heavily. 'Any luck with the software –'

An insistent beep interrupted him. He and Ed turned to one of the many computers in the workroom. A message flashed onto the screen.

'Another call on Hunter's phone.' Beckett reached out and flicked a switch, transferring the call to the computer's speakers.

'Colonel Easterhaus, sir?'

'That's the Colonel's trained Dobermann,' Beckett said. 'What was his name? Hex?'

'Good news,' the voice continued. 'I'm with Doctor Hunter now. He believes that his work on tri-meserone is finally complete. He can now deliver what we want.'

Another voice crackled from the speakers. 'Good,' was all it said.

'Easterhaus,' Ed confirmed. Beckett nodded.

'I'll meet you at the Ninth Avenue station,' Hex said. 'I'll bring the whole new batch with me.'

95

'Excellent,' Easterhaus replied. 'What time?'

'One hour.'

'I'll see you there.'

The phone went dead.

Beckett glanced at Ed. 'Sounds like they've fixed the drug.'

Ed tried to suppress a smile. It was bad news, but it meant he didn't have to sit in front of the screen any more. 'Better check it out,' he said, trying to sound grim.

Beckett drove. Ed didn't mind too much. He was just glad to get out of the office.

It took them ten minutes to get to their destination. The Ninth Avenue station was part of the overhead railway network that acted as the backbone of the city. Beckett parked his jeep as close as he could get, with the station poised above them on ten concrete legs. Neon lights glittered off its curved metal and glass sections, making it shine in the darkness like a phosphorescent beetle. The overhead rail-track curved away from it in both directions: a solid ribbon of cloud hanging above the empty streets, shuttered shops and concrete walkways of the Ninth Street area. An escalator linked the station to the street below, a steep flight of moving metal encased in a toughened glass tube. It looked rather eerie to Ed, moving steadily with nobody around and little visible means of support.

The nearest leg of the station to the stairs also contained a lift, for those people worried about escalators. The doors were open at the bottom, spilling out a welcoming light, but after his experience climbing the shaft in the half-built office block Ed thought he might be developing a phobia about lifts. The escalator looked fine to him. A lot easier to climb if it stopped working.

As Beckett switched off the engine, a shower of sparks from above illuminated the scene with a fitful, jittery light. Ed flinched, thinking someone was firing at them, but the familiar screech of metal against metal told him that a train was just pulling into the station. He glanced up. The blue light from the train's interior spilled around the edges of the suspended track. Doors hissed open, then hissed closed a few moments later. Nobody got onto the escalator, and the lift doors remained open at the bottom of the concrete leg. The train pulled off, accelerating with a high-pitched whine.

Beckett got out of the jeep, his binoculars in his hand. He raised them to his eyes and slowly panned across the scene.

'Anything?' Ed asked, getting out of the car and joining Beckett. The wind cut into him, and he zipped up his leather jacket.

'Quiet as the grave.' Beckett passed the glasses over to Ed. 'We've got half an hour. Let's check the place out – try to find a vantage point where we can watch them meeting up.'

'And what then?' Ed asked as the two of them began the walk across the tarmac towards the bottom of the escalator.

'I don't know. Try and disrupt it, I suppose. Get the working batch of drug from them.'

Beckett stepped onto the escalator. Ed joined him. As the metal steps carried them up through the transparent tube, Ed turned and scanned the area. Apart from their vehicle, he couldn't see anything out of the ordinary. Just shuttered shops and empty streets.

'You know,' he said, 'this would be an ideal spot for an ambush.'

Beckett nodded. 'The thought had occurred.'

In the distance, a set of traffic lights suspended on a long arm over the street changed from green to red.

As if it were a signal, the glass behind them exploded into a blizzard of razor-edged shards.

« Six »

Ed and Beckett frantically scrambled up the escalator steps, barely ahead of the deadly wave of destruction.

A stuttering flash of light to one side caught Ed's attention. He glanced over the escalator rail and saw that a man had stepped out of the shadows. It was Hex, and he was carrying a matt-black assault rifle, complete with telescopic sights and silencer. The light that Ed had seen was the muzzle-flash of the gun as he hosed the stream of bullets up the escalator towards them.

Beckett had seen Hex too. He dropped to his hands and knees and scrambled towards the sanctuary of the station. Ed copied him. His hands hit the cold metal steps just as the glass tube above his head shattered into a million whirling fragments with a noise like Armageddon. Sharp slivers of toughened glass fell around and on top of him as he moved. It was like being inside a razor-blade snowstorm. He could feel the sting of cuts on his hands. Blood slicked the metal – crimson on silver.

And Ed slipped on a fragment of glass.

His shoulder hit the edge of the next step up, and a jagged spike of pain shot down his arm. The motion of the steps carried him forward as the final few feet of the tube exploded ahead of them. Beckett sprinted to the top of the steps and turned to see what had happened.

Ed tried to pull himself to his feet, but his arm gave way nervelessly beneath him. His cheek slammed down onto the ridged metal of the step. The escalator kept moving, and as Ed's head cleared the top of the rise he could see along the last few feet of escalator, where the steps were flattening down to form a level section . . .

Before vanishing beneath the sharp metal teeth of the anti-litter mechanism.

The remorseless motion of the escalator, like a waterfall in reverse, carried Ed towards the teeth. One of them was on a level with his eye. He tried to get his arm beneath him to push himself up, but he'd hit the nerve on the first stumble, and it wouldn't move.

The third step ahead of him slipped beneath the metal teeth, ready to make its return journey.

His entire body was laid out on the level section of escalator now. His feet scrabbled on the metal, but the glass fragments crunched and slid beneath them and he couldn't get any purchase.

The second step ahead abruptly vanished from sight.

And then Beckett was leaning down towards Ed, his hands burrowing beneath his jacket, taking Ed's weight before he yanked Ed away from the end of the escalator and pulled him onto the safety of the station.

Ed quickly glanced around as he caught his breath. They were at the beginning of a short walkway, shielded from Hex by a metal arch at the top of the escalator. The rest of the walkway was glass. No balcony. No protection. Just fifteen feet of concrete floor shielded by another toughened-glass tunnel. And then the safety of the station.

Behind them the escalator was open to the cold night air. Steadily, shards of glass were being piled up at their feet by the motion of the steps.

Hex had stopped firing. Probably waiting for them to come out of cover. He knew they couldn't stay where they were for ever. Backward or forward; either way he had them.

Ed looked at Beckett. Beckett looked at Ed. They both looked along the walkway.

'You think we can make it?' Ed said through his gasps for breath.

'I'm not the fifteen hundred metres champion,' Beckett replied. 'But what option do we have?'

'Count of three?'

Beckett nodded. 'Count of three.'

'One –' Ed said, tensing.

'Two –' Beckett responded.

'Three!' they shouted together, and burst out onto the walkway, accelerating as fast as they could towards the station, feet pounding in time with their heartbeats. Ed could see the sudden flicker of Hex's machine-gun in the darkness outside as he caught sight of them. The glass tunnel exploded. Great jagged cracks travelled like lightning along its length, racing them to the end. Hex's silencer must have been almost used up, because Ed could hear the *chakkachakkachakka* of the gun beneath the splintering of the glass. The walkway shuddered under the hail of bullets, and great chunks of concrete blew up behind them as they ran.

And then they were in the station, slowing to a halt. The ticket hall was deserted. Machines stood sentry, ready to dispense tickets to travellers. Three small shops – a newsagent's, a fashion boutique and a flower shop – were closed for the night. A wide opening gave out onto the station platform. Apart from a shoulder-high glass barrier that ran around the edge to stop people falling off, and four rain shelters too far to run to, it was unprotected. If they went out there, Hex could pick them off like fairground ducks.

And if they went back: the same.

Beckett gazed back at the ruin of the walkway. 'Armour-piercing bullets,' he said.

'No kidding,' Ed replied. 'He's not taking any chances, is he?'

'If I was him,' Beckett said, 'I'd give it five minutes, then come up the escalator to get us.'

'If you were him we wouldn't be in this mess.'

They gazed around the small hall, looking for some means of escape.

Something moved in the window of the fashion boutique. Ed tensed, ready to fling himself to one side, but he relaxed when he realised that it was just a pair of robot dummies with blank faces, dressed in sharp lizard-skin suits and frilly blouses, jiggling from side to side and raising their arms to attract passers-by. They must have been activated by the presence of Ed and Beckett.

A thought flickered across his mind.

Perhaps the two of them didn't need to escape.

Perhaps they just needed to make Hex leave.

'Beckett!' Ed crossed over to the closed doors of the boutique. 'Here, give me a hand.'

'They're not your style, Ed,' Beckett said, looking at the blouses modelled by the dummies.

'Be serious! I think we've got a chance here. All we need to do is –'

'I'm ahead of you,' Beckett said, taking his lock-picking set from his pocket.

Once the door was open, it took only a few minutes to strip the two robots and dress them in Ed's leather jacket and Beckett's waxed coat. The hardest thing was forcing the sleeves over their still-waving arms. Cautiously, the two of them carried the robots over to the station. Ed knew they didn't have much time – if they left it too long, Hex might come after them. They needed him down on the ground, too far away to see what he was shooting at.

They paused at the edge of the station platform. Ed took a deep breath, grabbed his robot firmly around the waist and edged it out onto the station. He angled it slightly, so that to the waiting Hex it might look like someone looking around the edge of the ticket hall.

Nothing happened.

He pushed it slightly further out, tensing against the expected impact of the bullets. The robot flexed in his arms as its arms waved and its legs scissored.

Still nothing.

Perhaps Hex hadn't seen it.

Perhaps Hex was already on his way up the escalator.

In desperation, Ed pushed it as far out as he could without exposing himself as well.

The armour-piercing bullets blew its head into an expanding ball of plastic dust and metal wiring. Ed jumped as if electrocuted. The stream of bullets hosed downwards, fragmenting the robot's chest and sending one arm spinning into the night, still waving.

Ed threw the robot down and backed away, wiping splinters of plastic from his face. Beckett took his place, dropping to his knees and pushing the robot into the open as if it were trying to recover its companion's body. Its arms and legs moved in a bizarre parody of swimming.

The impact of the bullets sent the robot jerking away from Beckett, cogs spilling from its sparking innards. It sprawled in an ungainly position across the floor.

And then, silence.

Ed watched as the haze of plastic dust settled across the station platform. 'Whoever gets off the next train will think the mannikin mafia's been at work,' he whispered.

'Sssh!' Beckett made hushing gestures with his hands.

More silence.

Then footsteps, harsh against the pavement.

A car door slamming.

And then a car driving off into the night.

Ed peered around the edge of the ticket hall. The limousine that they'd seen whilst outside the half-finished office block was pulling up to the traffic lights at the end of the road. The lights went to green, and the car turned the corner. The growl of its engine hung on the air for a while before fading like a bad dream.

They were safe.

Ros drove through the dark streets, Easterhaus's gun pointed at her left ear.

'You know the way,' was all he said during the journey.

In the back, De Freitas and Hunter both looked out of their respective windows, caught up in their own thoughts. Hunter had a metal briefcase on his lap. It was filled with vials of a green liquid, each nestled in its own foam-rubber cocoon. Ros had seen him pack them.

Tri-meserone. The improved batch.

As they approached the dark, skeletal bulk of the office block, Easterhaus removed a control unit from his pocket. He aimed it at the hidden door to the underground car park and pressed a button. The door swung up smoothly, and Ros swung the car down the ramp. Coasting across the shadowed car park, she pulled up by the lift-shaft. Easterhaus aimed his control unit at the mushroom-shaped sensor above the lift doors from inside the car. Lights flickered and came on in an increasing circle around them. The lift hummed into life.

Ros watched Easterhaus carefully, noting which button he pressed, and for how long. It might come in useful.

If.

If she ever got the chance to get away.

The lift doors slid open. Easterhaus gestured Ros and Doctor De Freitas inside with a minute motion of his gun. He waited until Hunter joined them, then walked into the lift facing them. The doors closed behind his back, and he felt for the controls with his left hand. The gun never wavered from its aim point midway between De Freitas and Ros. A small motion in either direction would be enough to hit them, point-blank. He could probably shoot them both within a second.

Interestingly, Easterhaus was careful to ensure that Hunter was always in front of his gun. He never made it obvious, but Ros could tell that he didn't trust Hunter. Intriguing. Intriguing and possibly exploitable.

If.

If she ever got the chance to.

The lift shuddered to a halt, and the doors opened again. Easterhaus backed out confidently. He obviously knew the layout. He knew there was nothing to trip over or bump into.

Ros glanced around. They were on the twenty-second floor. The gym equipment – exercise bikes, jogging machines, weight-training nautiluses and rowing machines – still looked out of place in the office environment. They reminded Ros strangely of fair-ground rides after the fair had closed. They had that unoccupied and slightly forlorn air.

The tent of plastic sheeting in the distance glowed with its own internal lighting. The plastic sheets billowed slightly in a regular rhythm, as if the tent was breathing. Ros could still recall the comatose bodies of Jason Rupta, Kane and the other two students. The other two victims. Would she end up like that? Unfeeling? Unseeing? Unthinking?

She would rather be dead.

'Let's get started.' Easterhaus waved his gun towards the gym equipment. 'We haven't got long.'

Ros scowled at him. He was altogether too self-contained for her liking. She was used to ranting megalomaniacs and insane criminals. His calmness unnerved her. This was just a job to him. All in a day's work.

He could kill her in a moment and not even blink.

Hunter scurried across to a jogging machine and switched it on. The matt-black running belt jerked slightly as the machine went through its self-test routine. Lights flickered on its waist-high control panel. 'I'll need some monitoring equipment from . . .' His voice faded as he gestured towards the plastic tent. He didn't seem to want to look at it. 'From in there.' Perhaps he was ashamed of what had happened to his four test subjects.

Ros found it incredible that he could still proceed with his experiments knowing what he had done, what damage he had caused, but then scientists were like that. They could invent the atomic bomb and then be shocked that anyone might want to use it on other people. They got so tied up in their own genius that they could quite deliberately blind themselves to the ramifications of what they were doing. It didn't excuse their actions, but it did explain them.

'Then you'd better get it,' Easterhaus said.

Hunter pouted like a child. Glancing across at the tent as if it were a haunted house, he took a deep breath and bustled across to it. His hand plucked at the edges of the plastic flap, then withdrew. He darted a quick glance back at Easterhaus, then grimaced and ducked inside.

'Nervous, isn't he?' Ros said to De Freitas.

'But he's a biochemical genius,' she replied. 'I thought I was lucky to get him to work for the academy. He must have had much better offers from bigger institutions.'

'But they wouldn't have given him the freedom that

you did.' De Freitas looked away, and Ros added, 'Don't blame yourself. You couldn't have known what was going to happen.'

De Freitas glanced over at Easterhaus. 'I'm sure Doctor Hunter's consoling himself with the same thought,' she said quietly.

Hunter re-emerged from the tent, wheeling a rack of monitoring equipment. He was sweating, and cast nervous little glances over his shoulder, as if he expected Rupta and Kane to lumber after him.

'Take off your raincoat and stand on the jogging machine, please,' Easterhaus said to Ros. He punctuated the words with a small wave of his gun, just to remind her that it was there.

Sullenly, Ros stepped onto the rubber belt. It was about a metre wide and two metres long. Rollers at either end looped it back inside the machine's base. Two waist-high rails ran parallel to the belt, and an arm holding a control panel emerged from the machine's front.

'Tie her to the rails,' Easterhaus told Hunter. 'Then inject her with the new batch of tri-meserone.'

Hunter looked as if he might protest, but he decided against it. Obeying, he lashed Ros's wrists to the rails using electrical flex.

When Easterhaus was sure that Ros couldn't escape, he turned to De Freitas. 'On the weight-training equipment, I think, Doctor De Freitas.' He pushed her back with the barrel of the gun until her knees hit the edge of the padded bench and she sprawled backwards onto the flat surface. Quickly, before she could react, he lashed her arms and legs to the equipment struts with more flex.

And then he leaned over her and went to work.

Ros craned her neck to see what Easterhaus was doing, but Hunter came in from one side and pressed something cold and metallic to the skin of her upper

106

arm. She tried to jerk away, but he pressed a button. The metal device hissed, and a cold sensation spread through her arm as if someone had pressed an ice cube against it.

'That shouldn't hurt,' Hunter said, not meeting her accusing gaze. He turned his back on her and bent down to his open metal case. The vials of tri-meserone nestled in their niches like jewels. He retrieved a palmtop computer from a compartment in the lid of the case and switched it on.

'So is this new improved tri-meserone?' Ros gasped. Her arm felt suddenly warm. Sweat prickled across her back and face.

Hunter nodded. 'The previous versions often caused problems for athletes as their heart rates reached one hundred and eighty. You can keep track of your heart rate on the machine readout there.' He indicated the rack of equipment, where a red LED display flashed 90 at her. 'That's just increased pulse rate due to stress, of course,' he added reassuringly. 'When we start you running, it'll shoot up a lot higher than that.'

'Thanks,' Ros muttered.

Hunter bustled around Ros, still talking while he attached electrodes to her skin and plugged the wires into the equipment rack, but his words were coming from a long way away. Her stomach churned suddenly, and she felt as though she was going to be sick, but the feelings passed as quickly as they had appeared. She rested her arms on the rails and gathered her strength.

'We're ready,' Hunter said.

Easterhaus straightened up from the weight-training equipment. Concerned, Ros tried to see what he had done. De Freitas seemed to be in one piece, albeit angry, but it looked as if Easterhaus had been reconfiguring the equipment around her.

And as Ros realised what he had done she felt a sudden chill.

Easterhaus had rerouted the metal cables and weights so that ten fifty-kilogram weights hung directly over De Freitas's face, suspended only by a single cable. They were matt-black, like lead bricks, and they rotated slightly as the cable twisted and untwisted. If they fell, they would crush her head.

The cable holding the weights ran up and across a series of pulleys to an anchor point. Easterhaus had attached a box to the anchor point. It looked to Ros like a small explosive charge with an integral radio receiver.

Easterhaus walked over to where Ros was standing and placed a transmitter on top of the equipment rack. He ran a cable from it to the back of the equipment rack.

'You may be wondering what I'm doing,' he said to Ros as he programmed instructions into the equipment. 'In point of fact, I am ensuring your full cooperation.'

'Let Doctor De Freitas go now,' Ros said, trying to keep her tone reasonable. 'I said I'll do your stupid test, didn't I?'

He smiled, briefly. 'I'm afraid I still have a need for Doctor De Freitas. How do you feel?'

'How do you expect? Like a hamster on a wheel.'

Easterhaus turned to Hunter. 'What dosage has she had?'

'A hundred millilitres,' Hunter replied.

'Start the machine.'

Hunter touched a button on the jogging machine's control panel. The treadmill jerked into life. Ros was forced into a brisk walk to avoid having her arms pulled out of their sockets by the electrical flex.

On the LED display her heart rate went up: *91*. Then *92*.

Hunter made a note on his computer and pressed another button. The treadmill speeded up. Ros tried to keep her speed to a fast walk, but the machine was going too fast for that.

95.

She had to break into a run. Her breath was coming in short gasps now. Her head throbbed in time with her heart.

97.

'What will the tri-meserone do to me?' Ros gasped, trying to speak through her panting.

100.

Easterhaus glanced from her face to the readout, then back again. 'We really don't know. You may live – you may die.' He paused, relishing the panic that flashed across her face. 'Either way, you will *not* be in any position to further inconvenience my plans.'

Ros glanced over at the readout.

105.

Hunter pressed the speed button again, and Ros felt the treadmill shift beneath her feet. She accelerated to keep pace with it.

110.

Hunter typed comments into his computer. His eyes flickered from Ros's face to the readout on the equipment, then down to what he was writing. His fat tongue licked at the corner of his mouth. He didn't seem concerned. Only excited.

The readout changed to *120*, then quickly to *130*. Ros could feel the staccato thud of her heart, as if it were the drumbeat on the fastest dance track ever recorded. Sweat poured down her face, stinging her eyes and soaking her clothes.

144.

'One further thing,' Easterhaus said. 'I need this test to be conducted for real – I don't want you giving me second best.'

151.

Ros glanced at him sceptically. Sweat ran into her eyes, making her blink.

166.

'I've linked your treadmill to the piece of equipment Doctor De Freitas is tied to,' he continued. 'If your heart rate falls below one hundred and forty a small explosive charge will fire, severing the cable. The weights will fall and Doctor De Freitas's face will be crushed to a pulp. I doubt that she will survive the experience, but if she does, she will never be able to look in the mirror again.'

170.

Hunter increased the speed of the treadmill once more. Ros was sprinting faster than she had ever run in her life. Her feet were pounding into the belt like twin jackhammers.

162.

The control panel on the end of its arm was bouncing in time with her footsteps. The wires connecting her to the monitoring equipment whipped frenziedly. Her vision was hazy. Darkness encroached around the edges, pulsing in time with her heart.

170.

'This is the danger zone,' Hunter murmured. His tongue flickered out, coating his lips with saliva.

177.

Ros forced her gaze over to De Freitas. The Doctor's face was white. Her eyes were fixed on Ros, oblivious of the weights hanging over her head.

178.

Ros couldn't distinguish her individual heartbeats now. Her chest was filled with a continuous buzzing pressure.

179.

180.

'Yes!' Hunter whispered to himself. 'Yes! She's done it!'

Easterhaus nodded in satisfaction. 'Excellent.'

'With or without tri-meserone she can't take much more,' Hunter warned, plucking at Easterhaus's sleeve.

Easterhaus turned his attention to Ros. 'You'll be pleased to know that Doctor Hunter's drug has passed the test with flying colours,' he said.

'Good,' Ros panted, forcing the words out of her burning chest. 'What . . . about . . . me?'

'I think you can do more, don't you?' He reached out and placed his finger on the button that controlled the speed of the treadmill. Ros watched with sick fascination as he paused to appreciate her reaction.

Then he pressed it.

The treadmill felt like a rug that someone had pulled out from underneath her feet. Looking down, she could see only a blur where her legs had been. She couldn't even feel them any more. Everything below her chest was just a haze of heat and motion.

188.

The black tunnel around her vision crept further inwards, cutting off her sight of the control panel and Doctor De Freitas. She had to turn her head to see the glowing red letters of the readout.

195.

Jason Rupta's face floated in front of her eyes, filling whatever vision she had left. His face was contorted into a death mask of pure agony. Blood trickled like tears from his eyes. The crimson droplets traced the lines of pain in his expression. Her vision blurred, and it was Kane's face floating in front of her. Was that anger on his face, or fear?

She could smell burning rubber. The machine was being pressed to its limits. It couldn't take much more.

And neither could she.

From a million miles away she heard Hunter saying,

'Her body's giving out! I never claimed tri-meserone would work at this level of energy output! She can't take it!'

'Let's see, shall we?' Easterhaus replied laconically.

Ros shook her head violently, feeling red-hot drops of sweat spray in all directions. By sheer force of will she forced the visions away, and wrenched her head around until she was staring at Easterhaus.

'She's already running fast enough to do a two-hour marathon. What more do you want?'

'I want to take the new tri-meserone to the limit,' he said gazing unflinchingly into her eyes. 'She's expendable.'

'What?' Hunter cried. His face crumpled in disbelief. 'Was there any truth in what she told me? About you? About some invasion plan?'

Easterhaus turned away dismissively.

'*Are* the military interested in my research?' Hunter pressed.

'My foundation is funding your research,' Easterhaus snapped. 'That's all you need to know. Just carry on with the test.'

Ros could see the glowing red display in the corner of her vision. It dragged her gaze like a magnet. She couldn't help but look.

202.

How fast could a heart beat before it burst under the strain?

« Seven »

Hunter shook his head, jowls quivering. 'The test is over. Tri-meserone works. I'm stopping this *now*.' He reached for the control panel in front of Ros, and then turned towards the weights machine. 'And I'm disconnecting Doctor De Freitas.'

The black tunnel pushed insistently back, regaining lost ground and advancing until all Ros could see was Easterhaus's eyes. His cold, cruel eyes.

The treadmill slowed. Unprepared, Ros lurched forward. The control panel impacted her stomach, and she doubled over, resting her weight on it. Pain shot through her. The treadmill carried her feet back until her toes were dragging on the rubber.

Slowly it came to a complete halt.

Ros couldn't breathe fast enough. Her lungs were burning, trying to pump as much oxygen in as possible in the shortest possible time. The room spun around her like a carousel. She couldn't tell whether she was standing, sitting or lying down.

'How do you feel?' Hunter's voice said with concern.

Ros pushed herself away from the control panel and stood for a moment. She tried to focus on Hunter, but he was just a swimming blob of colour.

'Fine,' she whispered. 'I can come off my diet now, with all this exercise.'

Everyone was looking at her. She could sense it. What was it she had told Beckett, back before he put the bugs in place in Hunter's office? *Nobody will ever suspect you're up to no good if you're highly visible.*

This was her chance.

Ros deliberately let her eyes flutter upwards for a moment before crumpling to the rubber treadmill. The flex tying her wrists to the rails held her arms up, making her look like a ballet dancer doing the Dying Swan.

She had to endure the position only for a moment. Hunter rushed up and began untying the flex with one hand while he supported her weight with the other.

'Hunter!' Easterhaus barked. 'All you've done is push the failure threshold back. The drug is useless.'

'Help me get her to a bed,' Hunter pleaded.

Through half-closed eyes, Ros could see the blurred shape of Easterhaus approach. 'We can put her with the others,' he growled, 'and then we have to talk about her future.'

He leaned over and put his arm around her waist, ready to pull her up.

Ros slumped: a dead weight, pulling him off balance.

And elbowed him in the groin.

As Easterhaus doubled up in agony she shoved Hunter away and tried to wrestle the gun from Easterhaus's other hand. He resisted, but she tugged at it, trying to prise his fingers off the butt. At the last moment, when it seemed certain that she would succeed, he shouldered her away and threw the gun across the room. It clattered against the lift doors, and Ros sprinted towards it. Easterhaus tried to follow, but his foot caught in one of the exposed cable-run trenches. He pitched forward, sprawling full length on the floor. Hunter just gawped at them both.

Ros reached the lift and bent down to pick up the gun.

The lift doors opened.

Warm metal touched the back of her neck. She halted, still crouching, hand half outstretched, and turned her head.

Hex stood behind her. He held an assault rifle cradled in his hands.

'Sorry,' he said, 'no exit.'

Easterhaus limped over to them. His face was flushed, but he didn't seem angry. He looked Ros up and down, then turned to Hunter. 'I owe you an apology, Doctor Hunter. Tri-meserone *does* work.' He turned to Hex. 'Report?'

'Mission objectives achieved,' Hex smirked.

Easterhaus turned back to Ros. His face was still calm but, as she stared deep into his eyes, Ros could see a tiny spark of anger flaring within them. 'I do hope you weren't expecting your friends to rescue you,' he said.

'What do you mean?' Ros asked, but she had a terrible feeling she knew *exactly* what he meant.

'Both targets erased,' Hex added helpfully from behind her. Ros could still smell the stench of nitro-cellulose propellant that clung to his jacket. Her heart was still beating fast, but suddenly they were leaden beats, like the tolling of some great bell. She couldn't take it. The truth was too large, too indigestible. Not Beckett and Ed. Cynical, committed Beckett and boyish Ed. They couldn't be –

They couldn't be –

She couldn't even think the word.

Easterhaus led the way back to the treadmill. He didn't look back, expecting the others to follow him without argument. With the encouragement of Hex's rifle behind them, they did. Ros was still turning Hex's words over in her mind, looking for some flaw, some ambiguity, some escape route. They just *couldn't* be –

Easterhaus stopped and picked up Hunter's palmtop computer from where the man had dropped it. 'All the data is in this?' he asked, powering it up to check it wasn't damaged. 'The new formula – everything?'

'Yes,' Hunter said, looking like a child whose toy was being taken away. 'Everything you'll need is on there. There and . . .' He waved a flipper-like hand at the open briefcase containing the vials of green drug, looking like tiny glasses of crème de menthe.

'Excellent.' Easterhaus nodded once, as if he had made a decision. He caught Ros's eye and indicated Doctor De Freitas with a slight nod of his head. 'Free the good Doctor,' he said. 'I would hate to have her meet her end in such an . . . undignified position.' He smiled at Ros's hesitation. 'Don't worry about the explosive charge – as long as you don't touch the weights or the charge itself, you'll be safe. And please confine yourself just to untying her. I wouldn't want you getting any ideas about using the charge as a weapon – I can explode it in your hands quicker than you can throw it.'

Easterhaus powered down the palmtop as Ros walked over to pull the knots loose from De Freitas's wrists.

'How are you feeling?' De Freitas asked, massaging the blood back into her hands. 'I was worried – you looked like your heart was about to burst!'

Ros considered the question seriously. She had felt bad, but not as bad as she would have expected, given her level of energy expenditure. Tri-meserone obviously worked. 'Don't worry about me,' she replied, tugging the flex loose from De Freitas's ankles. 'The important thing is to get out of here.' She nodded inconspicuously towards the corner of the building in which she and Beckett had found the stairwell. 'There's a door over there. Be ready for my signal.'

De Freitas nodded. Ros had no worries about her. She was an athlete: she should be able to make it to the stairs quickly once Ros incapacitated Easterhaus and Hex. Ros, of course, still had the tri-meserone zooming around in her blood. On a good day she could outrun anyone she knew. With the tri-meserone she should just be a blur.

Ros was just about to alert De Freitas to her plans when Easterhaus clicked his fingers. 'Come with me now,' he barked. 'I want Hex to be the first to have some of the' – he paused, and smiled – '*new* tri-meserone.' He walked away again: arrogant, confident, certain that things would go the way he wanted them to. Ros and De Freitas followed, shepherded by Hex's rifle. Hunter picked up the metal briefcase and scurried after them.

Easterhaus led them over to a corner of the building, where a row of large glass bell jars stood on a desk. They contained a blue-tinged fluid. An acrid smell made Ros's nostrils prickle.

'Home brewing?' Ros couldn't help asking. 'Or are you hoping to market tri-meserone as a fizzy drink?'

Easterhaus didn't even glance her way. She shrugged. Never trust a man with no sense of humour.

She didn't like the look of the liquid in those bell jars, though. Given Easterhaus's record, it had to be something explosive or poisonous.

Or both.

Next to the bell jars was a transparent box. Inside the box was one of those black plastic ball-bearing clocks that Ros had seen in up-market designer catalogues. A motor raised an arm, once a minute, carrying a ball-bearing to the top of a series of ramps. Each ball-bearing rolled down like a blob of mercury, dropping through holes and reversing direction until it clicked against its fellows ramped at the bottom. Beneath each ball-bearing was a numeral – representing hours and minutes. If you could be bothered to figure it out, you could work

117

out the time from the numerals. Or you could just look at your watch. Ros had never understood the attraction of ball-bearing clocks – surely the whole point of technology was that it removed as many moving parts as it could, on the basis that they were the ones that always went wrong. A high-tech clock that went out of its way to introduce as many moving parts as possible was anathema to her.

Twin wires led from the clock to a pair of terminals that had been screwed through the transparent casing of the box. A timing mechanism? Looked likely. And that would explain the design – if Easterhaus was going to leave them alone with it, he wanted something that couldn't be picked up or tampered with.

He might have been barking mad, but he was clever with it.

'Get ready to pull out,' Easterhaus said to Hex.

Ros tensed, but Hex's rifle was still pointed halfway between her and De Freitas; his finger was still on the trigger and his eyes didn't even flicker towards Easterhaus.

The soldier nodded. 'Destroy all evidence, sir?'

'Completely,' Easterhaus replied, removing his own gun from his pocket and aiming it at Ros. The laser sight on top distorted the line of the gun, making it ugly and strange. No need of a laser sight at that range, Ros thought bitterly. He could close his eyes and work by hearing, and still hit us both first time.

Hex set the rifle down on the bench and went to work, connecting the bell jars to each other and to the terminals on the box with a cat's cradle of wiring.

Ros was appalled. 'What about those kids in the tent? They haven't done anything apart from test a duff batch of Hunter's drug! Can't you let them go – assuming they ever recover?'

She was pleased to see a flicker of anguish cross Hunter's face. She'd been aiming her words at him

118

more than Easterhaus. The colonel was a lost cause, but Hunter could still be turned.

If . . .

If she played her cards right.

'Casualties of war,' Easterhaus sneered. 'Hex is just setting up a series of explosions to clear all trace of our presence here. We have enough explosive to completely wipe out the floors that we've taken over.'

'Isn't that a rather untidy way to kill us?' Ros asked, more to buy time and keep Easterhaus talking than anything else.

'Oh, don't worry about the explosion,' he said with a thin, cold smile. 'We'll shoot you first. The explosion will just incinerate your bodies, and the four failures in the medical area. Messy it may be, but it's effective.'

And Ros couldn't help agreeing with him.

Hunter's flabby frame suddenly pushed in front of Ros. 'Is this really *necessary*?' he asked. He sounded as if he was seeking reassurance, rather than questioning Easterhaus's decision. Ros had met his sort before. He'd wandered blindly so far down the path to damnation that he would grasp any justification, no matter how slender, to continue rather than turn back. 'Only following orders' was an excuse created by people like Hunter.

Easterhaus must have been able to see how badly Hunter wanted to be convinced that what he had done was right, but it didn't matter. Ros could see from the flash of irritation that crossed his face that he was too busy to invent implausible justifications. 'Yes,' he said baldly, 'it is necessary.'

Hunter subsided like a pricked balloon. One more slight, Ros reckoned, one more chink in his armour of excuses, and he would turn. She was sure of it.

Easterhaus took a remote control from his pocket and aimed it at the ball-bearing clock. At the press of a button, the device whirred into life. The black plastic arm swung up, carrying its little metal sphere, and deposited it on top of the ramp. The ball began its descent. Everyone watched it go, their eyes moving like cats' watching a ping-pong ball.

Click, it went as it hit the other balls.

'This is a ball-bearing timing device,' Easterhaus said, rather redundantly. He gestured towards the bell jars. 'And this is sixteen gallons of highly volatile di-nitro-benzene. I've set a trip-switch so that when fifteen ball-bearings have run their course ... Well, let's say there might be some discussion about where the top few floors of this building went.'

'You're mad,' was all Ros could find to say.

'No,' Easterhaus said with a quiet intensity that only Ros could hear, 'only losers are mad. I'm a winner, so I must be sane.' He shivered slightly, then glanced over at Hunter. 'Doctor – time to prepare our first *übermensch*.'

Hex rolled up his sleeve. Hunter opened the metal briefcase, removed a vial of tri-meserone and fitted it into his air-hypo. Scurrying over to Hex, he hesitantly pressed the device against the bare flesh of Hex's forearm. The hiss cut across the click of the second ball-bearing as it rolled down its prescribed path. Hex swayed slightly, and Ros noticed a flush creep across his cheeks. If he was feeling the same way she had then he was covering up very well. Military training, she supposed. Pretend everything's OK up until the moment you pass out.

'Hex,' Easterhaus said loudly, as if for the benefit of posterity, 'you are honoured: the first of a new breed of soldiers.'

Hunter's hand froze as he moved the air-hypo away. 'You really *are* going to start a war,' he breathed. Ros felt like cheering. 'But you told me we would help people win gold medals. Now you're talking about super-soldiers.' He shook his head, still trying to fit

120

the mutually incompatible pieces together to form a coherent picture.

'What is sporting conflict but a pale imitation of the glories of combat?' Easterhaus sneered. A fanatical light had flared up in his eyes. Perhaps it had always been there, and Ros had just never noticed it before.

Hunter shook his head. His jowls juddered like jelly. 'But that's why we have sports,' he protested. 'It's harmless conflict – a safe form of rivalry, aggression channelled into peaceful competition.'

'Peaceful competition that you wanted to cheat at,' Easterhaus crowed. 'At least war is *honest* combat.'

Hunter reacted as if he had been slapped. *'Honest!'* Ros could almost see his thought processes reflected in his expression. He glanced around in bewilderment, and his eyes latched onto Ros and De Freitas. 'Look,' he said to Easterhaus, hands outstretched, 'you've used me and you've got what you want. Let them go, please. They're no threat to you.'

'I'm afraid that won't be possible,' Easterhaus replied coldly.

Hex shoved Hunter over towards Ros and De Freitas. His assault rifle didn't waver. With only a small movement of his hand, he could shoot any of them.

Or all of them.

And that, of course, was the plan.

Using Hunter's moving bulk as a cover, Ros took two steps forward. Hex caught sight of her just as her leg was sweeping up. He swung the rifle around, but her foot caught the barrel and knocked it up as he pulled the trigger. 'Run!' she shouted as his finger tightened in a reflex action.

Doctor De Freitas leapt up, wild-eyed, and dashed towards the door to the stairs.

The rifle juddered in Hex's hands and a spear of flame leapt towards the ceiling. Noise thundered in

Ros's ears. She shouldered Hex aside and rushed towards Easterhaus, but his gun was already up and tracking her. Death was in his eyes. She could see his mind calculating the decision. Live or die? She slewed to a halt, concrete chips stinging her face as Hex's bullets chewed through the ceiling. A bullet glinted in the darkness of Easterhaus's barrel. Her bullet. Live or die?

From the corner of her eye, Ros could see that De Freitas was halfway to the distant door. Her style was smooth and powerful, like a caged panther suddenly set free.

And she wasn't going to make it.

Hex swung the assault rifle down without taking his finger off the trigger, wrestling it like a man fighting an anaconda. The stream of bullets hosed across the room, turning the yellow back of De Freitas's tracksuit top into a churned-up field of crimson. She cartwheeled across the floor in an impromptu gymnastic display. Hex's rifle chattered its applause. She hit a pillar and stayed there, held upright by the pressure of the bullets. Chunks of concrete and chunks of flesh spewed indiscriminately in all directions.

Then Hex took his finger off the trigger, and De Freitas's body slid mercifully to the floor.

Ros turned away, sickened to her core, and found herself looking at Hunter. His mouth was flapping open and closed. He stumbled backwards. The expression in his eyes was an uneasy mixture of horror and betrayal.

Easterhaus turned to look at Hunter, who must have read his own death in Easterhaus's face, because he turned and lumbered towards the lifts. Hex stepped forward and aimed his rifle at the unmissable target of Hunter's broad back, but Easterhaus stopped him with a murmured, 'No – I don't want the tri-meserone damaged.'

Hex reluctantly lowered his rifle.

Hunter reached the lift. His fat fingers stabbed at the call button, shoulders tensed waiting for death to catch up with him.

Easterhaus took careful aim with his automatic. A red laser dot sprang into life on Hunter's greasy hair.

Hunter spun around almost unwillingly, like a puppet, briefcase clutched across his chest like a shield. His horrified gaze locked with Easterhaus. The red dot was the still centre of a turning world, a third eye in the centre of Hunter's forehead.

Easterhaus's finger tightened on the trigger. 'Goodbye, Doctor,' he murmured. 'Thank you for your help.'

The lift doors slid open with a muffled chime and Hunter half-fell into the dark interior. The gun bucked in Easterhaus's hand and a red flower bloomed and died on Hunter's shoulder. He whirled around with the impact, screaming shrilly.

The sound was cut off by the closing lift doors.

Easterhaus turned to Ros. His face was a careful, expressionless mask.

'That was stupid,' he said through gritted teeth. 'Really stupid.' He turned to Hex. 'Get down to the control room on the second floor. Use the stairs. I need to know where Hunter is.'

And beside him, the clock went *click* as another ball-bearing rolled down the slope.

The office was brightly lit, making the darkness outside the window look like the empty void of deep space.

Ensconced in his little bubble of light and warmth, Patrick Marcel gazed happily at the list of company names on his desk. There must have been fifty of them: each a small, struggling company on the verge of collapse; each a specialist supplier in a particular field. Electronics, armaments, guidance systems, aerodynamics, CAD/CAM, bulk transport . . . Pieces of a jigsaw puzzle that he was assembling.

He placed a neat tick next to three of the names. As predicted, they had come around to his point of view. Of the three, Belhampstead Enterprises had been the easiest. The owner of the company had signed ownership over to him straight away. Sensible woman. The other two had required . . . measures to be taken to ensure their cooperation. Serious measures. Measures that had meant some changes in the management structure.

Patrick shuddered slightly. He didn't like making threats. He had always been the sensitive one. Researching new business opportunities, creative accounting, planning major operations – that was his area of expertise. Violence wasn't his field. Jean-Daniel, on the other hand, had a positive talent for it. Thank God Jean-Daniel was there to help him.

At the thought of Jean-Daniel, Patrick's gaze inadvertently flicked across the office, past the half-unpacked cases of abstract artwork, to where the crate sat. The crate containing Death. His brother treated it like a pet, but the very thought of that sleek, devastating weapon made Patrick's pulse race slightly faster.

Sometimes, his brother frightened him, just a little bit.

Thank God Jean-Daniel had all these uncooperative directors, chairmen and chief executives to deal with. Otherwise, Patrick shuddered to think what he might get up to.

Patrick ran his finger down the list of names. Most of them didn't need any action yet. Now the Marcels controlled them they could go about their business quite happily, using the money that Patrick had paid into their accounts to make themselves solvent again. Their time would come later. There were ten companies on the list, however, that he had underlined in red. These were the ones with tasks to complete. Products to deliver to him. These were the important pieces of the jigsaw.

And two of them hadn't been ticked off the list yet.

Patrick felt a surge of anger within him, and suppressed it. Very deliberately, he smiled, although there was nobody around to see him. He couldn't allow his mask to slip. He had a part to play: he dressed the part, he acted the part, he looked the part. It didn't matter that sometimes he felt daunted at the responsibility put upon his shoulders. It didn't matter that sometimes he just wanted to smash everything around him into little pieces. He had a job to do.

Newsom's Coachbuilders and WeaponWorks. Two very different companies: one making advanced lorries, the other making high-tech weapons. Two companies who normally wouldn't even be talked about in the same breath, and yet he needed them. He needed them both.

Newsom's Coachbuilders. Run by Jim Newsom – an engineer of the old school: abrupt, short tempered and dedicated to making a go of his company. Patrick had approached him several times with no success. Time to clear him out of the way and hope his replacement was more amenable to reason. Time was running short.

WeaponWorks. Run by Claire Bishop – a woman who had kept the company going after the death of her husband. Again, approached several times. More willing to talk, or just more desperate for money, but unwilling to commit. Patrick didn't have time to wait for her to make up her mind. He had to force her hand.

Time to send Jean-Daniel in.

After all, he hadn't killed anyone for hours.

Beckett glared at the office block as if it was a personal enemy. 'Something tells me,' he murmured, 'that getting in this time won't be quite so easy.'

Ed nodded his agreement. His face had been scratched by the flying glass of the overhead railway station: he looked like he'd been attacked by a flock of budgies.

Together they made their way around the featureless façade of the building. Two floors were lit up, high above them, but the rest of the building was a black shape against the night sky. Beckett noticed in passing that the building-materials chute through which they had made their rapid escape earlier was missing. Even the window that had been shot out had been replaced.

Eventually they found the door to the underground car park. Ed ran his hands around the almost imperceptible seam.

'There has to be a way of opening this,' he said, more in hope than knowledge.

'Probably activated by a coded microwave signal,' Beckett agreed. 'Fortunately' – he pulled a device from his pocket and waved it at the wall above the door – 'I picked this up when we went back to the office to look for Ros.' Slowly, the door opened.

'It's one of her boxes of tricks.'

'So how come she knew the particular code the door sensor was looking for?' Ed asked, puzzled. 'And how come we didn't use it before?'

'The answer to the first question is: she doesn't – this box reprograms the entire sensor package with a code of our choosing. The answer to the second question is: we didn't know we'd need it the first time we came here.'

Halfway up, the door suddenly stopped and reversed direction, closing again. Ed and Beckett exchanged panicked glances, and sprinted for the narrowing gap. Ed managed to scramble beneath the descending edge and make it into the car park. Beckett had to hit the ground and roll. For a split second his head was beneath the door and he was looking straight up as it dropped, and then he was rolling past and into safety as the door hit the ground where his head had been. Hard.

'What happened there?' Ed gasped.

'Safety reset,' Beckett answered between deep breaths. 'The security system registered the fact that the code had been changed, and changed it back again. Very sophisticated software.'

'Nothing more sophisticated than having a door drop on your head, is there?' Ed grinned. Beckett just grimaced.

The car park was flooded with sterile neon light. Beckett felt like a fly walking across a sheet of paper as he and Ed approached the lift-shaft, but there was no cover they could use. Unfortunately, there was no other way in. This was the only entrance, and they had to pass through it. Ros wasn't back at Gizmos, and she wasn't at the academy. This was the only other sensible option.

Come into my parlour ... Beckett mused grimly.

'The power's on all right,' he muttered. 'We're probably being scanned by all sorts of sensors at the moment.'

'Like that thing?' Ed asked, pointing at the mushroom-shaped sensor projecting from beneath the lintel of the lift doors.

'Not a million miles away,' Beckett said.

Ed reached for the sensor. 'Easily fixed – I'll just rip it out. They won't be able to see us then.'

'No!' Beckett shouted.

Ed's hand froze a few inches away from the sensor. 'Keep your hair on, Beckett! What's the problem?'

Beckett indicated the thin strip of metal that ran around the concrete doorway and across the floor. It was impossible to get to the sensor or the lift doors without crossing it. 'I don't like the look of that,' he said.

'Didn't do anything before,' Ed pointed out.

'The power was off then. You want to risk it now?'

Ed gazed at the strip. Beckett had to admit that it looked innocuous. Perhaps too innocuous.

And there wasn't any dust on it.

Odd, that.

'I think,' Ed said, withdrawing his hand, 'that I'll take your advice.'

'That'll be a first,' Beckett growled.

The weightlifting bench retained the warmth of De Freitas's body. Which, Ros reflected as Easterhaus pushed her backwards on to it, was more than De Freitas's body did.

She could see De Freitas's death replaying through her mind in an endless loop. The way her body danced to the tune of the bullets. The way her blood polluted the crisp yellow fabric of her tracksuit. The way her eyes seemed to fix on Ros's as she died.

Easterhaus was going to pay for that.

With his life.

Easterhaus pulled the electrical flex savagely tight and straightened up, a snarl on his face. Ros was comforted to know that his imperturbability was already dented. Oddly, he had left her arms free. Ros racked her brain, trying to work out what he intended to do – why he hadn't tied her arms – but came up blank. It obviously wasn't a mistake, though, because Easterhaus didn't strike Ros as the sort of person who would make mistakes.

'Let me out of here!' she protested, not because she thought he would, but because she wanted him to remember that she was a human being, not an object. As a soldier, he was no doubt used to dehumanising the enemy. If she kept talking, kept imprinting her personality on him, maybe his finger would hesitate on the trigger.

As it had with Hunter? a little voice asked inside her head.

As it had with Doctor De Freitas?

Well, it was worth a try. After all, what other options did she have?

'Save your strength,' Easterhaus snapped. 'You'll need it.'

He reached across and removed a pin from the equipment like a man priming a hand grenade. The handlebars that stuck out on an arm above Ros's body – the ones that weightlifters would use to pump up their pectoral muscles – suddenly slammed down onto her chest. She felt her ribs creak under the pressure. Wriggling her hands beneath the rubber grips she tried to take the weight, but no matter how hard she pushed she could lift the bars only an inch or so. She tried to breathe, but the effort made black spots swim before her eyes.

'I've adjusted the weight on that bar,' Easterhaus said, leaning closer. 'Not even three body-builders on tri-meserone could lift it. I was going to shoot you outright, but you've caused me so much trouble that I want you to suffer. I want you to struggle to pull every single breath into your body. I want your lungs to burn, and as you fight to stay alive I want you to know that the timer is ticking, and every breath you take is a countdown towards oblivion.'

Ros had a cutting retort ready, but she couldn't get it out. All her energy was dedicated to holding the bar a precious inch above her chest: just far enough to allow herself to breathe.

And she knew, from the tremor in her muscles, that she wouldn't be able to hold the bar for long.

« Eight »

Easterhaus's radio crackled. 'Speak to me,' he queried irritably, picking it up.

'It's Hex, sir,' a voice said through static. 'I'm in the control suite now. Over.'

'Any sign of Hunter?'

'He's still in the lift, sir. He's alive – shivering like a wet dog. Too scared to leave, I think. Just keeps going up to the top of the building and back down again. Over.'

Easterhaus nodded as if Hex could see him. 'I must have that tri-meserone.'

'And sir? We have two intruders on the car park level. It's the two men who broke in earlier. Over.'

Suddenly Ros found it a lot easier to breathe. They were alive! She'd known they had to be, of course – how could Beckett and Ed ever die? – but it was nice to have it confirmed.

Easterhaus didn't look so happy. His clenched fist was thudding metronomically against his leg. 'You told me they were dead.'

'I'm sorry, Colonel, I thought –'

'Activate the ESF barrier,' Easterhaus interrupted. 'That'll keep them out of the building. We'll worry about them later. It's Hunter I want now.'

He deactivated the radio as Hex was halfway through signing off. Without looking at Ros, he strode off towards the stairs.

Click.

One more minute gone.

Beckett was crouching on the car park floor, examining the metal strip that encircled the entrance to the lift. He'd been all the way around it, and couldn't find any clue to its purpose, apart from a logo embossed into the strip at eye level – two intertwined Ws. Apart from that there was nothing, except the absence of dust and a slight smell of singed metal.

'So what do you think it is then?' Ed asked.

'Nothing nice,' Beckett replied. He sighed. He didn't like the look of that strip. Not at all. Not in the slightest.

'What's that?' Ed was pointing to the logo.

'The maker's mark?' Beckett shrugged.

Ed's face was screwed up into a caricature expression of puzzlement. 'I could swear I've seen that logo somewhere before,' he murmured, then shrugged. 'What the hell! We can't stay here forever, not if Ros *is* in here.'

'I know.' Beckett stood. 'I know.'

'Then let's go,' Ed said decisively, and made as if to walk through the metal hoop and press the button to summon the lift.

Perhaps it was a sound just below the threshold of hearing. Perhaps it was a faint tingle of ozone in his nostrils. Perhaps it was the way the hairs on the back of his neck began to rise. Whatever it was, Beckett suddenly grabbed hold of Ed and yanked him backwards without thinking.

'What the –?' Ed cried.

Lightning arced between opposite sides of the metal

131

hoop, top to bottom, side to side, corner to corner. A coruscating grid of actinic blue energy. A web of death so bright that Beckett had to screw his eyes up into slits to have any hope of seeing anything. He could smell something burning, and it took him a moment before he realised what it was. The air. The air itself was burning.

'What the hell –?' Ed breathed.

'Some kind of electrical generator,' ventured Beckett. 'Must take a hell of a generator to produce that much power. Megavolts.'

Something moved beyond the crawling lines of raw power. Beckett took a step backwards, trying to see through the glare. He raised his hand and, through his parted fingers, saw that the lift doors had opened. Ed had seen it too, he glanced sideways at Beckett, seeking guidance. Beckett shrugged. What use was running?

'Thank God!' a voice cried, 'you have to help me!'

It was Hunter: Beckett recognised the man's petulant voice. He sounded tired and panicked, and, from what Beckett could see of his plump figure through the searing arcs of energy, he'd been injured.

Oblivious of the threat, Hunter staggered forwards, towards Beckett and Ed.

'Hunter, don't!' Beckett shouted, putting as much authority as he could muster into his voice. 'You're just about to walk into some kind of electrical field!'

'Field?' There was a tone of childlike bewilderment in Hunter's voice. 'I don't know what you mean.'

He took a step forwards, hand outstretched in appeal.

'Don't touch it!' yelled Ed.

Hunter's hand intersected one of the electrical arcs.

A blinding discharge of sparks raised him off his feet and flung him backwards into the lift. Beckett expected him to scream but all he did was whimper, like a dog that has been hit too many times.

The smell of burning meat filled the air.

Hunter's undamaged hand scrabbled up the side of the lift for the control panel. On some deep, instinctive level he had obviously decided to go somewhere safe. *Safer*, at least.

'Hunter – Hunter, come back!' Beckett called. 'We can help –'

'No,' Hunter sobbed. 'If he finds me, he'll kill me.' He looked at his blistered, burned hand as if he had never seen it before.

The doors closed.

'No prizes for guessing who he's talking about,' Ed murmured.

Ros leaned her head backwards and frantically examined the weight-training equipment through blurry eyes, looking for some weakness or flaw that she could use. Her lungs were screaming for air, and the muscles of her arms were trembling with the strain of holding the weights off her chest. She couldn't hold out much longer. Either her arms would give way and the weights would fall, crushing her ribcage, or she would black out and the same thing would happen. The strain was incredible. Without the tri-meserone, she would already be dead.

Of course, without the tri-meserone, she wouldn't have got into this situation in the first place.

What she saw of the equipment didn't make her feel much better. The handlebars crushing her chest were attached to the machine by a long arm. A set of weights was attached to the other end of the arm by a series of cables. The weights ran in their own set of grooves, like trams on a track, and Easterhaus had added on all the spare weights from the other exercise equipment. Ros couldn't see any way of removing the weights, or snapping the cable, or detaching the arm.

She was well and truly trapped.

Click, went the timer. The noise sent a cold spike down her spine. So definite. So precise.

So final.

The arm she was trapped beneath would normally be prevented from descending too far by a metal pin that slotted into the frame, but Easterhaus had removed the pin. Worse – he had taken it with him. If he'd left it somewhere within reach of her feet then she might have been able to retrieve it and slot it back in, but –

A thought flashed across her mind, but the pain of the handlebars cutting into her chest was so intense that she almost lost it. Deliberately Ros tried to clear her mind of the pain, the distractions and the recurring images of De Freitas's wrecked body. She closed her eyes and concentrated. Recapture that thought. That image. That memory.

A pin. She had seen a pin somewhere in the equipment.

Craning her neck backwards again, Ros scanned the equipment. Struts. Cables. Weights. And . . . there! Another pin!

The bench she was strapped to was just one piece of equipment on a multi-purpose frame. Another bench projected out of the frame at a ninety-degree angle to the one she was lying on. That one was designed for people to sit facing the frame, and the projecting arm was correspondingly shorter. The handlebars were higher up, designed to exercise a different set of muscles from the ones that were about to rip themselves to pieces inside Ros's body. And they had a pin too, preventing the weights from pulling the bar too far down.

Without giving herself time to think, Ros lifted her feet into the air and swung them as far over her head as she could. The handlebars dug painfully into her stomach, and the position put even more strain on her

chest, but it was the only chance she had. Quickly she
canted her legs towards the other bench, twisting her
entire body sideways. Her feet hovered tantalisingly
close to the second set of handlebars. She couldn't
breathe at all now. Her chest pounded with the frantic
pulsing of her heart. She felt as if her head was about to
explode with the strain. Two inches more. Just two
inches, but she was stretching as far as it was humanly
possible to stretch.

So she stretched further.

Ros didn't know whether it was the tri-meserone
or just her own cussed determination, but her legs
seemed to lengthen, the tendons extending and the
joints relaxing to give her the precious few inches she
needed. Her toes made contact with the looped end of
the pin. Carefully – oh so carefully – she brought her
toes together, pinching the loop. She could feel the
ridge of metal through the soft leather of her shoes.
Gently she withdrew it.

Click.

Another ball-bearing rolled down the incline to join
its friends. Another minute gone.

The pin rasped against the metal edges of the hole.
Ros ignored the sound, ignored the ever-present whirr
of the motor in the ball-bearing clock, ignored everything except the pin, the hole and her toes. That was
the entire world. Nothing else existed.

Her biceps and triceps screamed with the pain of
holding the bar away from her chest. Her leg muscles
screamed with the pain of holding position and pulling
the pin gently out of the hole. Her lungs screamed for
air.

But she was oblivious. Nothing existed but the pin,
the hole and her toes.

The pin came free.

Ros hadn't been expecting it, and almost let it drop
in shock. The pin was shorter than the one Easterhaus

135

had removed from her side of the multigym! What sort of imbecile made multigyms with different-sized pins? It was stupid! Irresponsible! Almost criminal!

She pulled herself together. Fuzzy red edges were creeping into the sides of her vision. This was no time to succumb to hysteria.

Smoothly, Ros swung her legs back to her own bench. The pin dangled a few inches above her nose. The hole she needed to get it into was above her head and six inches back. No problem to a gymnast. Well, no problem to a gymnast who hadn't been starved of oxygen for five minutes.

And she still had to raise the bar far enough to slip the pin into the hole. Otherwise the pin would be *above* the bar, not below it, and she would die.

A slight tremor started in the muscle of her left thigh. The pin vibrated. Jerked. Slipped slightly. Ros tightened the grip of her toes, but it was no good. The pin was going to fall.

Deliberately, Ros relaxed her guard and summoned up a mental image of Doctor De Freitas. Of her body, spinning like a dancer under the impact of Hex's bullets. Of her face. Her eyes. Her shocked, pleading eyes.

Anger washed through her body, pushing pain and fatigue aside. It washed down into her legs, and the tremor stopped. It flooded up into her arms, and the bar seemed to rise as if it were made of balsa wood. Somewhere in the back of her mind, Ros knew that she couldn't maintain this for more than a few seconds, but it was a gift from whatever deity looked after errant computer hackers and she wasn't going to waste it.

She lunged with her legs, and the pin vanished above her head. Her vision had narrowed to a small circle surrounded by a red mist, but by craning her neck she could just make out the hole between two struts that the pin had to go into. She twisted slightly until the key was as horizontal as it was ever going to be, and then she edged her legs sideways.

The pin clanged against the strut.

Ros could taste the metallic tang of defeat in her mouth. The red edges were encroaching across her vision now, and behind them followed blackness. The blackness of death. She had to succeed. She *had* to, for De Freitas.

Without looking, trusting to blind luck, she slammed her legs sideways.

The pin slipped so neatly into the hole that it might have been on an invisible thread.

That last, desperate rush of strength suddenly gave out and the bar came crashing down onto the pin.

And the pin held.

Ros brought her legs back over her head and down to the bench. She let gravity pull her head back against the padded surface of the bench and gratefully sucked lungful after lungful of air into her chest. She had never come that close to death before. And she never wanted to again.

Click.

She wanted just to lie there all night. She wanted just to go to sleep. But she had a job to do, so she swung her protesting legs over the edge of the bench and sat upright. The ball-bearing clock was sitting happily in its little box, its little plastic arm swinging happily up with another ball-bearing. She had been paying attention to Easterhaus's little lecture earlier on, and she couldn't see any way of stopping it. Perhaps Beckett and Ed . . .

Beckett and Ed.

They were downstairs, in the car park, and something called an ESF barrier had been activated. She had to get to them. Now.

Her radio was inside her coat pocket. She pulled it out and activated it. 'Beckett? Beckett, are you there?'

'Ros?' Beckett's voice responded instantly. 'Ros, we were – Are you okay?'

The relief in his voice gave her a warm, fuzzy feeling, but she quickly suppressed it. Time for the full story later. 'Where are you?' she asked.

'Stuck in the underground car park,' he said. 'There's a kind of force field we can't get past.'

She thought for a moment, shaking her head angrily to clear the fatigue away. 'Look up in the ceiling, just by the lift doors. There's a mushroom shaped sensor there.'

Silence for a moment. 'Yeah, got it. It's the other side of the barrier.'

'No problem. It's a remote on/off for the entire building's power supply. I don't suppose you –?'

'Picked up your code changer from the office? Of course we did.'

'You read my mind. Use it on the remote.'

'The building's got a reset function, Ros – it'll reject the new code straight away and go back to the old one.'

'Well,' Ros said grimly, 'you'd better be quick then.'

Ed glanced at the sensor, then at the crackling electrical field, then back at Beckett. The intensely blue lightning illuminated his face like the random flashbulbs of paparazzi. 'We're not going to have much time, Beckett,' he said.

Beckett nodded. 'We can do it in two. The first time, we just press the button and call the lift. The second time, we jump in.'

'And what if there *is* no second time?' Ed glanced at the sensor again. 'I mean, we might get away with it once, but what if the system's clever enough to ignore a second attempt to reset the code.'

'If that's true then we already alerted it by using Ros's box of tricks on the car park door. The security system might just freeze us out this time.'

Ed shook his head. 'Separate circuit, remember? The car park door had power when this lift didn't. They're not controlled by the same computer.'

Beckett opened his mouth to deliver a smart answer, but nothing came out. Ed was right. Computers could be built to be that clever. They might be able to deactivate the field once for a few seconds, but perhaps not twice. They had only one chance to get this right.

'OK,' he said decisively, 'we just do it right first time. How much clearance do you reckon there is between the lift doors and the field?'

Ed shaded his eyes and tried to gauge the distance. 'A foot. Two maybe?'

'And how flat do you think you can get your body?'

'I'm not a contortionist, Beckett!' Ed laughed in disbelief. 'You're not seriously suggesting that we use Ros's box to switch off that cattle fence, call the lift then plaster ourselves to the door until it arrives, are you?'

'That's *exactly* what I'm suggesting,' Beckett said grimly. 'Unless, of course, you have a better idea?'

Ed thought for a moment. 'No,' he said finally. 'Then let's do it.'

Beckett positioned himself one step from the electric field. Even with his eyes closed he could see the flickering sparks. He could feel his hair rising and his skin prickling at the proximity of all that raw energy. He heard Ed take up a position beside him. Before his better judgement could talk him out of it, Beckett pointed Ros's control box at the sensor hanging underneath the lintel of the lift doors and pressed the button. Lights flickered and died all around the car park. For a long moment the electrical discharges hung in the darkness like an abstract painting, then they vanished leaving bright afterimages across Beckett's vision.

'Go!' he yelled.

It was the longest two steps that he had ever taken.

He flung himself against the cold metal lift door. It shuddered as Ed hit the other door. Less than a second later, lightning sliced the air apart behind them.

Beckett felt his jacket burst into flames at the same time as the car park lights came on. 'Ed! Ed! My jacket's on fire!'

Ed squinted sideways at him. 'The light's too bright, Beckett – I can't see anything. What do you want me to do?'

'Just hit the button. Call the lift!'

'I *can't*! The button's on your side!'

Beckett could feel the hairs on the back of his neck shrivelling. 'It's on *your* side! I saw it!'

Ed's hand scrabbled across the door frame. 'There's nothing here.'

Perhaps he'd been wrong. Perhaps it *was* on his side. As the heat on his back increased past *cosy* and into *painful*, he slapped his hand against the wall on his side and brushed it up and down. Nothing! The button *had* to be on Ed's side. It *had* to be.

And then he felt a curved metal rim beneath his questing fingertips. He punched the button, punched it again and punched it a third time for good luck.

The door vibrated as the lift started its descent.

Beckett could hear the crackling as the material of his jacket blazed. He knew Ed couldn't risk beating the fire out. Ed only had to move his hand a few inches backwards and it would be barbecued. Like Hunter's.

The lift doors shuddered. The lift must have come to rest behind them.

He could smell burning cloth. The heat in the centre of his back was like the worst sunburn he'd ever had.

'Just our luck,' Ed muttered, 'if Hex is in the lift, waiting for us.'

For a moment Beckett forgot his burning jacket. Easterhaus and Hex! It had never occurred to him that they might have been in the lift when he called it.

Nothing he could do. There were dramas and there were crises, and having your back on fire was a crisis. A man with a gun was just a drama.

The doors opened. Slowly. Gradually. Massively.

As soon as he could get his fingers in, Beckett wrenched them further apart and forced himself in through the gap. The lift was mercifully empty, and he dropped to the floor, rolling about as fast as he could. Ed followed him and helped to pull the jacket off. While Ed beat it against the walls, Beckett ran his hands over his back looking for blisters but it looked as if the fire hadn't penetrated that far.

When he turned around, he found Ed holding his jacket out to him. There was a charred patch in the centre of the back, about the size of a floppy disk.

'It felt a lot more dramatic,' he said lamely.

'You know,' Ed said, grinning, 'I never had you figured for a hot dresser.'

Beckett smiled wanly. 'I never liked this jacket anyway.'

Glancing around the small space of the lift, Ed said, 'Hunter must have left. What do you reckon he's doing?'

'Wandering around in a daze, judging by the way he looked earlier. I think he took a bullet.'

'A little falling out among thieves?'

'Yeah, that sort of thing. Still, he's not the primary threat. It's Easterhaus and Hex we have to worry about.' He reached out and pressed the button for the twenty-first floor. 'We'll get out below Ros and go up the stairs, just in case Easterhaus and Hex are waiting for us.'

Ros's voice crackled out of Beckett's radio just as the lift doors closed. 'Beckett? Ed? Are you guys past the barrier yet?'

The lift lurched upwards. 'It was a close shave,' Beckett replied, 'but yeah.'

'Hunter's got the tri-meserone and the data. Easter-haus is stalking him. I think Hex has gone down to the control suite on the second floor – the one we ran through when we were escaping last time.' She paused. 'And Doctor De Freitas is dead.'

Beckett felt a cold hand tighten on his heart. He glanced at Ed, whose face had drained of colour. 'Why?' he heard himself saying, 'What did she do?'

Ros's voice was grim, even through the static. 'Nothing except get in the way. These people are mad.'

Beckett's mind raced. So much to do – so little time. 'OK, I'll get after Easterhaus. Ed – you handle Hex.'

'Be careful,' Ros interrupted, 'Hunter gave Hex a dose of the new tri-meserone.'

'Terrific,' Ed said with a twist of his lips.

'And we've got a time limit, guys. Easterhaus has two incendiary bombs set up. The one I'm staring at is meant to wipe out this floor and the one above. There's one on the second floor as well, but I don't know whether Hex has set it or not. They're both tamper-proof.'

'When's the bomb set to go off, Ros?' Beckett asked.

'Ten minutes.'

'And Easterhaus is still wandering around the build-ing looking for Hunter?' Beckett was incredulous. How stupid was this guy?

'So long as he's not on the second, twenty-second or twenty-third floors, he'll probably get out alive,' Ros replied. 'After all, it's the evidence he wants destroyed, not the building. And I guess he needs that tri-meserone badly enough to risk it.'

'Rather him than me,' Ed muttered, then frowned in thought. 'Although I guess if I'm stupid enough to go in after Hex, that makes me as stupid as he is.'

The lift suddenly jerked to a stop. The doors opened halfway, then jammed.

'They've stopped the lift,' Beckett said, half to Ed and half to Ros. 'They must have an override –

probably down in the control suite. And that means Easterhaus and Hex are in communication with each other. OK, Ros – we know what we've got to do. You try to get the four sleeping beauties out of the building before the bombs go off.'

'Why do I always get the easy jobs?' Ros complained. The radio went dead as she switched it off. Beckett slipped his own one back into his pocket.

Ed gave Beckett a mock salute, then slipped out of the half-open lift doors. Beckett was about to follow him when he had an idea. Hex and Easterhaus were communicating. That meant they were using radios. That meant –

He pulled his radio receiver out again and checked the frequency setting. It was a digital unit, which meant he could search for bands that were in use. Neither he, nor Ros, nor Ed was transmitting at the moment. And *that* meant –

He smiled, and triggered the search function on the radio.

'Hex?' Beckett jumped. Easterhaus's voice echoed around the lift, so loud that for a moment Beckett thought he was outside the doors. 'Hex, I'm on level twenty-six. I think Hunter's heading for the roof.'

'Understood, Colonel.' Hex's calm voice. 'Our intruders disabled the ESF barrier but I've isolated the lift power. They're on level fifteen.'

'Deal with them yourself. I'm going after Hunter.'

Easterhaus cut the connection before Hex could reply. He didn't sound happy. Beckett wasn't surprised – if he was up near the roof then he was above the bomb. Both bombs. He must *really* want that tri-meserone, if he was prepared to risk everything to get it back.

Beckett checked the lift display. He was on the fifteenth floor. Easterhaus was on the twenty-sixth. Eleven floors, and the lift was out of action.

Hadn't he been here before?

« Nine »

Ros stared down into Kane's face. Slack. Vacant.
Almost innocent. She tried to recall some of the sheer
mind-numbing terror she'd felt when she was fleeing
through the corridors of the International Sports
Academy, but it had gone. Too much had happened
since.

She'd been more scared since.

A breeze caressed the back of her neck. She glanced
behind her, but the flap of the plastic tent remained
undisturbed. For all she knew, Easterhaus and Hex
could be standing outside waiting for her, but the tent
was in a world of its own. She felt safe here. And at
least it shielded the noise of that damned timer clicking
away.

The medical equipment attached to Kane was familiar. She'd seen specifications and handouts at medical
technology exhibitions, and she had an almost eidetic
memory for operational functionality. That, after all,
was how she kept ahead in the fast-moving, cut-
throat world of computer technology. She ran her
hands across the control panel, calling up details of
his condition. The more she saw, the more puzzled
she became. His blood pressure and oxygen levels

appeared to be normal, and the heart monitor didn't show any abnormalities at all. To all intents and purposes, Kane might just be asleep.

A clipboard of notes hung at the foot of his bed. The medical details had all been written in Doctor Hunter's meticulous handwriting. The dates and times were irregular: no doubt he'd only popped in occasionally. When Doctor De Freitas wouldn't suspect anything, perhaps. Or, more likely, when Easterhaus would let him. In the early stages of Kane's treatment there was, as far as Ros could see, evidence of massive heart tachycardia and the presence of toxins in the bloodstream. His brain functions had been severely depressed, with evidence of deep coma. Despite the irregularity of Hunter's observations there was, however, clear evidence of improvement. Hunter had even written a marginal note speculating that, once the toxins had cleared from the system, Kane and the others might make a complete recovery.

Perhaps . . .

Perhaps he *had* pulled through.

Perhaps they had *all* pulled through.

Ros checked all four of the comatose students, and found them all the same. No sign of the heart and brain problems that they had originally displayed. No toxins in the blood. They were sleeping. They were all sleeping.

So, even in its early stages, tri-meserone had worked. Almost.

She checked the last page of each clipboard. Hunter had been administering sedatives to the four students, keeping them unconscious so that their bodies could metabolise the toxins. The last dose had been several hours before. That meant –

Ros activated her radio. 'Ed? Ed, are you there?'

'Yeah Ros – I was just creeping up behind Hex in his control suite. Thanks for interrupting.'

Ros was mortified. 'You're joking, aren't you?'

'Yeah, I'm joking. But I might not have been. What do you want?'

'Listen, the kids up here are all sedated, but otherwise they're fine. I think I can revive them.'

'So when were you at medical school, then?'

'It's OK, Ed,' she snapped, angry at his automatic assumption of authority, 'I know what I'm doing.'

'All right, Doctor Ros – do your stuff.'

Ed stashed his radio away and stepped out onto the second floor. The security monitors stretched away into the shadows. He listened, but there was no sound. If Hex was here, he was keeping very quiet. That meant that he knew Ed was here. If he was here. *If*.

As quietly as he could, Ed walked along the row of monitors. Each displayed a different shot: stretches of half-carpeted floor; rows of columns like a concrete Stonehenge; dizzying expanses of stairwell. None of them were labelled, and with nearly thirty floors to choose from it was almost impossible to work out which monitors were showing what floors.

At the end of the row a trolley had been parked. On top of the trolley was an odd device, like a miniature multi-storey car park made out of black plastic, with ball-bearings for cars. It was inside a plastic box. A wire ran from it to a set of glass bell jars. Each bell jar was filled with a blue-tinged liquid, and was connected to the next one by a wire.

The bomb timer that Ros had talked about? It seemed like a fair bet. Ed watched it for a moment, but nothing moved. The ball-bearings remained where they were. No levers swung up or down. Nothing ticked. Nothing tocked. Nothing went boom. Looked like Hex hadn't started it up yet – probably waiting until Easterhaus had tracked Hunter down. Sensible guy.

146

But the one upstairs was still counting down.

OK. Time to get to work.

Ed chose one of the monitors at random, and sat down. The screen was showing the empty, sterile car park. Close up, he could see that the monitor was actually a computer workstation, fed from some central mainframe core. There was no keyboard. No mouse. No means of inputting instructions.

Except . . .

Except that the screen was set a few inches back from the surrounding frame. That was interesting. Very interesting. Ros had shown him something like this before. It was something they used in places like nuclear power stations and centralised train-route control rooms. Touch-sensitive screens: infra-red beams, criss-crossing a few millimetres in front of the glass, with sensors to detect whether a beam had been broken.

Ed poked experimentally at the screen with his forefinger. Before his finger touched the screen, a menu appeared, outlined in white on top of the picture of the car park.

'Yes! Easy!'

One of the menu options was *Change location?* He pointed his finger at it. The menu disappeared, and was replaced by a schematic of the building. As Ed waved his finger up and down, the floors in the schematic were highlighted in red, one by one.

He chose the twenty-second floor. Another schematic sprang to life, this time of the floorplan of the twenty-second floor. There were twenty-five red spots scattered about the schematic. It took Ed a few moments to realise that they must be camera locations. He stabbed his finger at one near the centre of the room – the closest one to the medical tent where Ros was rousing Hunter's experimental subjects.

The screen darkened. The menu vanished. And then Ed was staring at Ros from a position a few feet above her head and slightly behind her. She was injecting something into a guy who was lying on a bed. A stimulant, Ed assumed.

The guy stirred, blinking in the harsh neon light. Ed grinned and settled back in his seat. This had to be the ultimate in voyeurism.

Ros helped the guy to a sitting position. Her lips were moving, but Ed couldn't hear what she was saying. Belatedly he noticed a red box in the corner of the screen. In the box were the words *Audio Off*. He poked the box with his finger, and the words changed to *Audio On*.

'Whe –?' the guy was saying.

'Don't say it – "Where am I?", right?' Ros interrupted.

The man nodded.

'Good question,' Ros continued. 'Very long and complicated answer, though.' She handed him the hypodermic. 'I'll need your help with rousing the others.'

The guy pulled back the blanket covering him and cautiously got out of bed. It was only then that Ed recognised him.

It was Jason Rupta.

For a moment Ed was back in the *dojo*, fists thudding into his ribs. A strange, unreal feeling began to wash over him and then receded, leaving him empty and confused. He shivered.

On the monitor, Ros and Jason Rupta were both working on separate beds. Ed could see their hands moving, but there was something else moving on the monitor. Something midway between them, in the centre of the screen. Something dark and vague. Amorphous, but purposeful. Ed squinted, trying to make it out. It looked like a shadowy figure holding something metallic in its hands but it was fully three or four times as big as Ros, and it was overlaid on the beds and the medical equipment as if it was only half there.

With a sudden, cold shock, Ed recognised who the figure was.

Hex.

And he wasn't on the monitor.

He was reflected in it.

Ed flung himself to one side as Hex fired his assault rifle. The monitor exploded, sparks flying like burning insects across the room. Hex pivoted on his heel, spraying bullets after him. Monitor after monitor burst into shards of glass and flashes of flame. A transformer detonated with a bang, sending cables writhing away like fire-headed snakes.

Ed dived to the floor and rolled beneath one of the benches. Shards of glass from the monitor screens rained down onto him.

Same man.

Same gun.

Same silence for a moment. Ed glanced left and right, but he couldn't see where Hex had gone. He scuttled sideways as quietly as he could. Nothing. Head flicking left and right. Ears straining for the faintest sound. Nothing.

He stood up slowly: every muscle in his body tense.

Hex had to be around here somewhere.

The sound of a firing pin hitting a cartridge made Ed whirl around. Hex stood behind him, assault rifle pointed at Ed's chest. His finger was on the trigger. The smile on his face was sliding into a frown of bemusement.

Misfire.

Before Hex could clear the dud cartridge, Ed lashed out in a roundhouse kick. His foot caught Hex's rifle, sending it spinning away into the shadows. Hex watched it go, then whipped his gaze back to Ed. The tendons in his neck were taut, and Ed could see a pulse in his temples. White-hot rage was in his eyes. No mercy. No chance.

'Who needs weapons?' he snarled.

Ed punched him twice in the chest, aiming for the nerve junctions, trying to paralyse Hex's arms. No good. The man's muscles were like slabs of slate. Ed backed off, but Hex followed. Inexorable. Unstoppable.

Hex swung backhanded at Ed's head. Ed ducked, feeling Hex's fist slice through the air above him. Taking the chance he stepped in close and punched Hex in the stomach. Hex didn't even blink. He just threw his hands wide and brought them crashing together on Ed's ears.

The world exploded into an inferno of agony.

Ed fell to his knees. He couldn't hear a thing. His head throbbed like a rotten tooth. Through a blood-red mist he could just make out Hex reaching down to him. Fingers clenched around his throat, but it was all too far away to worry about. Another world. Another time. Muzzily, Ed wondered if he should do something about the encroaching darkness, but it was all too much trouble. Too much trouble.

No.

No, he never gave up.

No matter what the odds.

No matter how hopeless the cause.

He *never* gave up.

Never.

With an inarticulate cry of rage, Ed clenched his fists together and slammed them up into Hex's chin. Hex's head snapped backwards with a click that echoed across the entire floor of the building and his hands exploded away from Ed's throat, sailing wide as his body became airborne. He flew away from Ed and across the nearest bench, legs flailing, body jerking, coming to rest on the spluttering remains of the transformer that he had shot earlier.

Sparks fountained around him and his body convulsed as if he had fallen into a pit of vipers. His limbs

150

whipped back and forth hard enough to snap tendons and break bones. Blisters formed and burst on his blackening skin, but he didn't scream. He just kept staring at Ed, murder in his eyes, until his eyes curdled and burst.

Ed rubbed at his throat, hypnotised by the grotesque sight until the rising smoke blocked his view.

When the throbbing in his head died down enough for him to think properly, Ed walked away, leaving Hex's body still jerking like a clockwork toy.

Dead, but still moving.

The sun was coming up when Beckett emerged from the twenty-sixth floor into the open air. The sky was a delicate shade of salmon-pink, and the taller buildings were casting long fingers of shadow across the city. The wind whipped his hair across his eyes and made it difficult to hear anything.

The twenty-sixth floor was effectively just a windowless block about half the size of the previous twenty-five. One door led out onto a broad balcony that ran around the edge of the building. That was the door Beckett had just come through. Twin tracks for a window-cleaning cradle bordered the edge, although the cradle itself wasn't visible. The other half of the roof, on top of the windowless block, was accessible via ladders on each side.

Hunter stood at one end of the building, close to the edge. Too close to the edge. He held a metal briefcase at the end of his extended arm – the uninjured one. There was nothing beneath the briefcase but twenty-five floors of air, followed by hard tarmac. Blood had soaked through his jacket. Some of it was dry, but some was still bright and wet. He'd been hit badly.

Easterhaus was halfway along the edge of the windowless block – about twenty feet from Hunter. His gun wavered between pointing at Hunter and pointing out into the void. It looked to Beckett as if he had come in halfway through some kind of confrontation. Hunter had got himself into a perfect defensive position – Easterhaus couldn't shoot him without losing the tri-meserone over the edge, and, no matter how well it was packed, all he'd scoop up off the road would be powdered glass and damp foam-rubber. On the other hand, Hunter had no bargaining position. Even if he came to an agreement with Easterhaus and handed the briefcase over, he became redundant the moment he let go of the handle.

'Hunter – stop!' Easterhaus shouted. The wind carried away his words. Beckett had to strain to hear him.

'Shoot me and you'll never get your hands on this!' Hunter shouted back with false bravado, waggling the briefcase. He almost overbalanced, and had to steady himself for a few seconds.

Easterhaus deliberately brought the gun down to his side. 'We can talk about this,' he said, obviously trying to inject as much sympathy as he could into his voice. It didn't work: he just sounded like an insurance salesman at the end of a bad day.

'Stay back or it goes!' Hunter screamed, taking a step back. One more step and he would vanish over the edge, assuming that the weight of the briefcase didn't take him sideways first.

'Don't throw away the work you've spent years on!' Easterhaus sounded almost convincing. He must have been really worried. 'Let's talk about this!'

Beckett weighed up the options. He couldn't just wade into the situation – Easterhaus would just shoot him where he stood and Hunter might just take another step backwards by accident. On the other hand, he couldn't just stand there and watch the drama play out. He had to do *something*.

He glanced at the scenery and the props he had to

play with. The block of the twenty-sixth floor was windowless, and that meant he could get all the way around without Easterhaus seeing him. And the window-cleaning cradle might make an effective weapon, if he could find it. And if he could get the villain of the piece into the right position.

It was worth a go.

Beckett moved away from Easterhaus and Hunter, towards the nearest corner, trusting to the wind to cover any noise he made. He moved as fast as he could, knowing that anything might be happening behind him. Easterhaus might make a grab for the case, sending both him and Hunter plummeting towards the ground. Or Hunter might faint through loss of blood. Or the bomb might go off, four floors below, rendering all other options null and void.

He skidded around the corner and broke into a run. No sign of the window-cleaning cradle on this side. He had to slow down at the next corner in case he overshot and went over the edge. The third side of the block was as featureless as the rest. Still no sign of the cradle. Beckett hoped that it hadn't been dismantled and taken away for repairs, otherwise his entire plan would be up the spout. As he approached the third corner he came to a halt, offered up a quick prayer and peered around the edge.

Hunter was still standing at the fourth corner. The briefcase was in his left hand, hidden from Beckett by his body. Easterhaus was out of sight behind the block, which meant that he couldn't see Beckett.

And the window-cleaning cradle sat on the tracks about halfway along the side of the building, reminding Beckett oddly of a lifeboat on the edge of a ship. It took up most of the space on the balcony, its heavy rear end counterbalancing the twin cranes that swung over the edge and supported the cradle. All the better.

Beckett walked as fast as he could along the fourth

side of the building, towards Hunter. He hoped and prayed that Hunter wouldn't see him or, if he did, wouldn't react. Fortunately the doctor was standing slightly forwards of the line that Beckett was taking, meaning that he would have to lean slightly backwards to see along the side of the building.

Beckett sidled past the cradle and got to within ten feet of Hunter before the doctor caught sight of something moving out of the corner of his eye. He whirled around, panicked, assuming it must be Hex who was creeping up on him. Too late for subtlety now. Beckett lunged for the man and grabbed his jacket, pulling him around the corner before he could release his grip on the briefcase. He spun around and pushed Hunter before him, past the cradle and out of harm's way. Then he turned and thudded his shoulder into the bulk of the cradle. For a moment it resisted him, but the track was well oiled and the cradle began to move. Once it had got started it picked up speed quickly.

Easterhaus came around the corner, gun raised, just in time to get the cradle full in the chest. He flew backwards, his face a mask of astonishment. His shoulders hit the ground while his legs were still in the air, and he skidded towards the edge of the roof. It was a fifty/fifty chance that he would go over, but Beckett wasn't going to make any assumptions about the outcome. He took hold of Hunter's uninjured shoulder and pulled him round the corner then sprinted for the door into the block, towing Hunter behind him.

The door slammed in their wake and Beckett made straight for the lift. If Ed was on the case then it would be quicker than the stairs. Whether it was Easterhaus they were escaping from or the bomb on the twenty-second floor, quick was good.

'Ed?' Beckett yelled into his radio, 'Ed, have you got control of the lift yet?'

'Keep your hair on!' Ed's voice came over the radio. He sounded out of breath.

'Are you all right?' Beckett asked.

'Nothing that a month's cruise around the Adriatic wouldn't fix,' Ed said with a short laugh.

'What happened to Hex?'

'Just like any soldier who makes a mistake – he's on a charge.' It sounded like a joke, but Ed wasn't laughing.

'Ed, I *really* need that lift up on the twenty-sixth floor.'

'No problem,' Ed replied. 'Don't go away.'

Beckett switched the radio off. He glanced sideways at Hunter. The doctor's face was ashen, and his eyes were half closed. He looked like someone on the verge of passing out.

'Your friend shouldn't worry,' a voice said from behind Beckett. He turned slowly, knowing what he was going to see.

Colonel Easterhaus was standing a few feet away from him. Armed. Armed and very, very angry.

'Why's that?' Beckett queried with a calmness he didn't really feel.

'Because neither you, nor he, nor your exceptionally annoying female colleague will be going anywhere ever again.'

While Kane and Rupta administered the stimulants to the other two students, Ros turned her attention to the bomb.

It couldn't be tampered with.

That was her first conclusion. The clock mechanism was battery-powered, and the batteries, the clock and the detonator were all sealed inside a transparent box. The box was made from a scratchproof, heatproof glass first developed for the US space-shuttle cockpit – Ros had seen examples of it before, and nothing short of a class-three laser beam could cut through it. Ros *had* a class-three laser beam generator, but it was back at Gizmos and it wasn't exactly portable. No, she couldn't get to the clock.

It couldn't be disrupted.

That was her second conclusion. For reasons known only to himself, Easterhaus had chosen to use a designer ball-bearing clock mechanism, and Ros had initially thought that all she had to do was turn the box over and let the ball-bearings fall off their little rat-run ramps. Unfortunately, Easterhaus had thought of that. Four trembler mechanisms were connected to the clock. If she so much as tilted the box by the thickness of a credit card, the whole thing would explode. The detonators, which took the place of stoppers in the bell jars, were also fitted with tremblers. Everything there was tremble-proof. Except Ros, who was trembling like crazy.

It couldn't be dismantled.

That was her third conclusion. The wires connecting the clock to the detonators in the bell jars passed through a small hole in the box. After that they were unprotected. A pair of nail scissors would be enough to cut them, but it was too obvious. Easterhaus would have thought of that. The detonators were probably fed a small charge from the battery inside the box. When the clock finally reached the pre-set time, the chances were that the charge would be cut off. It was the *lack* of current that would cause the detonators to trigger, not the sudden *presence* of current. Cutting the wires would just set the whole thing off early. That was what Ros would have done, and she had to assume that Easterhaus would have done the same.

It looked like she was out of luck.

That was her fourth reluctant conclusion. All the vulnerable points were covered. Every weak link was protected.

The little arm swung up to the top of its trajectory,

carrying a gleaming metal sphere. The ball-bearing rolled down its predetermined path like a rat running through a maze, until it reached the bottom.

Click.

Ros sighed, and stood back from the trolley containing the bomb.

That was the way she usually dealt with problems. Stand back. Don't get caught up in detail. Take a global perspective. Look at the big picture.

Ros deliberately blanked her mind of all thought. The bomb was there, filling her vision, but she shied away from thinking about it. She just looked. The clock. The batteries. The tremblers. The box. The wires. The jars. The detonators. The blue-tinted liquid. The trolley. All pieces of a puzzle. The answer was in there somewhere.

The trolley.

The entire thing was on a trolley.

Ros did something she had only ever read about in books: she smacked herself on the forehead with the heel of her hand. A trolley! How could she have been so stupid?

How could *Easterhaus* have been so stupid?

All she had to do was wheel it to safety.

Ros glanced over to the medical tent. Kane, Rupta and the two others were still occupied. She had to do this herself.

Crouching, she clenched her hands on the edge of the trolley and began to wheel it very carefully towards the lift. If she could get it up to the top floor, the explosion might just dissipate into the atmosphere. It was a long shot, but it might just work.

The hundred yards between her and the lift doors seemed more like half a mile, and every inch was booby-trapped with exposed cable-runs, missing carpet tiles and loose wires.

Each time the trolley jolted, Ros's heart missed a

157

beat. She didn't know how sensitive those tremblers were. Just breathing on them might be enough to set them off. She wanted to race to the lift as fast as she could, pushing the trolley as fast as its little wheels would take it; but that would have been disastrous. Slow. Slow and easy. That was the way to do it.

Click.

The noise almost stopped her heart, but it was only one more ball-bearing having its moment of glory.

After an eternity of trundling, she looked up to see the lift doors just a few feet away. Gratefully she leaned forward and pressed the call button. According to the display above the doors, the lift was already on its way up. If she was lucky, Ed was controlling it. If she was unlucky then it was Hex, but at the moment she didn't care. Just as long as she could get rid of the bomb.

The lift came to a halt. The doors opened. Ros tensed, but the lift was empty. She pushed the trolley to the back of the lift, praying that the doors wouldn't close on it when she was halfway in and blow her to kingdom come. They didn't, and she breathed a sigh of relief. All she had to do now was send the bomb up to the top of the building and warn Beckett that he should get down as soon as possible.

What could possibly go wrong?

« Ten »

The barrel of Easterhaus's gun was a long tunnel into oblivion. Beckett could feel the sweat trickle down his back. He'd given it his best shot, and it hadn't worked. Life was like that: no guarantees.

But he was glad there was fresh blood soaking through Easterhaus's polo-neck shirt. The window-cleaning cradle had done some damage, at least.

Easterhaus held his left hand out, palm up. 'Doctor Hunter – the briefcase please.' His eyes didn't flicker. Neither did his gun.

Hunter, pale as death, handed him the briefcase.

'Now move away from the lift.' Easterhaus, Beckett and Hunter performed a strange gavotte, all circling around the same point until Easterhaus was standing with his back to the lift doors. His gun was trained on Beckett all the time. He obviously didn't rate Hunter as a threat. Pulling a small radio transmitter from his pocket, he said, 'Hex – send the lift to the twenty-sixth floor. I have the tri-meserone. Set the timer on your own bomb and join me in the car park. We're evacuating the building.'

There was no reply from Hex. Easterhaus frowned.

Beckett tensed. If Easterhaus realised Hex was dead

159

and Ed was controlling the lift then all hell might break loose. As it was they still had a chance, assuming that Ed and Ros were on the ball.

The lift doors slid open, and Easterhaus's frown disappeared. Thank God for that, Beckett thought. Easterhaus had fallen for it. He assumed Hex had sent the lift.

Easterhaus stepped backwards, past the doors. 'I believe this is goodbye,' he said with a cruel smile. 'I would shoot you but, after the trouble you've caused me, you don't deserve an honourable death. You and your friends can burn along with the building.'

Something glinted in the harsh fluorescent light of the lift, catching Beckett's eye. Something small and metallic. Small, *round* and metallic. It was part of something larger. Something made of black plastic and blue-tinted glass. He tried not to look. He had to fight to keep his eyes on Easterhaus's face, because he had a terrible feeling he knew what was in the lift with Easterhaus and he didn't want the man to see it. Not until it was too late.

He could feel the success balancing on a knife-edge. Win or lose, live or die, it all depended on whether Easterhaus turned round.

Hunter suddenly seemed to pull himself together, shaking his head and sighing heavily. It looked like the last rally of a dying man. Beckett risked a quick glance sideways, and was horrified to see that the doctor had noticed the object in the lift. Easterhaus reached out to the control panel.

Hunter's pale, sweating face creased into an exaggerated frown. He raised a trembling hand and indicated a point just behind Easterhaus. 'Isn't . . .' he slurred, and trailed off, '. . . isn't that . . .?'

Beckett held his breath.

Easterhaus frowned, and pressed a button.

Hunter sighed, and slumped to the floor as the doors started to close.

Beckett relaxed, and allowed his gaze to move to the trolley, and the black plastic device wired up to the bell jars of fluid that was sitting on it.

And the little black arm that was swinging up, carrying a ball-bearing.

Click.

Easterhaus's head snapped around. Through the narrowing gap, Beckett could see the incomprehension and the dawning horror that washed across his face. His hand lashed out for the door-open button on the control panel, but he was too late. The doors slammed shut with echoing finality.

And the lift started its descent.

Beckett backed away from the doors, dragging Hunter with him. It wasn't going to be healthy, standing in front of them. The concrete lift-shaft would absorb most of the force of the explosion, channelling it upwards and downwards, but there was a good chance that the doors would be blown off their tracks.

The lift passed the twenty-first floor, and Beckett breathed a sigh of relief. If Ros was still there, she was safe.

Beckett held his breath, waiting. Perhaps the bomb wouldn't go off at all. Perhaps Easterhaus knew a way to defuse it. Perhaps –

The building shook. Beckett fell to his knees. He could feel a deep vibration travelling towards him like a tidal wave. Girders screamed. Light fittings shook, sending fitful shadows dancing across every surface. The lift doors blew outwards on a wall of flame, crumpling and melting as they flew across the room. Beckett felt as though he'd stepped into a furnace. The moisture on his eyeballs dried up and the hairs on his arms shrivelled and . . .

. . . And then the wave passed. They were alive. Alive and safe.

Beckett gazed down at the unconscious Hunter.

Considering the man's build, he had held out against pain, exhaustion and loss of blood for longer than Beckett had expected. It was amazing what people could do. Even without tri-meserone.

He looked back at the lift. Or, rather, where the lift had been. There was just a hole there now. Smoke billowed from it, and, from what he could see, the walls of the shaft were charred and cracked. The rungs that he had climbed up the night before had melted, leaving small stubs of red-hot metal. Small fires had started on the carpet by the hole, but the major force of the explosion had been dissipated upwards, through the roof and into the air above the building.

'I don't know about you,' Beckett murmured to Hunter, 'but I think we're going to have to use the stairs.'

It was a long way down, especially with Doctor Hunter walking like a zombie beside him, but Beckett made it. His feet hurt, his lungs burned, his head swam, but he made it.

Hunter was probably in worse shape, but at least he wasn't complaining.

Ros and her pyjama-clad group of tri-meserone guinea pigs joined him on the twenty-second floor. Ros didn't say anything when she saw him: she just smiled with relief that he was still alive. He smiled back as she fell into step beside him. The martial-arts students, bright-eyed and bushy-tailed after their long sleep, clustered around Doctor Hunter and guided him down the stairs.

Ros was very obviously avoiding walking anywhere near Kane, and Beckett couldn't blame her.

At every third level Beckett cautiously opened the door from the stairwell into the building itself and peered inside, checking for signs of imminent collapse or conflagration. The lift doors had in each case been blown halfway across the floor, most of whatever glass was in the windows had been blown back out and small fires guttered on the carpet or across the ceiling tiles, but the structure of the building was safe. The lift-shaft had channelled the explosion vertically, preventing the whole thing coming down.

From outside it must have looked like the world's biggest Roman candle when the bomb went off.

Ed was waiting for them on the second floor. He was battered, bruised, scratched and scuffed, but he was still grinning.

'Congratulations, Ed,' Ros said when she saw him. 'You finally look as distressed as your leather jacket.'

For once, he was too tired to come back with a snappy answer.

The stairwell terminated on the second floor, and they had to hunt around for the exit that they had missed last time they'd tried to leave the building. Beckett for one didn't relish having to use a building-waste chute again.

Fortunately, the pressure of the explosion had blown the access door open. Beckett expected Ros to make some sarcastic comment about the wisdom of hiding the door to the emergency exit, but she was too tired.

The stairs led them down to a hidden exit near the car park ramp. Easterhaus's limousine was sitting by the kerb. The air was cool and fresh on Beckett's skin. He stood for a moment, gazing around at the empty streets of the city, grateful for the fact that he was still there to see them. He never wanted to stare death that closely in the face again.

Well, not for a while at least.

Something was moving, up in the dawn sky – a black, cigar-shaped object that rose steadily into the air. With a pang of memory, Beckett realised it was the airship restaurant where they had talked with Doctor De Freitas, taking off for its breakfast cruise. How long ago had that been? How many lifetimes?

Ros patted him on the arm. 'Come on, Beckett. We'd better get back to the office.'

He nodded. 'Jeep's in that direction.' He nodded across the street. 'The pyjama party here can get back to the academy in Easterhaus's car,' he said, thinking the logistics through. 'You, Ed and me can get back to the office in mine. Ed? You coming?'

When there was no immediate answer, Beckett turned around. Ed was looking uncertain. 'I'll be back in a minute,' he said, and began to walk in the opposite direction.

'Ed, where the hell do you think you're going?' Beckett called after him.

'I need to check something in the car park,' he called back over his shoulder

Ros looked at Beckett. 'What was that all about?'

'Search me.'

Ros steered the students and Hunter towards the limousine. 'Are you OK to drive?' she asked Jason Rupta, avoiding Kane's eyes as much as she could.

Rupta nodded.

'Then take them all back to the academy,' she continued. 'Say Hunter collapsed, and don't tell anyone about what happened here.'

Kane and another student gently loaded the semi-comatose Hunter into the back of the car, and then the rest of them squeezed in around him. Rupta looked from Beckett to Ros and back again, then shrugged.

'Thanks,' he said, 'for . . .'

Ros nodded. 'It's our job,' she said.

Rupta climbed into the driver's side and fired up the engine. Within a few moments, the car was cruising away down the street.

A cold breeze cut straight through Beckett's jacket, where it had been torn by flying glass and debris. 'Let's wait in the jeep,' he said. 'It's cold out here!'

They walked over to his jeep together in silence. Ros climbed into the passenger seat. As Beckett was about to get into the driver's seat, he glanced back at the building.

Three black vans with polarised windows had drawn up by the kerb. A group of men wearing black coveralls and radio headsets had climbed out of the back, and were walking down the car park ramp. As Beckett watched, feeling the cold hand of paranoia clutching at his heart, a woman in a long overcoat got out of the passenger-side seat. Retrieving a wide-brimmed hat, she shut the door and watched her companions vanish into the gloom of the building.

Beckett felt a sudden adrenalin-fuelled surge of concern. Ed. Ed was still inside.

What was going on?

Just as Beckett was about to call Ed up on his radio, the woman turned and smiled at Beckett. 'Wait here,' he said to Ros, and walked towards her.

The jeep shifted on its suspension as Ros got out again. 'Problem?' she called after him.

'I don't think so,' he said, 'but if I'm not back in three weeks, assume I'm not *coming* back.' He was joking, but for a moment he wondered how close to the truth he might be.

Ros nodded, and watched as he walked off towards the van.

As Beckett got closer to the woman, he couldn't help noticing that she was stunningly attractive, with skin so pale it was almost translucent, large green eyes and copper-coloured hair. In the golden light of dawn, she looked like an angel. 'Mr Beckett,' she said in an almost musical voice before he could say anything. 'Good work.'

'And you are –?'

She shrugged. 'If you have to think of us as anything,' she said, 'then think of us as a clean-up team.'

Beckett felt his grip on the conversation beginning to slip away. It hadn't been the best of nights, and what he wanted most right now was a cup of cappuccino and a croissant. 'Cleaning up what?' he said, rather more snappily than he had intended.

She glanced up at the building. 'What have you got? Laboratory equipment, guns, bodies, bombs ... You made quite a mess in there, but all the evidence is still intact. We wouldn't want an insurance investigator accidentally sitting on a hypodermic syringe full of tri-meserone, now would we?'

'You *know* about tri-meserone?' he shouted, suddenly angry. 'And about Easterhaus? Then why didn't you do anything?'

'The key to good intelligence work is never admitting how little you know.' She smiled. When Beckett didn't react, she continued, 'We knew *who*, we even knew something about *how*, but we didn't know *when* or *where*.' She turned her head and glanced at the column of smoke that rose from the roof of the building. 'By the time we found out *when*, it was too late to do anything, and you've very kindly told most of the city *where*.'

'Are you from the Hive? The Bureau?'

She just smiled. 'Go home, Mr Beckett. Get some rest. Leave the details to us.'

He opened his mouth to say something, but the words just weren't there. He stared at her speechlessly, deep into her deep green eyes, and somehow a message was exchanged, an acknowledgement of a job well done, a thanks of sorts, and a warning.

He turned and walked away, and didn't look back.

As he got to the car, and the waiting Ros, he heard Ed's voice behind him. 'Beckett!'

Ed jogged up to the car. He held a twisted piece of metal in his hand. 'Who are the goons?' he said, jerking his thumb back over his shoulder. 'They're swarming all over the car park and working their way up the building.'

Beckett shook his head. 'Don't ask,' he said quietly, trying to project the impression that *he*, at least, knew who the newcomers were. The secret of good intelligence work.

His eye was caught by the piece of metal in Ed's hand. 'What's that – a souvenir?'

Ed glanced down at it. 'You remember I thought I recognised a logo on that metal strip?' he said hesitantly. 'The strip that created the barrier?'

'Yeah.'

He chucked the piece of metal at Beckett, who picked it out of mid-air and examined it. There wasn't much left, but it looked as if it had come from the same strip. And there was a logo embossed into it: two Ws intertwined.

'WeaponWorks,' Ed said. 'It's an armaments company. They make all sorts of things – including security barriers.'

'OK,' Beckett said carefully, 'but why is it important? Easterhaus probably picked all sorts of things up on the grey market. We can't chase all of them down.'

Ed wouldn't look at Beckett. 'WeaponWorks is run by a friend of mine from Oz. Claire Bishop. I thought she ought to know that one of her products almost killed me.'

Beckett nodded. Ed didn't talk much about his life before Gizmos. It was tempting to assume he hadn't ever had one, but then every so often a part of it surfaced again. Like that gold medal lark Doctor De Freitas had mentioned in the restaurant, when the whole thing started. And now this Claire Bishop.

'OK,' Beckett said, 'but at least come and have some breakfast first. I think we all deserve it.'

Claire Bishop felt fatigue lapping at the edges of her

mind. The figures on the screen blurred into an impressionist mess. With a conscious effort she pushed the fatigue away. She didn't have time for it. Not now, of all times.

She had a company to rescue.

The light from the Anglepoise lamp on her desk cast strange shadows across the room. Shadows of a stapler, a coffee cup, a clock in a chunk of onyx. Shadows of the weapons that hung on the walls – her wares, her display pieces. Shadows of the future. Shadows of failure and despair.

The bottom line on the spreadsheet projections showed that she had a few weeks of grace left before her lines of credit ran out. WeaponWorks was almost dead on its feet, like a boxer too punch-drunk to realise that the referee had stopped the bout.

Bitterly, she rehearsed the options again in her mind. She could declare herself bankrupt, but that would be an admission of defeat. She could try to arrange a refinancing package, but that would just be staving off the inevitable. She could sell the company to any one of her competitors, but she would rather perform an appendectomy on herself with a plastic spoon than let any of those bastards have the satisfaction of swallowing her up. Or . . .

The letter was still on her desk. Face down. She put her hand on it, stroking the paper gently with her fingers. Fine-quality paper. Blunt, direct message.

Pulling her hand back she checked her watch. Seven o'clock in the morning! Her employees would be arriving soon! She had worked through the night, weighing up the options, comparing frying pan with fire to see which looked better.

Claire glanced across her office to where a blanket had been draped over a computer table. In the tent beneath, she could just make out the tousled hair of her daughter. Katie was fast asleep, a book still open in her outstretched hand. A wave of bitter guilt washed over Claire. She was doing this all for Katie, to give her some kind of future, but was she doing it at the expense of the present? What kind of kid was Katie going to grow up to be?

When she looked away from Katie, something had changed. The office was different, and it took her a moment to work out what it was. The shadows had changed.

And then one of them stepped forward.

He was a small man, but his elegant raincoat bulked him out and made him look larger. A cashmere scarf was wrapped around his neck, and a gold Rolex was clamped around his wrist. 'My name is Patrick Marcel,' he said, cutting across her instinctive 'Who are you?' He smiled, and tapped the letter on her desk. 'You've had my offer for several days now, Ms Bishop. Is something wrong? Was I not clear enough about the terms and conditions?'

Claire weighed up the distance to the nearest weapon on the wall, and decided that she might just make it. 'I'm still thinking,' she said, gathering her legs beneath her.

'Please,' the man said, 'let's not be melodramatic.' She wasn't sure whether he was talking about the offer or her plans to make a dive for the gun. 'And besides,' he continued, 'you don't want to wake your daughter.'

He had known. He had seen her preparing to move. And he was threatening her daughter.

'Who *are* you?' she said, meaning, *Who the hell do you think you are?*

'Take my offer,' he said. 'Do what I ask. I need your contribution to the grand plan.'

'I need to –' Her voice dried, and she coughed. 'I need to . . . to consult with my employees. Check with my bank. I can't . . . make any decisions now.'

He nodded, just like a reasonable man. 'I understand.

I'll be back later for your answer. And it had better be yes.' Smiling, he turned and walked towards the door.

Followed by a huge chunk of shadow that had been standing by the wall.

By Katie.

Heedless of where they had gone, Claire rushed over and gathered her daughter in her arms. As Katie blinked and murmured, 'Mum?' in a half-asleep voice, all Claire could do was choke back tears of rage, frustration and fear.

When they got back to Gizmos, the first thing Beckett did was to sink back into a chair with a cup of coffee in his hand.

'Bad for you,' Ed said, bouncing into the office. He looked bright and breezy, despite the bruises on his face.

'What is?'

'Too much coffee. It's a stimulant.'

'Thank you, Doctor Ed.'

'Come on, Beckett – haven't you learned anything from the past few days? Healthy mind, healthy body? Peak of physical fitness? Am I ringing any bells?'

'If I've learned anything from the past few days,' Beckett said heavily, 'it's that too much sport is bad for your health.'

'So is too little sport,' Ros said, walking in and throwing her coat across the back of a chair. 'I was thinking of buying a skiing machine for the office.'

Beckett smiled. 'Not a jogging machine then?'

'A skiing machine sounds great, Ros,' Ed enthused. 'Best aerobic exercise you can get, skiing.' He held something bright up in his hand. 'Hey Beckett, if you really try hard you might win one of these!'

Beckett squinted at the object Ed was holding. It glinted with a soft, golden light, and it seemed to be attached to a ribbon. It looked like ... It couldn't be!

'Ed, is that the gold medal you told us about?'

Ed tossed it up in the air and caught it as it came down, a grin plastered across his face. 'All it takes is a little dedication.'

'That's easy for you to say,' Beckett grumbled. 'Even your muscles have got muscles.'

'And they're all one hundred per cent natural,' Ros said, clapping Ed's bicep and squeezing. 'No additives, no artificial stimulants –'

Ed's face fell. 'Well, almost . . .' he said, blushing. He fiddled with the gold medal for a moment. He looked to Beckett to be peeling some kind of covering off it.

When he had finished, he held it up. It wasn't gold any more. It was dark brown, almost black.

'I do like my chocolate,' he said, and popped it into his mouth.

« Eleven »

The gun was a series of smooth, rounded metal tubes with a short shoulder stock at one end and a widely flaring nozzle at the other. It was matt-black, of course. Ed had noticed that most guns were either matt-black or had a brushed-metal finish. Just like stereo units.

And this one had a discreet WeaponWorks logo embossed in gold on the stock.

He lifted the weapon off the projecting pegs that held it on the wall and turned to face the office, holding it like a tommy-gun. 'When I heard you'd become a weapons designer, Claire,' he said, 'I thought you'd be coming up with different colour schemes. Mauve mortars, polka-dot pistols, that sort of thing.' He laughed, despite himself, at the sudden image of an entire army in coordinated colours. 'Not this sort of thing.' He jerked his head at the wall behind him, which was so chock-full of bizarre weaponry that it looked like the armoury for an invading force of Martians.

Claire Bishop glanced up from the paperwork scattered across her desk. A fan on top of a nearby filing cabinet lifted the corners of the papers as it turned. 'Very funny,' she said. 'Next you'll be asking me if the funnel on the end of the weapon you're holding is used

172

for pouring icing sugar into the barrel.'

Ed picked up on the edge in her voice. 'Point taken. There's no reason why you *shouldn't* design weapons, it's just that I remember the times you used to find beetles rolling around on their backs, waggling their legs in the air, and you used to turn them over so they could run away.'

Ed turned away again. He could imagine the look that had come over Claire's face all too well, and he didn't want to have to see it. Regret. Wistfulness. A little guilt, perhaps. Beckett might have pressed home an attack at that stage, while the other person was off balance, but Ed didn't work like that. He had to feel his way through conversations, hoping to sense a weakness, a vulnerability. The problem was, Claire was an old friend. He knew her vulnerabilities. She knew his. Ed could hit the buttons that would make her open up to him, but he didn't want to wallow in it.

Then again, if the only expression on her face was irritation then he didn't want to know. It would mean she had changed. It would mean she wasn't the girl he remembered.

'Perhaps I grew up, Ed,' she said quietly, but he could tell from her voice that she was lying. 'And perhaps you didn't.'

'Perhaps you just went into the wrong business,' he said, just as quietly. He could feel the warmth rising in his face, and he was grateful for the cool air from the fan.

The silence resounded between them like the tolling of some huge bell.

Eventually, Claire sighed. 'If it's any consolation, I'm printing a new catalogue. I'm taking out all the things that kill people. I want to concentrate on selling non-lethal weapons.' She laughed bitterly. 'If that's not a contradiction in terms.'

'Non-lethal?'

173

'You stop your enemy, but you don't kill anyone. I've got the suppliers lined up. Now all I have to do is convince the customers it's where the future is.'

Ed raised the matt-black weapon he'd picked up. 'You're not telling me that *this* is non-lethal?' he said. 'It looks so dangerous it should have yellow stripes and wings.'

She smiled. 'You think so?' Her eyes scanned the room, and fixed on the fan. 'Aim the weapon at that,' she said, 'and squeeze the trigger.'

'Are you sure?'

She nodded. 'Go ahead.'

Ed raised the weapon and snuggled the stock into his shoulder. He felt slightly stupid, aiming at something so close, but he gazed through the telescopic sight on top. Might as well do this properly.

The fan was dead in the centre of the scope. Digital information flickered around the edges of the field of view.

Ed squeezed the trigger.

He braced himself for a recoil that never came. Instead, the weapon bucked slightly against his shoulder as if someone had just given the barrel a little tap with the palm of their hand.

And the fan stopped. Dead. The motor whined in a rising note of panic that culminated in a burst of sparks from the back of the unit.

All Ed could think of to say was, 'Oh, wow!'

When he lowered the weapon, he found Claire standing by his side. She took it away from him and replaced it on the wall. 'An electromagnetic accelerator inside the barrel fires a titanium casing,' she said. 'A radar in the weapon itself calculates the range and sends a signal to the casing when it's near the target. The casing breaks open and releases a cloud of monomolecular filaments that expand rapidly.' She crossed the room and switched off the defunct fan at the wall. 'They're designed to wrap themselves around rotating objects and tangle up, stopping them from turning.'

'Rotating objects like helicopter blades,' Ed said, a rising note of understanding in his voice. He was a pilot. He knew what would happen if the blades locked. The helicopter would drop, rotating like a sycamore seed, until it hit the ground. Hard, but not fatally hard. And the guys inside could still bail out.

'Or propellers on boats,' Claire added. 'Or wheels on armoured cars. Or tracks on tanks. It's a very versatile little weapon, and a good example of the sort of field I want to move into.'

'It's amazing,' Ed said. And he meant it.

'I work to a simple principle. Make the deal while everyone else is still laughing at the idea. Mostly they don't work out. But someday one of them will.'

Ed laughed boyishly. 'This ain't the arms trade. It's the magic toyshop.'

'Toyshop's about the size of it,' Claire replied with a touch of bitterness. 'The big companies keep the big markets to themselves. It's a hard one to crack.' There was something beneath the words, some shade of meaning that Ed spotted but didn't recognise.

'Sorry about the fan, by the way,' he said, knowing the words to be inadequate to the situation but unsure what else to say.

'That's all right – I can still afford to buy another one.'

Ed caught sight of another weapon hanging from the wall. This one looked something like a flame-thrower – a tube with handgrips front and back, with a flexible hose leading from the back to a separate unit that was obviously meant to be worn on the body. 'And what's that?' he asked. 'Looks like something you might use to keep the weeds down in your garden.'

'That's an immobiliser,' she replied. 'It fires glue

175

bombs that expand when they explode and then harden on contact with the air. Come on, Ed. This is small talk. You came here for a reason.'

He took a deep breath. 'Do the initials ESF mean anything to you?'

She nodded. 'Yeah, we market a high-intensity electrical barrier along those lines. ESF stands for Electrical Separation Field. Ground units can set them up as perimeter fences – reduces the need for guards. 'Why?'

'Ever sold any to a man named Easterhaus?'

Her face hardened. 'What is this – some kind of interrogation?'

'I was trapped behind an ESF barrier earlier this morning,' Ed said, meeting her challenging gaze. 'It had your logo on. Someone got hurt, Claire.'

A shade of concern crossed her face. 'The ESF isn't licensed for sale in this country. Are you –' She caught herself. 'Of course you're sure. Let me check my customer database. Easterhaus isn't exactly a common name. Who is he?'

'International mercenary,' Ed replied.

Claire's mouth twitched into the beginning of a smile. 'Funnily enough, Ed, when I ask my customers what they do for a living, very few of them say "international mercenary".'

Claire moved back to her desk and started accessing her PC. Ed turned and glanced around the room. The strange weapons did make it look like a toyshop, but the extensive and expensive security procedures Ed had gone through to make it to Claire's office would prevent even the most determined shoplifter. Even the door to Claire's office, right in the heart of the building, could be opened from outside only with a magnetic card and a four-figure code.

It still didn't ring true to him. Not Claire. Not this. He still remembered her as an idealistic young girl. He hadn't changed. Why had she?

176

Something moved behind the glass panels in the security door. Ed turned to look, and jerked back in shock. A midget with a grotesquely distorted face was staring at him, hands cupping its head.

A ponytail.

The midget had a ponytail.

Ed breathed out a silent sigh of relief. 'Claire – I think your daughter wants in.'

Claire triggered a button beneath her desk and the door slid open. Katie walked in. Without her fingers to stretch her lower eyelids down and her mouth wide she looked like a normal eight-year-old girl.

'Hi, Katie,' Ed said brightly.

Katie just stared at him.

'Remember me?' he tried again. 'Uncle Ed?'

Katie didn't react for a moment, then she nodded slightly.

Ed glanced over at Claire. She was absorbed in whatever her screen was displaying. 'Mum's working,' he said. He glanced around the office, looking for something to distract the child with, and spotted a PC on a desk in a corner. The packet of dinosaur-shaped biscuits next to the keyboard suggested that Katie had already been playing on it, and Ed had a shrewd suspicion that she hadn't been practising her abilities to manipulate spreadsheets. 'Ah – you want to play a game?' he asked.

Katie nodded again.

While Claire worked, Ed pulled up a second chair for Katie and sat down in front of the PC. He had a nose for games, and it took him only a few seconds to find them on the hard drive. Claire had a whole range of things – flight simulators, shoot-'em-ups, strategy games – but the one that caught Ed's eye was an old shareware game called Anti-Ballistic Missile Defence, in which the player had to fire missiles into the paths of incoming warheads, exploding them before they could reach the bottom of the screen and progressively reduce the cities there to rubble. It was simple, it was fun and Ed hadn't played it for years.

'Is this OK?' he belatedly asked Katie as he started the game.

She didn't even look at him. She just stared at the screen. Ed wondered briefly if she was OK. The Katie he remembered – the five-year-old Katie – had been bouncy, energetic and full of life. You couldn't shut her up. This Katie was so different that she could almost have been another kid.

'See?' he said as the first few warheads came arcing in and he aimed his launchers at them, 'you have to knock 'em out before they hit the ground.' Missiles climbed on pixels of flame from his launchers and exploded into globes of light in front of the incoming warheads. 'What do you think?'

Three warheads avoided the expanding globes and dropped on his cities. Small mushroom clouds sprouted from the bottom of the screen and cleared to reveal a broken wasteland.

Katie nibbled on a dinosaur biscuit. 'What's the point of that?' she asked.

That was a poser. Ed was willing to bet that a real missile-defence commander had never been asked a question like that before.

Still, at least she was talking now.

'What's the point of it? Well, what's the point of dinosaur biscuits? It's fun. Have a go.'

Katie slipped in front of him and took hold of the mouse. The second wave of warheads appeared from the top of the screen. With practised skill, Katie whizzed the mouse across the screen, clicking away. Her missiles launched, straighter and truer than Ed's, and detonated like time-lapse flowers. When the screen cleared, the warheads had vanished. Completely.

Katie smiled a small, secret smile.

Nonplussed, Ed turned and walked over to where Claire sat, working on the computer. As he approached, Claire turned several pieces of paper face down on her desk.

'No luck, I'm afraid,' she said, not meeting his gaze. 'If your man Easterhaus bought an ESF barrier from us then he was using a different name. Sorry.'

'Is that easy?' Ed asked. 'I mean, don't people who buy sophisticated defence systems need some kind of identification?'

'Ed, in this business it doesn't pay to be too scrupulous about checking the credentials of the people you deal with. You tend to accept the names they give you; and let's face it, any customer who can afford to buy our kit can afford to have an end-user certificate faked.'

'You're in a dirty business, Claire,' Ed said, looking over at where Katie was engrossed in the game.

'I have to be,' she snapped. 'I have to survive. There are plenty of other firms who would be glad to take what few scraps of business I've managed to keep.'

'Financial problems?' Ed guessed.

Claire jumped as if stung. She reached out automatically to cover the pieces of paper on her desk with her hands. 'Look, just because I have to refinance Weapon-Works, it doesn't mean I'm failing.'

Ed held up his hands placatingly. 'Nobody even mentioned failure.'

'I really don't want to discuss it. I'm going to make this work, but whatever I end up doing, it'll be on my terms and no one else's.'

'That,' Ed said grimly, 'is where I get worried.'

'I'm not the wreck I very nearly was. I can handle it. The company and the kid are the two things that held me together when –' She caught herself. 'They fill up the time twice over.'

'Well, I hope you can make it work. Jack couldn't

179

have asked for a better memorial.'

She looked down at the desk at the mention of the name that had hung between them, unspoken, since Ed had arrived. 'Look,' she said finally, 'if I think for one minute that I'm getting in over my head, who's the first person I'm going to run to?'

Ed smiled and shrugged. What more could he do? 'I'm sorry I bothered you, Claire.'

She nodded. Her eyes were moist. She opened her mouth to say something, but –

Buzzzz.

Claire reached out to flick a switch on her desk. 'Sorry, Ed – I've got a meeting planned and it looks like the guy's turned up early.' Her expression was a strange mixture of sadness, apology and –

Fear?

Ed shook his head slightly. He was getting jumpy. Claire was a practical, calm woman. What could she be frightened of?

'Go let them in,' he said. 'Don't worry about me – I can find my own way out.'

She nodded gratefully and got up. She took a step towards the door, then returned and swept the papers on her desk into a neat pile and picked them up.

As she walked past Ed's chair she reached out and tousled his hair.

'You know I hate that,' he said. Quietly. Too quietly for her to hear.

As the door slid shut, Ed turned towards the girl at the computer. 'Katie?'

Katie remained hunched over, pretending to be absorbed by the screen.

'Katie?' he repeated, then cupped his hands around his mouth. 'Earth to Katie, Earth to Katie . . .'

Still no reaction, but he could see her shoulders shake as she tried to suppress the giggle that was threatening to break out.

'Seeya, kid,' he said, and walked out.

The pass that Claire had given him when he arrived served to take him through several booths, turnstiles and manned checkpoints to the foyer. Sunlight shone through the glass doors and refracted off the polished stone floor. Two uniformed guards stood by the door, just silhouettes against the light. With his skills of observation honed by his Gizmos experiences, Ed could also make out the video cameras and movement sensors hidden around the plain but impressive space of the foyer.

It cost a lot of money to protect premises to that extent, Ed knew. A *lot* of money. The problem was, if you were in the armaments business, then you had to pay for the protection. You could cut corners on a lot of things, but never security. The last thing you wanted was to have half your stock stolen by a ram-raider. Very embarrassing, and quite tricky to explain away.

Especially when muggers and gangs started using your kit on the streets.

Poor Claire. Committed to the protection but without the orders to pay for it.

As Ed crossed the foyer, leather jacket slung over his shoulder, he noticed Claire. She was shaking hands with a short man in a sharp suit. They were both standing by the reception desk where Ed had been given his pass. Claire was gazing into his eyes, talking nervously. Ed felt a pang of jealousy.

'Mr Marcel, it's a . . . pleasure to meet you again,' he heard her say.

'Please,' he replied, with a hint of a Continental accent, 'call me Patrick.'

Ed left them to it, and walked out of the doors into the bright sunlight. His motorbike was parked just outside. A limousine had pulled up alongside it, almost blocking him in. The chauffeur, sitting in the front seat, was so large that the car might have been built around him. Ed gave him a dirty look, but the man didn't react. He just sat there, staring straight ahead.

Through the glass doors.

Into the lobby.

At Claire and her visitor.

For a moment Ed felt a chill run up his back, but he dismissed it, climbed onto the bike and roared off.

Beckett knew he wasn't the world's most intuitive man – as far as he was concerned, hunches were what Quasimodo had on his back – but something was wrong. Something was wrong with Ed. He hadn't been the same since arriving back from WeaponWorks. Moody. Out of sorts. And he hadn't cracked a single bad joke.

Around them, Gizmos hummed, clicked and beeped as usual. Ros was in the techroom building yet another device in a black box. Beckett had been checking on-line databases, trying to find out what had happened in the country that Easterhaus had been trying to overthrow. The answer seemed to be: nothing. The president had returned to find his government still in place and his palace still intact and in safe hands. Another job well done.

But something was wrong.

'What's up, Ed?' he asked. 'You've been pounding away at that keyboard for hours, and your face is so screwed up with concentration it looks like you've been sucking lemons.'

Ed leaned back in his chair and shook his head. 'It's nothing.'

'No,' Beckett replied, 'nothing doesn't cause you to wear your fingers to the bone doing something you normally hate.'

'Nah, it's nothing. Really.'

It was like pulling teeth, getting information from

182

Ed. Beckett tried again, as patiently as he could. 'Look, I could remotely log-on to the computer you're using, hack into all your files, trace back the file audit trail and work it out the hard way, but you could save me the trouble by just telling me.'

Ed frowned. He had the most transparent set of expressions Beckett had ever seen. Beckett could almost see the thoughts as they rippled the shallow pond of his mind.

'You have to admit,' Beckett prompted, 'you're not the world's expert on computers. Maybe there's something I can do to help.'

'I've got this friend,' Ed started.

Beckett bit back the obvious reply.

'She's in trouble,' Ed continued. 'Financial trouble. I've been trying to run a check on the people she's seeing about refinancing, but I don't like the picture I'm getting.'

'What sort of picture?'

'You get a company going to the wall and trying to stay afloat. An offer comes in from these people, but it means handing over control –'

'What's new in that?' Beckett shrugged. 'It's just business. Happens all the time.'

Ed's voice was bleak. 'But in all the cases I've found, within hours of turning down the offer, the chief executive of the company either died or disappeared.'

Beckett got up and walked over to where Ed was sitting. His interest had been piqued. Or rather, he welcomed any distraction from wading through a mass of turgid news about a country he had no interest in apart from the fact that he had stopped it from being taken over. 'Don't tell me – as if by magic, the deal gets done?'

'With the same person every time. Patrick Marcel. French family. French money.' Ed indicated the file on screen. Beckett began to speed-read it. The file was a list of company names, with a paragraph under each name detailing what had happened to the chairman, or the director, or whoever was in charge. Disappearances. Deaths. Crippling injuries. In some cases, fires or explosions. Three apparent suicides, including one man who had taken the lid off a vat of acid in his own factory and climbed in; and another who had locked himself into his office safe and suffocated.

Beckett didn't believe in coincidence.

'This is . . . incredible,' he breathed. 'Look at this one. Dominic Neville – sets out to attend a board meeting set up to discuss refinancing his company but never turns up. And nobody's heard from him since. Why hasn't anyone twigged until now?'

'No reason why they should.' Ed ran a hand through his close-cut, sun-bleached hair. 'No evidence of murder for the dead ones: no ransom notes for the missing ones. Guys are all in deep financial doo-doo – you kinda expect a few suicides and guys vanishing to start a new life.'

Beckett glanced sideways at Ed. 'And your friend's talking to this Patrick Marcel?'

'Yeah. Claire Bishop. Beckett, I'm . . .' Ed looked away. 'I don't want anything to happen to her.'

Beckett suddenly found himself at a loss for words, so he clapped Ed on the shoulder. 'Don't worry mate – nothing will. Leave it to Gizmos. We'll call Ros in on it and see what ideas she has.'

Ros felt dwarfed by the desk. It was like an oversized prop made for a film about people who had been shrunk by some mad scientist. The man behind it had to crane his neck to see her. He looked like a kid sitting in his dad's chair: an impression reinforced by his forced confidence. Underneath, Ros could tell that he was nervous.

According to the prism-shaped nameplate on the

desk, his name was Wilson Cook and he was the chief executive officer. The nameplate was the only thing on the desk, apart from a blotter the same colour and almost the same size as a pool table.

'The rumours are that you're on double your predecessor's salary, Mr Cook,' she said. Just to make it look good, she scrawled a few meaningless notes on the screen of her handheld electronic notepad with a lightpen.

'Stepping into the breech at such a . . . a delicate time for the company wasn't easy,' he said, his voice too firm, too practised. 'We had to send a message to the financial markets that we were healthy and we were here to stay. An increase in the CEO's salary was the right message.' He smiled. 'I'm sorry, I know you said you wanted to interview me, but did we establish who exactly this interview was for?'

Time to bait the hook. 'Now, Mister Cook,' she said as coyly as she could, 'I've hinted as much as I can. Shall I just say that . . . well, we've had too many examples of high honours being given to those of . . . unexamined backgrounds?'

Cook swallowed. 'How . . . high an honour are we talking about?'

Ros picked up the nameplate. It was heavy, and she had to strain to hold it. 'Well, you'll need a bigger one of these.' She locked eyes with Cook. He had taken the bait: hook, line and sinker. Time to whack him with the gaff. 'What happened to Dominic Neville?' she asked gently.

'He folded under the pressure,' Cook said automatically.

'Disappeared?'

'Ran away and sent his wife a postcard. Thanks to him the company was inches from total collapse. His plan involved downsizing, but I've secured backing for expansion.' He was obviously cruising for

185

compliments, and Ros tried to look impressed. It was almost as difficult as looking coy.

'So perhaps you can explain something to me, Mr Cook. You're a pharmaceutical company. You've got a very small share of a very big market. Your licences are running out and you have no new products to replace them. How on earth do you expect to survive, let alone expand?'

He opened his mouth to answer, and found there wasn't one. Not an easy one, anyway. He gaped just like a landed fish. 'My backers have a lot of confidence about the future,' he said, making a partial recovery. 'I –'

His intercom beeped, and the relief on his face was so obvious that Ros almost felt sorry for him. 'Yes, Gillian?'

'It's the call you've been expecting, Mr Cook.'

'Thank you.' He smiled apologetically at Ros. 'Excuse me. I've been expecting this. Perhaps we could continue this discussion at – at some later date?'

He wanted her out, and Ros knew she was unlikely to get anything else from him. He was running scared. She smiled sweetly and got up to go. Cook waited until she was almost through the door before he put the receiver to his ear.

'Hello?' he said. '*Ah, bonjour Monsieur Marcel. Ça va?*'

She pricked up her ears, but the closing door cut the conversation off like a guillotine.

Ed read the postcard again: 'Couldn't take the pressure any more. Had to get away. I'm so desperately sorry – Dominic.' No clues there. Short and to the point.

He was beginning to regret this. While Beckett was tracking down firms that hadn't been approached yet and Ros was approaching some of the ones that had, Ed had been given the task of working backwards and checking the backgrounds of the people who had died, or vanished. The problem was that Ed was hardly the most tactful of interviewers, and all of the interviews were turning out the same. No, he or she had no reason to do what he or she did. No, we're at a loss to explain it. Yes, the firm was in trouble, but it seems to be all right now.

Across the room, Fiona Neville wrapped another cup in newspaper and placed it gently into a tea chest. A fine dust of tea-leaves covered the carpet, and her hands were grey with rubbed-off newsprint. She had obviously been there for hours, filling chest after chest with her life. The room was almost bare, apart from the two chairs. And the chests.

'He loved his work,' she said. 'He'd never walk away from it. It was hard enough to get him to come home once in a while.'

'What about this?' Ed asked, tapping the postcard against the palm of his hand.

'Forged.' Mrs Neville smiled bitterly. 'It looks like his writing, but it isn't him. They did that to keep it all from looking too suspicious.'

'Who did?'

'If I knew who, then ...' She left the rest of the sentence unsaid. Perhaps there was no more to it than that.

Ed turned the card over. Clean sand. Blue sky. Women in skimpy bathing costumes. Candy-striped beach-brollies. Looked familiar: he'd probably slept there when he was younger. 'South of France?'

Another cup went in the chest, muffled in old news. 'We went there once. He'd no special feel for the place. Someone's killed him, and no one wants to listen.'

'Why would anyone do that?' Ed asked as gently as he could.

'Because they couldn't buy him. You want to hear my theory? They're drugs barons. This is a way to launder their money.'

Ed knew better, but he didn't say anything. It wouldn't help. 'I guess there could be something in that. But the thing that bothers me is –'

'Why pump money into businesses that are so obviously struggling?' Mrs Neville looked around the room. 'And it *was* struggling. Dominic had sunk all his money into the company – that's why I'm moving out. I can't afford the house any more.' Her eyes met Ed's. 'Although I hear that the company's fortunes have picked up since his – since his death.'

'He may still be alive,' Ed said, leaning forward. 'Don't lose hope.'

'He's dead,' Fiona Neville said firmly, almost as if she was comforting Ed and not the other way around. 'I *know*. Believe me, after fifteen years of marriage, I *know*.'

Ed looked down to where Fiona Neville was holding a sugar bowl in her hands. The bowl was fragile eggshell porcelain, and her knuckles were just as white as it was.

After checking through commercial databases, looking for companies that matched the profile of the ones Ed had found, Beckett had identified ten. Small. Run by one person. High-tech. Superficially successful. On the verge of collapse.

Newsom's Coachbuilders was the closest.

He was expecting the workshops of Newsom's Coachbuilders to be a dark, echoing place, filled with flying sparks and occupied by troglodyte workers in facemasks beating metal panels into obscure shapes. Instead it was a large, white room the size of an aircraft hangar. Air-conditioning pipes ran the length of the ceiling, flanking a suspended track from which a robotic crane dangled. An area of the building had been partitioned off and roofed over to provide office space. Near where Beckett stood in the doorway a row of bare chassis were stacked, bereft of anything above the tops of their wheels.

As Beckett watched, the crane silently zoomed down to the opposite end of the room. Extending insectile arms, it selected one of a row of twenty truck bodies and gently clamped its claws around the body's sides. The truck was streamlined, with a transparent bubble in front where the driver would sit and a fairing that ran all the way along the base, almost hiding the wheels, to optimise airflow. The wheels were missing, of course – the body was just a hollow shell, with everything below the level of the fairing yet to be fitted. The robot arms hoisted it in the air like an alien predator stealing its prey, and rushed it down towards Beckett.

Twenty feet from him it stopped, then lowered the body onto one of the bare chassis. The arms shifted position, as if they were looking for a vulnerable spot. For a moment they hesitated, then bright laser light illuminated the workshop as they soldered the halves together. The arms retracted towards the ceiling, leaving the unpainted but completed truck sitting in front of Beckett. Finally a person intruded on the mechanical ballet, a woman in a coverall who walked over with a clipboard in her hand and started inspecting the completed vehicle.

'Impressive,' was all he could say as Jim Newsom, the firm's owner, chairman of the board of directors and chief engineer strode towards him. Newsom's face was choleric. He looked to Beckett like the sort of man who worried too much, enjoyed worrying too much and worried even more if he didn't have anything to worry about.

'What can I do for you, Mr –?' he asked brusquely.

'Beckett.' They shook hands, and as Newsom's gnarled fist closed around his, Beckett knew how the coach must have felt when the robotic arms clamped

189

around its sides. 'I'm investigating a company called Computer Recall,' he said, disentangling his hand and resisting the urge to check for protruding shards of bone. 'It's run by a man named Patrick Marcel. Have you ever had any dealings with them?'

He could tell from the way Newsom's brows drew together that the answer was yes, even before the man snarled, '*They* sent you, didn't they?'

'No,' said Beckett, but Newsom was talking over him.

'How do they get their information? Tell me that? Because they seem to know more about my financial affairs than *I* do, and I do the bloody accounts!'

'I was hoping,' Beckett said, speaking calmly and slowly, 'that you might be able to tell me that. I –'

'You can tell those Frogs,' Newsom growled, poking Beckett in the chest with a finger like an iron rod, 'to get back in the pond. All this is mine, and I'm not selling out to anyone!'

'Mr Newsom, I think –'

It was no use. Newsom was walking – no, *storming* – off towards the partitioned office area.

'I think you're a dickhead,' Beckett finished – *sotto voce*, just in case Newsom could hear him.

'Hard on the ears, isn't he?' a female voice said.

Beckett was proud of himself. He didn't flinch – he just turned around as if he had heard the woman approach. Her name badge said 'Lena Williams'. He recognised her as the person who had been checking the completed truck. Attractive, with a strong-boned face and green eyes. 'I asked him a simple question,' Beckett said in his most aggrieved voice, 'and he just explo –'

For a moment Beckett thought Newsom had crept up behind him, boxed his ears and shoved him in the small of the back. Deafened by an enormous impact, he lunged inadvertently towards Lena Williams. Her eyes were wide and her face seemed almost to be glowing. He tried to say something, anything to explain what was happening, but he didn't *know* what was happening. She was screaming something, but Beckett couldn't hear what she was saying.

It wasn't until the twisted scraps of metal and the daggers of glass came flying past them both that Beckett realised the offices had blown up behind him. A wave of heat rolled over his back as he hit the floor on top of Lena, knees and elbows taking the impact as he tried to protect her from the blizzard of deadly fragments. The back of Lena's head hit the concrete floor and her eyes were suddenly unfocused and wide. Beckett glanced back. The offices had vanished, apart from one wall, which had been bent backwards by the force of the explosion. Flames raged across the floor and the buckled outside wall of the workshop.

Alarms were going off dimly, far away. People were whispering, and there was a sound like wrapping-paper being crumpled in another room. Intellectually Beckett knew his hearing had been temporarily overloaded, but he couldn't believe how distant it made everything. How uninvolving. It was as if he wasn't really lying there, sprawled across Lena Williams's semi-conscious body: he was really somewhere else, dreaming it. Just dreaming it.

He blacked out.

191

« Twelve »

WeaponWorks was as dark as the sky when Ed's motorcycle thundered up the access road towards it. It looked as if everyone had gone home, but Claire's car was still sitting in the managing director's space, alone in the concrete expanse of the car park.

Ed kicked the bike onto its stand and sprinted for the door. It refused to open for him. There was a security-pass-reader, but no other way of opening the doors. The foyer was illuminated only by the red lights on the security cameras and the blue glow from a television screen recessed into the receptionist's desk. He looked around for some means of raising Claire's attention and found an intercom button beside the door.

'Come on Claire,' he muttered as he repeatedly thumbed it, '*be* here. Just *be* here.'

The intercom buzzed, then hissed with static. Someone was listening.

'Claire,' he said. 'Claire, it's Ed – look, we've got to talk. I've been –'

The intercom went dead.

He pressed the button again. And again. And again.

Nothing. If Claire was home, if it *had* been she who'd answered the first time, then she didn't want to talk.

Or couldn't.

And Ed had to know.

He was about to walk around the building, looking for a conveniently opened window or unlocked door, when he suddenly remembered something. He still had the security pass from his earlier visit. It may have been cancelled by now, but if Claire was preoccupied . . .

Seconds later he was skimming the pass through the slot of the reader. For a few heart-stopping moments nothing happened, then the doors slid open. He moved quickly into the darkness, every sense alert for danger.

The corridors were lit only by the EMERGENCY EXIT signs. He slipped down them like a ghost. His pass still opened any security door he came to. The building seemed empty – even the cleaners had packed up and gone home. He retraced his steps until he came to Claire's office.

She wasn't there. The room was dark.

Where else? Ed started searching the building, checking the areas he hadn't previously been to, looking for signs of life. It took him ten minutes to find the lift down to the basement, and another five to find the right corridor, but eventually he came to a double door with a sign across it reading: WEAPONS DEMONSTRATION RANGE: AUTHORISED ACCESS ONLY.

Why, he wondered irrelevantly, do you never see a sign that says UNAUTHORISED ACCESS ONLY?

He pushed it open. He may not have been *technically* authorised, but he felt pretty sure that he was *morally* authorised.

The range was a long, thin room with a set of targets at one end. Despite Claire's assurances that she was moving into non-lethal weaponry, the targets were all cut-outs of men with guns. A bench at the end closer to Ed had ear-protectors stacked on it. Signs around the walls described weapons safety and first-aid procedures.

One of the targets at the other end of the room had been reduced to smouldering splinters of wood.

Claire was standing near Ed. She was holding a sleek weapon with a massive magazine. And it looked as though she'd been using it.

'Claire?'

She didn't turn. 'What are you doing here, Ed?'

'I came to warn you about the people you're getting mixed up with,' he said, feeling suddenly unsure of himself. There was something wrong. She didn't want to face him, didn't want him to see her face. What had happened?

What had Patrick Marcel done?

'I'm not mixed up with anyone,' she said. Ed knew that tone. He'd heard it before, years before, when they'd both been younger. She was close to tears. 'How did you get in?' she continued, and this time he could hear the wobble in her voice.

'Claire, we have to talk.'

'There's nothing to talk about. Please go.'

He took a step towards her, then halted impotently. What could he do? 'Claire!' he cried. 'This isn't some stranger here, it's me!'

'You've got to leave, now. Please. Or I'll call security.'

He felt his heart turn to ice. 'What have they said to you? What have they done?'

She turned even further away. He could see her shoulders shaking as she sobbed.

'Claire? Claire – where's Katie?'

She didn't answer.

Ed couldn't remember how he got out of the building. He just remembered the rage and the frustration burning like acid inside him. When he got to his bike he just straddled it, kicked it off its stand and let it rip, bombing down the highway over a hundred miles an hour until the world blurred around him and the slipstream dried his tears before he even felt them.

It didn't help.

It didn't help at all.

Later, after the sprinkler systems had doused the fire; after the shocked employees had been taken off in ambulances; after the statements had been taken and the insurance assessors had filled in their forms; after his hearing had returned and he knew where he was and what had happened, Beckett stood in the rubble and gazed at the place where the office had stood. Everything had gone. Desks. Computers. Filing cabinets.

And, of course, Jim Newsom.

'One hell of an office party,' Ed's voice twanged from behind him. He'd already heard the crunch of glass over the ringing in his ears as Ed approached, so he didn't react.

'You'd be surprised what a lick of paint and a quick vacuum over the carpet will do,' Beckett replied. The joke was forced, but he felt he had to make the effort.

But he would remember. He hadn't liked Newsom, but the man hadn't deserved what happened to him. Nobody deserved that.

'A bomb?' Ed asked.

'I'd put money on it.' Beckett shook his head and turned to where Ed was standing. Ed's expression was unusually rigid. 'We'll never prove it, of course. If this is Patrick Marcel's work, and if he's responsible for all the other deaths and disappearances of businessmen and directors, then he's good. Very good. Nobody's suspected anything until now.'

Ed nodded. 'You know what?' he said.

'What?'

Ed gazed at the wreckage. 'I just hope Claire had the

195

good sense to give in. I hope she agreed to whatever this Marcel wanted.'

'You've tried to warn her?'

Ed's mouth tightened. 'She's not answering her phone. Mobile's switched off as well. I managed to get to see her, but she wouldn't talk to me. Ordered me out. She's scared, Beckett. More scared than I've ever seen her before.'

'It's time we went on the offensive, if we're going to stop this guy,' Beckett said decisively. He looked around. Across the other side of the workshop, a series of partitions were being erected under Lena Williams's supervision. Desks were being carried in and computers were being connected up to power sockets. 'I'm assuming that if the head of the firm won't cooperate, and Marcel bumps them off, then he'll approach whoever takes over.' He began to walk over towards Lena Williams.

'And you're going to be that person?' Ed said as he followed.

'If Lena will cooperate.'

As they got closer, Beckett could see that Lena's face was dark with smoke and dried blood, except for a few lines running down from her eyes where the tears had wiped the grime away. She turned at his approach. Beckett indicated the computers. 'Getting up and running quickly?'

'We've got orders to fulfil,' she said defiantly. 'I know it might seem ghoulish, but it's what Jim would have wanted. By the way, I never thanked you for getting in the way of that explosion. If you hadn't shielded me –'

'He knows it's the only way he'll ever get close to a beautiful woman like you,' Ed said with his typical blunt Australian charm. Lena smiled despite herself.

'This is Ed,' Beckett said. 'He's just leaving.'

Taking the hint, Ed nodded his goodbyes and left.

Beckett turned back to Lena. 'Can I ask a favour?'

'Of course. What is it?'

'There's no pleasant way to put this, but the explosion was no accident. I think it's tied up to a takeover bid for the firm, and I think whoever made the bid will make another offer now that the stumbling block is out of the way.' Lena's face was shocked, and Beckett pressed on before she could interrupt with questions. 'Lena, I want to pretend to be the new head of Newsom's. It's necessary if we're ever going to bring this bastard to justice.'

To her credit, she didn't waste time by asking if he was sure, or saying that he must be mad, or asking for details of who and how and why. She just nodded. 'No problem. If you think it will help, we'll give you an office, a desk and a PC.' She glanced over at the partition walls. 'Just as soon as they're ready.'

'Don't worry about anything,' he reassured her. 'We'll tap all the phones and wire the place up, and when the next approach comes we'll field it. Is that acceptable?'

She nodded. 'I'll tell the staff that you're in charge for now. We can pretend it's an insurance thing.'

'Good. We're going to need everyone's cooperation. You've all got to keep working as normal. They're trying to scare you.'

She half-smiled. 'I'd say they'd been pretty successful so far,' she said.

An hour later, everything was set up. Beckett had his desk, his chair and his PC. A couple of cloth-covered partitions separated him from the rest of the workshop. He'd fixed bugs to the telephone, the desk, the Anglepoise lamp they'd found for him and, just in case he went walking about, to his jacket as well. Everything was well and truly covered.

So why was his heart beating so fast?

Must be the after-effects of the explosion. Yeah, that was it.

He leaned back, a cup of coffee on the desk, and closed his eyes. Cocooned in his little space he could almost believe that nothing had happened.

Except that he could still smell the explosion.

And his ears still rang.

'Will you be all right?'

Beckett snapped his eyes open. Lena had poked her head round the partition.

'Sorry?'

'I'm the last one left – everyone else has gone home. It's late. Are you going to be all right?'

'Yeah.' He nodded with more confidence than he felt. 'No problem. You go and join Ed and Ros in the car. Just make sure they're listening in.'

'OK.' She turned to go, then turned back. 'Good luck.'

'Thanks.'

He closed his eyes again, listening to Lena's footsteps as she walked across the workshop floor to the door. The slam of the door behind her echoed through the cavernous space.

And then there was silence. Perfect silence, undisturbed by traffic, people or the hum of computers. The sort of silence that Beckett rarely heard. Even the airconditioning was quiet.

He swung his feet up onto the desk and leaned back. Gradually, he felt his muscles relax.

He ached. His knees and elbows were raw from where he'd scraped them on the floor, and his back was bruised from the debris that had been blown against it by the explosion. His ears *still* rang. Sleep beckoned him like a lover. He just wanted to sink down into its comforting, welcoming arms, surrender to the darkness, drift out on the retreating tide . . .

'I'm sorry – am I disturbing you?'

Beckett jerked awake. His feet slid off the edge of the desk and hit the floor with an audible thump, swinging

198

him upright before he knew where he was.

A man was standing in front of the desk. A small man wearing a long overcoat of a thin, silken material over a beautifully cut suit. His hair was styled with the sort of precision that only a laser cutter could achieve. A gold Rolex was fastened ostentatiously around his wrist. The smile on his face was friendly, and slightly quizzical. 'I was looking for Mr Newsom,' the man continued. 'Please don't say I've woken you up.'

'It's been a long and difficult day,' Beckett replied, running a hand across his eyes.

'Yes, I noticed as I came in.'

Beckett's thoughts caught up with his actions. Was this the second contact or just a late-night business appointment made by Jim Newsom before he died? He hoped Ros and Ed were listening on the bugs. He'd hate to have to go through this with no backup.

Or, something whispered in the back of his mind, no record of what was said if he died.

'Mr Newsom is – indisposed,' he said cautiously. 'I'm the new management.'

'I see.' The man nodded. 'I'm Patrick Marcel.'

He said it with no special emphasis, but Beckett's heart skipped a beat. Patrick Marcel. The man who had been talking to Ed's friend Claire. The man who had visited all the other companies, before their little accidents.

Marcel reached into his jacket with his right hand. Beckett tensed, ready to dive for the floor if his hand came out holding a gun. Marcel's hand pulled half out. Beckett's fingers clamped on the arms of his chair.

With a smooth motion, Marcel pulled out a folded piece of paper and placed it in front of Beckett. 'I see a future for this company,' he said. 'Enough of a future to make you a very generous offer. I made the same offer to Mr Newsom, but he turned me down. Foolish. Very foolish. I hope you won't be as foolish.' He didn't look at Beckett as he was talking, and his voice was as friendly as that of a man petting a cat, but Beckett's blood was running cold. 'I'm going to need my answer right now. Are we alone here?'

The question took Beckett by surprise. Why did Marcel want to know? Did he intend killing Beckett as well? 'Everyone else has gone home,' he replied.

'Good.' Marcel shrugged. 'Please – read the offer. I think you'll find it's one you can't refuse.'

Beckett opened the sheet and scanned the text. The first paragraph was a short but concise statement of Newsom's Coachbuilders. He had no idea whether it was accurate or not, but if it was then the company was within two weeks of bankruptcy. Massive loans and a thin order book. Not a good combination.

The second paragraph was an offer. A very tempting offer. A large cash injection in exchange for chairmanship of the board of directors. Straight, simple and to the point. 'You know this company better than I do,' said Beckett. Something made him add, 'And I do the bloody accounts.' He shivered.

'Let me explain the prospects to you this way,' Patrick Marcel said. 'What if –' He reached out with his hand and grasped a handful of empty air. 'What if a small and struggling fish were suddenly to find its main competition' – he clenched his fist violently – 'dead in the water, so to speak.' His hand opened, palm up, revealing nothing. He smiled.

'Then,' Beckett said, following the obvious trail, 'a company like ours would acquire a *lot* of value overnight. What exactly are you proposing?'

'I have access to inside information on some of the biggest players in the game. Don't ask me how. I'm buying up a whole range of small companies, ones I've chosen very carefully to fill the gaps if any of these big players should happen to' – he shrugged – 'fall.'

There it was. The lure. The bait on the end of the line.

Best not to make it too easy. Marcel might suspect something if Beckett gulped the bait right down.

'What?' he said in a tone of voice that was meant to convey interest but uncertainty. 'Huge businesses going bust, just like that?'

'It can happen. Especially if there's help.'

'How?'

Marcel reached into his pocket again. Beckett tried not to flinch. Marcel's hand emerged with a CD-ROM disk encircling his forefinger like a silver halo. 'Partners – yes or no?'

Beckett let his gaze flicker towards where the bomb had gone off, hidden by the partition. 'I suppose it's got to be "yes", hasn't it?'

'Good choice.' Marcel flicked the disk onto the desk in front of Beckett. 'I'll have the paperwork drawn up. And to cement our new relationship, here's a small job I want you to undertake – a small contribution to the grand design.' He turned away, his overcoat curling around his legs like a cape, then turned back. 'You really would have regretted it if you'd said no,' he beamed, and walked off.

Midnight. Lena Williams slipped the CD-ROM into the tray and gave the tray a quick tap. It slid into the PC with a whirr. The PC itself had a high-resolution CAD/CAM monitor, twice the size of a normal PC monitor.

Ros stood over her, fingers itching. She wanted to be doing it herself. She wanted to be sitting in front of the PC, feeling the coolness of the keys beneath her fingers, figuring her way through unfamiliar software, but it would have been impolite. It was Newsom's Coachbuilders' computer, after all, and Lena was the *de facto* boss.

And besides, it was an old system. It would have been like driving a ten-year-old car – interesting while you got used to its idiosyncrasies again, but boring within a few minutes.

Beckett gave her a sympathetic glance, tinged with amusement. He knew what she was thinking. Ed was chafing – fingers tapping rhythms on his jeans. He wanted to be out there, doing things. He didn't like the standing around.

Lena used a lightpen to highlight options on a monitor. Within a few moments she had pulled up a list of the files on the CD-ROM. They all had the same three letters after the filename – some kind of standard format created by a specific piece of software.

And, judging by Lena's sudden intake of breath, she recognised the software that had created them.

'Do you know what they are?' Ros asked.

'Design files,' Lena answered. 'This is amazing. Whoever drew these plans used our own software to do it.' She backed out of the file-manager menu until she got to the top-level screen, then clicked on a virtual button to boot up another set of software. The screen cleared to blank whiteness except for a row of buttons along the top and a faint blue grid overlaid across the screen. She clicked on one of the buttons, and a file menu dropped down. She located the CD-ROM drive again and double-clicked on the first file.

The CD-ROM drive whirred, and a set of blueprints suddenly sprang into life on the screen. They appeared to show some kind of vehicle, with everything from basic chassis through suspension and pneumatics to superstructure appearing in levels, one after the other, until the sheer denseness of lines created the impression of a paint job over the top. It was an articulated lorry trailer, designed to be fitted to a standard cab. Ros quickly scanned the picture, trying to peer through the top levels to see what was inside.

Lena suddenly made it easy for her by using her lightpen to colour-code the various levels. Everything looked the way Ros would have expected, except for two angled racks inside the trailer with a whole load of excess wiring coming from them, and what looked like an angled blast plate at the back.

'What do you think it's for?' Beckett asked, leaning closer. Ros could sense his interest in Lena.

'Some kind of ski-jump?' Ed asked sarcastically. 'New attachment for a Swiss Army knife?'

Lena looked up into Beckett's face. It was only a few inches from hers, but she didn't move away. 'You're going to have to tell me what you want me to do with this.'

'Schedule the job and order the materials,' Beckett replied, gazing into her eyes. 'If we don't, they'll wonder why. They're bound to know – they seem to know everything else.'

Lena finally broke gaze with Beckett and said, 'I'll set it up.'

As she got busy with her lightpen, calling up order forms for components and setting up project management charts, Beckett moved back to talk to Ros.

'There's a lot more to this than just buying up companies for their investment potential,' Ros said before Beckett could speak. 'By the look of it, this Patrick Marcel is out to pull off something specific.'

'And,' Beckett said, 'it's pretty obvious Marcel must have access to a lot of commercial information.'

'Yeah, but how? No system's hacker-proof, but this is as good as any commercial outfit I've seen.'

Ed, who had been listening to the conversation, joined it with, 'Hacking wouldn't do it. These guys seem to have open access to everything.'

'Oops,' Lena said from her position by the screen.

The three of them crowded around her. 'What's the matter?' Beckett asked.

She pointed apologetically to the screen, where a large flashing sign read: *Please Wait: System Backup In*

Progress. 'Sorry – everything stops when the system backs itself up. It makes a full protection copy of everything, once every twenty-four hours. That way, we can still operate if a bomb hits the –' She stopped, looking a little sick.

'That's how you got up and running again so quickly,' Beckett said, patting the computer.

'That's right,' Lena said, grateful to be rescued from her *faux pas*. 'The office computer was wrecked when ... when it happened, and we lost all our orders, our invoices and our financial records, but this way we managed to retrieve almost everything within a few hours.'

Something flared in the back of Ros's mind. 'Break the connection,' she snapped.

'That'll abort the backup,' Lena protested.

'Break it.'

Lena tapped a few keys. The flashing sign vanished. In its place, another one appeared saying, *Backup Aborted*.

'Who makes the copy,' Ros asked, 'and where's it kept?'

Lena shrugged. 'It's downloaded through a dedicated telephone line to Computer Recall. They're one of the biggest of the computer backup facility houses.' She swivelled round in her seat. 'And before you ask, they're guaranteed secure. That's why so many companies use them.'

'Yes,' Ros said grimly, 'but who *owns* them?'

The Computer Recall building looked like some vast alien creature that had been turned inside out and left to die. Pastel-coloured panels, glistening with the same sheen as internal organs, had been bolted together to form the walls, while the bright blue and red external pipework covering them mimicked the branches of a circulatory system. Ed almost expected the building to swell slightly and then deflate in some grotesque parody of respiration as he drove up to the projecting portico that housed the front door.

He parked Beckett's jeep and stepped out into the early-morning sunshine. Birds were singing somewhere, but he couldn't for the life of him figure out where. The grass was so green, the flowers so bright that he assumed they were artificial. Perhaps the birdsong was, too – recorded noises on a chip triggered by the sun coming up.

The suit was tight under his arms and across his shoulders, and the tie almost made him choke. He hadn't wanted to wear it, but Ros had insisted. 'Young corporate executives don't wear leathers and ride motorcycles,' she'd said. 'So go and get your suit out of cold storage. And go on *four* wheels.'

'Can't I just be a motorcycle courier?' he had asked.

'Ed – we're running a risk as it is. Patrick Marcel may have seen you at the WeaponWorks building when he went to talk to Claire. You were wearing leathers then – if you wear a suit now, he might not recognise you.'

'Why can't you do it then?'

'Because I've got other plans.'

'Then why –'

'Ed – just do it.'

So here he was – just doing it. Ed leaned back into the four-by-four and pulled out the padded case. It was bigger and squarer than a briefcase, and the Newsom's logo had been stencilled on the side. He walked up to the front door, trying not to limp as the suit tightened under his crotch. The door – a smoked-glass affair impossible to see through – remained solidly closed. Ed spotted the intercom beside it, just where Lena had said it would be, and pressed the button.

'Please state your business,' an American voice snapped. Ed would have tried to engage it in conversation, but he guessed it wasn't real.

'Newsom's Coachbuilders,' he said. 'We lost our ISDN line in the middle of the backup routine last night, so I brought you the optical disks instead.'

Ed imagined the computer sorting through a list of possible responses until it found the one it needed. 'State your client ID number.'

'Three two nine, two four zero.' At least, he thought that was it. Lena had told him three times, and he'd repeated it back to her, but Ed and numbers didn't go together.

Something hummed by his elbow. He glanced down. In the wall below the intercom, a slot had opened to reveal a cylindrical metal chamber.

'Please deposit your data in the safe,' said the voice.

Ed crouched and pushed the case inside. The chamber was just large enough to accommodate it. Before the door could close again, he reached in through the case's partially open zip and pushed a button on the surveillance equipment inside. He'd already orientated the case so that the end of the fibre-optic camera cable would be pointing into the building.

Zipping the case shut, he withdrew his hands and stood up. The slot closed.

'Thank you. Now please leave the premises.'

'Whatever happened to "Thank you for your custom"?' Ed grumbled as he turned away. He didn't expect an answer, and he didn't get one. The computer probably wasn't programmed to respond to that particular question.

As he got back into Beckett's jeep, another vehicle swept up the access road and across the empty car park towards the portico: a snub-nosed, canary-yellow car with the distinct hum of an electric motor. Ros's car. It parked a few feet away from him, and Ros climbed out. She was in her power-suit – all classic lines and sharp shoulders – and she carried a small briefcase. She didn't look at him, and he tried not to look at her.

As Ed started the ignition and pulled away from the enemy's camp, he took one last glance in the rear-view mirror. The door had opened, and Ros was stepping into the darkness within.

Then the door closed, and she was swallowed up within the belly of the beast.

« Thirteen »

'Our biggest clients are in London and Switzerland,' Patrick Marcel said as he guided Ros through the corridors of Computer Recall. Marcel was charming. So charming that he oozed it from every pore. He obviously thought of himself as suave and sophisticated, but he just made Ros's skin crawl.

'Why's that?' Ros said, trying to show some interest in his boasts.

'Multinational companies,' he explained. 'You have to go where the power is.'

Superficial, Ros thought. That was another word distinctly applicable to Patrick Marcel. Superficial. Superficial and oozing.

They turned a corner, and Ros's nostrils caught the distinct tang of fresh paint and the fainter tang of scorching. She glanced around. That section of corridor looked slightly cleaner than the rest, and the carpet tiles a little less worn.

'You've had a fire,' she said, more a statement than a question.

Marcel's expression didn't change, but Ros noticed his hands clench. 'Nothing that affected business,' he said. 'All our clients' data is stored in mainframes in the data vault upstairs. The halon fire suppressor system dealt with the matter within seconds. We are protected against every eventuality.'

'Can I see the mainframes?' Ros asked.

Marcel shrugged, holding both hands up. 'Alas, security. We cannot allow anyone into that area, I'm afraid. It's one of the guarantees we make our clients.'

'Pity – that's the part I was hoping to see. In order to make an informed decision about my own company's needs, of course.'

He placed his hand across his chest. '*Je suis desolé*. It breaks my heart to disappoint you.'

Ros smiled. Marcel smiled too. Neither of them meant it.

'We offer a level of protection no one else can match,' he continued as they walked. 'Computer systems are so ... vulnerable. If you lose your data, you lose your business. We recognise that. We store updated copies of everything on a daily basis, and we offer a complete disaster recovery service.'

'Protection – for a price,' Ros couldn't help saying.

'Precisely,' Marcel agreed, missing the irony.

It struck Ros that Patrick Marcel was the first and, so far, the only person she had met. Apart from him there had been nobody in reception, nobody in the lift to the first floor and nobody in the corridors. Stranger still, the rooms they had been passing looked distinctly unused – furnished but unused, like hotel rooms between guests. There was no sense that anyone worked in the building at all. It had the feel of a stage set – but set for whose benefit? Ros wondered. 'Who works here?' she asked as they passed a large, open-plan office bereft of any signs of occupancy.

'Right here? Nobody. It's emergency office space – an overflow area that we can expand into as our business expands. Spooky, no?'

'No,' Ros said firmly. 'You say you're planning to expand your client list?'

'You're interested in our stability, of course. I can show you our complete client list. We have all kinds, from small companies to big multinationals. They come to us because we are the best, and because we are *very* competitively priced. We're bomb-proof, fire-proof, earthquake-proof, radiation-proof –'

'Bug-proof?'

'The entire building is a Faraday cage – no electro-magnetic radiation can get in or out.'

'What about telephone and power lines?' Ros asked as they entered a large office more cluttered with furniture and computers than any of the ones she had seen until now.

'You're worried about power spikes? Every line entering and leaving the building is filtered. Your requirements sound very stringent – what kind of business are you in, Miss Henderson?'

Ros looked around for something she could use to deflect the conversation, and saw the abstract artworks that covered the walls. No two matched in terms of style, colour or composition. 'Is this your office? It's very – cosmopolitan.'

'Oh, the place is so grim, I had to add a few comforts – my pictures, my sculptures . . .'

Something on Marcel's desk caught Ros's eye – something so out of place that it stood out even amid the clutter of abstract art and high-tech machinery. 'Your milk and dinosaur biscuits?' she asked.

Marcel's gaze followed hers down to the tray, the plate, the glass and the curly straw. 'My guilty secret,' he said, wide-eyed and innocent.

Ros smiled. 'Perhaps I could visit the restrooms before we get down to our discussions,' she asked.

Marcel nodded. 'Of course,' he said. 'Back down the corridor and it's the third door on your left.'

When she got to the restroom door, Ros turned around. Patrick Marcel was watching her from the door of his office. She looked away and entered the ladies' restroom. It was so pristine and white that she was almost blinded for a moment. The washbasins were dry, the taps gleamed and the mirrors were untarnished. Ros was probably the first person ever to use the facilities.

Quickly she turned on a tap to drown out any electronic ears, feeling slightly guilty at disturbing the perfection of the room, and looked around for security cameras. Seeing none, she rested her briefcase on the nearest washbasin and opened it. She had already stocked up with useful items before leaving for the meeting, and she thought for a moment before removing a box with an antenna on top. Dropping to one knee, she peered beneath the washbasins. As she suspected – as per building regulations – the water pipes were all earthed. Working fast, Ros pulled one of the earth wires free and attached it to a terminal on her box. Straightening up, she brushed her designer suit down, checked her hair, turned the tap off and headed for the door.

Then she came back and flushed one of the toilets. Just in case.

Beckett was watching the grainy output from the security camera when Ros arrived back at Gizmos. He'd been sitting there ever since Ros had put the radio relay for the TV signal in place. The camera itself had only a short-range transmitter and they had guessed that the building was shielded anyway, so it had been necessary to connect a longer-range relay somewhere near it. From then on, all Beckett had seen was a wall and part of a ceiling. He knew it was all being recorded, somewhere in the electronic Aladdin's Cave that was Gizmos, but he preferred watching it

211

live. Somehow, it was more involving. Just like cricket: what was the point of watching the test match next day on video? The fun had all leaked away.

'Poisonous little toad,' Ros exclaimed, throwing her overcoat onto a chair and crossing to the desk Beckett was sitting at.

'Who?' he asked. 'As if I couldn't guess.'

'Patrick Marcel. By the end of that meeting I wanted to lean across the desk and wipe that smirk off his face.'

'I know how you feel, but be careful of him. He's dangerous.'

'So are toads,' Ed said, entering the room. He was still wearing his suit. 'At least, the poisonous Australian ones are.'

'And presumably the non-poisonous Australian toads are harmless?' Beckett asked.

'That's right.' Ed tugged at his tie.

'So,' Beckett continued, 'what we appear to have established is that poisonous Australian toads are dangerous, and non-poisonous Australian toads aren't dangerous.'

'I didn't know you were an expert on Australian wildlife, Beckett.'

Beckett and Ros exchanged glances. 'So how,' Beckett asked, 'do you tell the difference between a poisonous Australian toad and a non-poisonous Australian toad?'

'Lick one,' Ed said.

Ros sighed. 'Meanwhile, back in the real world,' she muttered, 'what's happening with the camera in the bag? Are we getting a signal out?'

'Yeah,' Beckett replied, turning back to the screen. 'Did they search you going in?'

'No, but they didn't let me anywhere near the secure data vaults either.'

'So where did you put the radio relay?'

'On the building's earth wire.'

'Why do that?' Ed asked. Somehow, while the others had been looking away, he'd changed back into his jeans and leather jacket.

'The building's shielded against electromagnetic signals going in,' Ros explained. 'That means none can get out either. The relay will pick up the signal from the camera inside the building and smuggle it out on the earth wire to the mains supply. We pick it up from there.'

'Clever,' Ed said.

'That's our job,' Ros replied.

Something loomed into view on the monitor screen: something that looked like a skyscraper wearing a dark blue suit and a cap. A massively distorted hand – or perhaps, Beckett reflected, just a massive, distorted hand – appeared in view, then the camera's point of view was wavering all over the room before settling down into a steady bouncing rhythm. 'We're off!' he said, and the other two crowded around the screen. 'That's not Patrick Marcel,' Beckett added. 'Anyone recognise him?'

'He was outside Newsom's Coachbuilders when Patrick Marcel was inside, talking to you,' Ros replied. 'We thought he was the chauffeur, but he was acting more like a guard. Lena almost walked into him before I dragged her out of the way. He's built like a brick shithouse, and I think he was armed.'

The camera was being carried along a corridor, whose lines were distorted by the low angle and the camera lens. A pair of lift doors appeared ahead. The mysterious chauffeur carrying the Newsom's bag approached them and pressed a button. The doors opened.

'Going up,' Ed murmured, 'lingerie, stationery and kitchen utensils.'

'I'm beginning to develop a phobia about lifts,' Beckett said.

The camera swivelled round as the doors closed behind it. The three of them waited, not quite breathing, to see whether their ploy had worked. Would the bag be taken to the sealed data vaults, or just dumped into a skip?

The doors slid open again. The room the camera emerged into was a nightmare of perspective. It must have taken up most of the top floor of the building. Row after row of computer units stretched away into the distance, diodes flickering in meaningless code on their control panels.

'This,' Ros said redundantly, 'is the level I didn't get to see.'

The camera point of view turned away from the console and headed down an alley between two parallel rows of units. Beckett imagined the scene as looking like something out of a Japanese monster movie, with the man in the rubber suit striding between city office blocks, breathing fire and smoke.

'Those must be the mainframes,' Ed said.

Why, Beckett wondered, was everyone suddenly stating the obvious?

'That's a parallel-processing neural network,' Ros corrected. 'Those are the transputer nodes. Very expensive, cutting-edge stuff. These guys are serious.'

'Yeah, but serious about what?' asked Beckett. 'Not just archiving data, that's for sure.'

'Imagine what all the information in there could be worth,' Ed breathed.

'Updated nightly,' Ros added, 'and handed over free.'

The camera rounded another corner. Directly ahead of them, at the end of another row of nodes, was a crescent-shaped console. Above it loomed a large screen showing a map of Europe. Lights clustered together where the cities were located. It was like looking down from an aircraft at night.

'This must be where they break the data down,' Ros said.

The camera-carrier slung the camera onto the console. All they could see for a moment was a close-up of a few unlabelled switches and an embedded trackball, then the camera was rotated and they were looking up into the Neanderthal face of the chauffeur. He was sitting in the swivel chair, dwarfing it with his bulk. Bizarrely, he had a pair of half-moon spectacles perched on the end of his nose.

'Does anyone else get the impression,' Beckett said, 'that we've been barking up the wrong tree?'

Ros nodded. 'I was wondering about Patrick Marcel when I talked to him,' she said. 'He's very smooth, very convincing, but his knowledge is only superficial. It's like he's parroting lines that someone else has written for him.'

Beckett turned to face her. 'I think it's got to be that Patrick looks the part, so he plays it, but it's Mighty Joe Young here who's the brains behind the outfit.'

Ed tapped them both on the shoulder. 'Hey, guys – I think we've been rumbled.'

The chauffeur was frowning, and squinting at the bag. The picture tilted as he reached to pull open the zip.

'Had to happen eventually,' Ros said as the picture went to static. 'Still, we know more now than we did before.'

'Trouble is,' Beckett mused, 'if he's at all intelligent, he might be able to trace that camera back to us.'

'I didn't leave a calling card, Beckett,' Ros said, slightly annoyed.

'I know, but his brother saw your face, and he probably had a picture of Ed delivering the camera. He's smart enough to connect the two of you together – especially if he discovers the relay unit in the restroom. All he needs to do then is ask around. It's not like we have a secret base hidden in a volcano here – we're in the phone CD-ROM, for God's sake.'

Ros nodded slowly. 'OK – so what can we do about it?'

'I don't know.' Beckett was about to add something when he noticed that Ed was frowning. 'Something wrong?'

'Can you replay that last bit?'

'Sure.' He fiddled around with the mouse until he found where Ros had piped the raw data to, then pulled back the last thirty seconds before the signal went down.

Once again, the big man frowned and reached out for the bag. The picture tilted –

'Freeze it!' Ed said.

Beckett hit a button. The picture halted on a blurred sweep shot of the control console.

'Can you go a few frames forward?' Ed asked.

Beckett edged the picture forwards. Buttons flashed past. The edge of the desk. A dark area with light cross-hatching and a blurry pink mass that must have been something out of focus in the distance.

'OK,' Ed said, 'hold it there. Can you enhance the image – take some of that blur out?'

Beckett looked at Ros. She nodded. 'I've got some software I blagged from the International Security Agency – it's what they use to improve their satellite pictures.' She leaned over Beckett's shoulder and keyed instructions into the computer. A series of wipes travelled down the screen, altering contrast, sharpening edges and cleaning up noise.

Each one did little by itself, but the cumulative result was stunning.

The dark area was a wall.

The cross-hatching was thin metal bars.

The blurry pink mass was a face. A girl's face.

'Katie!' Ed cried in anguish.

* * *

216

Ed heard Claire approach long before she entered the office. She was almost running as she came down the corridor, and she dropped a pile of paper halfway along and cursed as she stopped to pick it up. Her voice was hoarse and halting, as if she was trying to fight back tears even when she was talking to herself.

She walked into the room and saw Ed straight away, sitting behind her desk. She jumped back a step, a little gasp of fright escaping just before her lips clamped shut.

'Before you ask,' Ed said, 'I burgled my way in. I knew there was no point asking to see you.'

'How did you get past my security systems?' Claire asked.

'There are ways. You know the line of work I'm in.'

'What do you want, Ed?'

He took a deep breath. 'Claire – where's Katie?'

'She's at home,' Claire replied too quickly, as if she'd rehearsed the answer so many times that it had lost all spontaneity.

'Can I see her?' Ed asked.

'No.' Flat. Stubborn. Frightened. No chance of negotiation there.

Ed tried to inject every last gram of sincerity he had into his voice. 'They've taken her, haven't they? That's the hold they've got over you.'

'I – I don't know what you mean.' She was fighting back hysteria: one more thing could send her spiralling over the edge. Ed had to deal with her as cautiously as he would with a coral snake.

'Claire, I can help you.'

'I don't *want* your help! Just *go*, Ed.' She tried to force her expression into an angry frown, but the fear was too deeply ingrained. Ed noticed her eyes flicker towards the computer on her desk, then to the onyx clock next to it.

Computer. Time. What was the connection? What was she expecting?

His eyes scanned the monitor. There was something odd about it – something that he wouldn't normally associate with computers. Yes! Sitting on top of the screen, like a smaller brother to the Anglepoise lamp she had on the desk, was a little device with a flexible stem supporting what looked like a disc with a lens in it. The whole thing was barely larger than Ed's fist. A digital camera? He'd seen Ros mucking around with similar things, and it hadn't been there the last time he visited. 'A little gift from Patrick Marcel?' he ventured, and knew he was right when Claire flinched. 'Expecting a conference call?'

'It's something private, Ed. *Please!*'

She was pleading, and he couldn't resist her. Besides, he'd already bugged the telephone. He rose to go, and as he did so he slid the telephone closer to the computer monitor. To distract Claire's attention, he said, 'After all the time we've known each other, I just wish you'd trust me.'

She wouldn't meet his eyes. 'I'm sorry, Ed.'

'So am I.'

He walked past her. He was almost at the doorway when she stopped him by saying, 'Ed – I *do* know the line of work you're in. Did you bug the room? Swear to me you didn't.'

He'd never lied to Claire. He'd always loved her too much for that.

'Of course I didn't,' he said.

And left, before she could see the expression on his face.

By the time Ed arrived back at Gizmos, Ros had a computer set up that was echoing everything on Claire's screen, with added static.

'How did you do that?' Ed asked, impressed. 'And

218

what did moving the telephone nearer have to do with it?'

Ros fiddled with a modem on the desk, trying to tune the frequency closer. The picture on the screen improved. 'Any phone line picks up stray radiation from any screen near it, unless the screen's heavily shielded,' she replied. 'With the right box of bits, you can take a signal off the line and reproduce the picture on the screen without even breaking into the wire. I put a repeater box on the line outside the office to direct the output here. Hyper-elegant, hyper-clever. Just like me.'

'In your dreams, Ros,' Ed scoffed, pulling up a chair beside her. Ros smiled. He seemed better now they were doing something. Less frustrated. Less angry.

She switched her attention back to the screen. Nothing much seemed to be happening: Claire had carried out some desultory spreadsheet work on Weapon-Works's finances – which were in a parlous state – and rented a delivery lorry, but it was obvious that her heart wasn't in it. She was waiting for something.

And, with a sudden flurry of activity, it happened. Icons sprang into life, windows opened up, and suddenly there were two faces on the screen. One of them was a woman of around Ed's age, although worry made her look older. The other was the same girl whose image had been captured accidentally by the hidden camera in the Computer Recall building just before it had been disabled. Katie, Ed had called her.

It looked as if Claire's software was configured to show her what her own camera was picking up, as well as the image that was coming in. Both images were being updated every half-second or so, making it difficult to read expressions or body language. The background was blocky and the edges of Claire's and Katie's faces were defined by irregular steps rather than smooth lines. So, some kind of on-the-fly data compression then. Ros did a quick mental calculation and came up with a good estimate of the bandwidth required to transmit that much information. Probably using good fibre-optic telephone links or a dedicated ISDN line.

'Mummy's here, Katie,' Claire said, holding back the tears.

'Mummy, I want to go home.' Katie looked scared, but not panic-stricken. Level headed.

'I'm working on it, sweetie.' Claire was working hard to seem bright and confident, but Ros could see she was only just hanging on by her fingertips. 'What are they giving you to eat?'

'Pizzas,' Katie said with a scowl.

'Just pizzas?' Maternal instincts momentarily overcoming concern there, Ros thought.

'They give me salad as well,' Katie admitted, 'but I leave that.'

'You shouldn't leave it. That's the best part.'

Ros could tell from Katie's face that she knew her mother was lying, but at least the trivial conversation was relaxing both of them. Some of the tension had gone out of Claire's shoulders, and Katie was even smiling slightly. 'At school we talked about giving things up for Lent,' she said primly. 'So I'm giving up lettuce.'

A sudden, vertiginous swing away from Katie made Ros's stomach lurch. On the screen, Claire's face looked horror-struck as Patrick Marcel's face appeared in the place of her daughter.

'Well, that's it for now,' he said. 'Do your job well and we'll have no more problems. You have the blueprints.'

Claire's mouth twisted in anger as she reached out to something out of shot.

The screen went to static as she switched her computer off.

Ros turned to say something to Ed, but his face was tight and the muscles of his jaw were clenched tight. She closed her mouth and looked away. This was a private moment. She had no right to interfere.

'Ros? Ed?' Beckett obviously had no such compunction. He came barrelling into the room holding a sheaf of colour laser copies. 'I've been on-line to news agencies in Paris, and I've collected the entire rogues' gallery. Look!'

He held up the pictures. They seemed to show front and side views of unshaven men with Gallic features. Given the unappealing nature of most of the faces, Ros would have been quite content with just one view rather than the two. The back of their heads for preference. Most of them looked so hard and, to be honest, so stupid that they might even mug themselves if they couldn't find anyone else.

'All members of the same family,' Beckett continued. 'All in different French jails for supplying and dealing in narcotics. Our two were the only ones not implicated, and the money was never recovered.' He let most of the prints drop to the floor, keeping two in his hands. The first was obviously Patrick Marcel, and with a flick of his wrist Beckett switched it with the second one. Ros recognised that flat stare – so uninterested it was almost insolent – and that great stubbled head. It was the man who had discovered their camera in the Computer Recall building. 'This is Jean-Daniel Marcel,' Beckett said. 'Brother to Patrick. Jean-Daniel is the *real* black sheep of the family. He's run through all of the seven deadly sins and started inventing his own. He joined the Foreign Legion but quit because it was full of sissies. When he heard that the family business was in trouble, he returned and took it over. *He* is the brain of the family, not Patrick.'

'So basically they gave him the family fortune to invest,' Ed said.

Beckett nodded. 'With instructions to think big and think crooked.'

As Ros skidded across the car park and up to the WeaponWorks building, Ed noticed that Claire's car was still in the car park. When Ros kept on driving past the entrance to the building and around the corner, he turned to her. 'I thought we were going in to confront her,' he said.

'I just remembered something.' Ros sped along the narrow access road running along the side of the building. 'Your friend rented a delivery truck while I was watching her screen – a self-drive truck. She did it all via e-mail, which is why I noticed it. The last thing we want to do is barge in the front door while she's heading out the back.'

The car came to the end of the building. Ros turned the corner, and almost crashed into a truck that was backed up to the loading bay. Skidding to a halt she leapt out. Ed followed. Coming around the rear end of the truck, he found Claire struggling to manoeuvre an open plastic crate on a wheeled trolley towards the van. Ros had stopped to watch her. Claire was so engrossed in her work that she hadn't noticed either the car or Ros.

Ros's attention was fixed on something inside the crate. From where he stood, Ed's view was blocked by Ros's body, so he stepped to one side, dreading what he might see. Part of his mind was whispering that the crate was about the size of a small coffin. A child's coffin.

The relief when all he saw inside was a metal tube with bits stuck on it was so palpable that he let out his pent-up breath. Claire heard the noise and whirled around, her face visibly paling when she saw the two of them. Ed was about to say something when his mind caught up with what his eyes had seen. He looked again, but it was still there: a metal tube as thick as his thigh and about four feet long. Two pairs of fins projected from its body on complicated gimbals, and it came to a point at one end. It had been spray-painted white, and the pointed end had been overpainted red. A yellow-and-black-striped ring emerged from a hole just behind the line between the different colours.

'It's a missile,' Ed said, knowing how stupid it sounded even as the words emerged.

« Fourteen »

'Is this what they wanted from you?' Ros asked Claire. Ros seemed quite comfortable with the idea that it was a missile, but Ed's mind was still gibbering. He tore his eyes away from the crate and found himself looking in the back of the truck, where a similar crate rested. With a similar missile inside.

Claire's eyes were darting from Ros to Ed and back again. 'Oh God, no,' she breathed. 'Get away from here! If I don't turn up with these, they're going to hurt Katie!'

'This must be what Lena's vehicle is for,' Ed said, suddenly realising. 'It's a missile-launcher!'

Ros nodded.

No doubt she'd figured that one out as soon as she saw the missile, Ed thought.

'What's the warhead?' Ros asked.

Claire didn't answer. Panic had paralysed her.

'Claire?' Ed prompted gently.

Claire slumped against the back of the truck. Ed thought she might faint, but she sighed and said, 'They're non-nuclear pulse weapons. They're designed to explode at a specified height and put out an immensely powerful pulse of electromagnetic energy.'

Her gaze sought out Ed. 'They're non-lethal. Nobody dies, unless they're within range of the explosion.'

'But every electronic device within range gets wrecked by the energy dumped in them,' Ros said bitterly. Ed could sympathise. This was Ros's worst nightmare brought to life: a weapon that targeted computers. 'Can we disable it?' Ros continued. 'Buy ourselves some time to work out what we can do to stop them?'

'No,' Claire said. There was something in her voice that Ed didn't like: a hard, final edge that didn't match up with the way she was slumped against the lowered tailgate of the truck.

And then he realised.

She was reaching behind the crate that had already been stacked.

Before Ed could warn Ros, Claire had straightened up with a gun in her hand. It must have been lying behind the crate, ready for an emergency like this. It looked like some kind of sculpture, and fitted into Claire's hand as if it had been designed that way. Which presumably it had.

Given the circumstances, Ed wasn't amused to see that it was matt-black.

'No risks,' Claire snapped. 'Not with my daughter's life.' She gestured towards the crate on the trolley. 'Just load that in the truck.'

Ros tensed slightly. Claire swung the weapon to cover her. 'I designed and built this before I moved on to non-lethal technologies. It's a flechette gun – it fires a cloud of razor-sharp needles, and it can shred you into chop suey where you stand. Now do it.'

Ros and Ed swapped glances, then moved to wheel the crate over to the truck's tailgate.

'This is a mistake, Claire,' Ed said as he hefted the crate onto the back of the truck, next to the first one.

Ros nodded. 'What do you think they'll do when

they get what they want – give Katie a party bag and send her home?'

Claire backed towards the cab of the truck, keeping Ed and Ros within clear line of sight all the time. 'I'm going to do exactly what I'm told and nobody's going to interfere.' She swung herself into the cab. 'I'm sorry,' she added.

Without closing the door she started the ignition, then, steering with one hand and keeping them both at gunpoint with the other, she managed to back the truck up and swing it around. Then she swung the door shut, threw the weapon onto the passenger seat and, before the two of them could do anything, drove off.

'Get Beckett,' Ros said grimly. 'I'll follow her and radio in.'

A buzzer sounded, somewhere in the clutter of the Gizmos offices. Beckett jumped, almost spilling his coffee. It took him a few moments to work out what it was – incoming fax, incoming e-mail, hacker security breech, attempt to tap into the protected phone lines or laser-beam bugging of the windows. In the end, he realised it was the door buzzer.

Shifting a mass of computer printouts, he located the monitor for the security camera above the door. He thumbed the button. Whoever was at the door must have been standing really close to the camera, because he filled the grainy screen from side to side and top to bottom: a blurred figure in suit and tie. A young corporate turk wanting to get one up on his office competition, no doubt – the usual Gizmos customer, and a type that Ros had no time for.

The figure leaned forwards and pressed the doorbell again. The buzzer sounded again, like a hornet in a jamjar. 'Yeah, hold on,' Beckett grumbled into the intercom. 'I'll be right –'

He stopped as something that had been subconsciously bothering him started intruding on his conscious mind. If the figure was far enough away from the door to have to lean forwards to press the doorbell, then how come he still filled the screen?

Unless . . .

Unless he was as big as hell and twice as wide.

Beckett's attention snapped back to the screen. Now he knew what he was looking for he had no trouble recognising the bald head and the calm expression of Jean-Daniel Marcel. As Beckett's mind raced through the range of options open to him – everything from 'hide until the man goes away' to 'invite him in and offer him a cup of coffee' – Jean-Daniel reached out of shot and retrieved something long and tubular with a flared nozzle and a handgrip. A part of Beckett's mind found a label for the object and stuck it on while another part was still arguing the toss, saying, 'Be serious, he can't *really* be holding a bazooka, can he?'

Jean-Daniel rendered Beckett's entire mental debate redundant by raising the long, tubular object to his shoulder, casually aiming it at the Gizmos door and firing it. In the moment before the backblast of smoke and debris engulfed Jean-Daniel, Beckett noticed that his expression didn't change from polite disinterest. Not for a moment.

And then Beckett had more important things to worry about.

The explosion in the front room rocked Gizmos to its foundations. Suspended neon strips fell as they jumped their chains. Monitors fell off desks and shattered with a noise reminiscent of repeated artillery fire. Dust and smoke filled the air and Beckett's eardrums felt as if they had been imploded so far that they formed a thin line down the middle of his skull. He clapped his hands to his ears and felt the stickiness of blood trickling out. Blinking the dust out of his eyes, he staggered to the workroom door and stared at the wreckage. He knew it was stupid. He knew he should have run for his life. But he did it anyway.

Jean-Daniel was standing in the centre of the room, the bazooka still slung over his shoulder. 'Hello?' he said brightly, like a neighbour who has just popped around to borrow a cup of sugar. Seeing Beckett in the doorway he swung the bazooka around one-handed and fired again.

Beckett dived to one side, twisting in mid-air to avoid the shattered remnants of a computer bench. He could swear he saw the bazooka shell actually pass through the doorway: a dark, sleek shape, like a steel-jacketed wasp on amphetamines. It hit the far wall and exploded, sending a titanic wave of concussion back into the room. The pain was a physical thing shoving its way into Beckett's head. He tried to push himself to his feet, but one of Ros's file cabinets was teetering on a shattered floorboard, and by the time he saw it he couldn't fling himself out of the way in time. The cabinet toppled, and he toppled with it, falling into oblivion.

The second from last thing he saw was the impassive steel face of the cabinet jerking to a stop half an inch from his forehead as it got caught on the remains of the destroyed computer bench.

The last thing he saw was the impassive fleshy face of Jean-Daniel Marcel looming over him and reaching out with a hand bigger than the universe.

The rest was darkness.

Ros stayed well behind Claire's truck as it drove through empty streets to its destination. If it went around corners then she drove slowly up and peered around the edge to check that it hadn't stopped at traffic lights or been slowed down by other traffic. If it was heading along straight roads then she stayed far enough back so that she was only a blur in Claire's rear-view mirror, without colour or shape.

All the time she was wondering what Claire thought she was doing. The Marcel brothers were never going to release Katie. They were never going to let Claire go, either, once she had delivered the finished product. Claire was playing right into their hands.

But, Ros thought bitterly, all that assumed Claire was thinking rationally. Ros always thought rationally, and she tended to assume other people did as well. They didn't. Especially when their kids had been kidnapped.

Ros hated it when people didn't act the way she would act. It made them so much harder to predict.

Eventually, Claire turned the truck into an access road leading into a large underground car park. The truck dipped out of sight. Ros hesitated for a moment, then parked her car by the side of the road and followed the truck down into the depths on foot.

The truck had stopped some distance away from the ramp. Columns reached for the ceiling like sterile trees, while spotlights made islands in the darkness. Somewhere in the distance, Ros could hear water dripping from a broken pipe. She sought the shelter of a nearby pillar and watched.

A growl echoed through the cavernous expanse of the car park, as if a wild animal were prowling the shadows, ready to pick off unaware drivers. Ros's head snapped round, trying to trace the source of the noise. It couldn't be something alive, surely. It had to be a trick of acoustics.

Her eyes caught a gleam in the dark. Twin gleams, like eyes staring unblinkingly at her. The growl echoed again through the concrete forests of the night, and the eyes grew brighter as the creature approached. The growl broke into a roar – a terrifying, tremendous roar that set atavistic tremors off deep inside her guts. The eyes blazed out, twin beacons of rage, and the creature crept forwards into the campfire of the nearest spotlight, teeth gleaming with spite.

And suddenly it was only a lorry, an articulated lorry with a bulbous, aerodynamically styled cab and a radiator made up of vertical metal bars. Its headlights picked out Claire's truck and its engine growled as it crawled towards her, towing a metal-sided trailer unit behind it and stopping a few feet away. Its engine died down to a contented purr. For a moment nothing happened, then the driver's door opened and a man leapt lightly down.

Patrick Marcel.

He pulled back the sleeve of his expensive suit and checked the time on a Rolex that Ros could see, even at that distance, was solid gold. Looking up at Claire in the front of her truck, he nodded sharply.

Claire got out of the truck, walked around to the rear and opened the doors. With a lot of effort, she pulled the missile crates out one by one, resting them on the truck's tailgate before letting them drop to the concrete.

Patrick Marcel, meanwhile, had vanished into the metal trailer unit. For a few minutes the only sound was Claire's heavy breathing as she lugged the crates to the side of the trailer. Then a sudden metallic whine cut through the air like a buzzsaw. The sides of Marcel's lorry were folding down like advanced exercises in origami, supported by pistons inside the trailer itself. Each side had a triangular section of the truck's roof attached, hinged so that the triangle ended up flat against the side as it came to the horizontal.

Ros just gaped. Whatever plan Patrick Marcel and his deceptively stupid-looking brother were working on, they were certainly committing all the resources they could to it. No half-measures here – this was about as professional as it got. Almost too professional

– as if they were more concerned with the way it all looked than the way it functioned. Ros suspected Patrick's influence there: he looked like he had seen too many big-budget thrillers.

Inside the trailer, revealed by the descending sides, was a twin-railed launcher connected by a thick bunch of cables to a control unit. A flat blast-plate had been soldered immediately behind the launcher. So, Ros thought, on the one hand we have two missiles with EM pulse warheads; on the other hand we have a mobile launch platform with two launch rails. Any guesses what the connection is?

Her radio beeped. Her arm flicked out reflexively to acknowledge the call before Patrick or Claire could hear it. 'Ros – go ahead.'

'Ros, it's Ed. I'm at Gizmos. The place has been wrecked, and Beckett's missing. I think they've got him.'

'Can you be sure?' she whispered.

'I've got a bombsite where my games console used to be, no Beckett and a visiting card in the middle of the wreckage that says Computer Recall on it. Now I know I haven't got the Nobel Prize for logic, but –'

'Point taken.' She thought for a moment. 'Any ransom demand? Terms of surrender?'

'Nothing. What do we do?'

'We do what Beckett would want us to do – we carry on and stop them.'

'You don't think he'd want us to mount a rescue attempt?' Ed asked.

'I tell you what – if we ever get him back, we can ask him. Ros out.'

She cut the connection. Claire had removed the two missiles from the crates and had fitted them to the launcher rails while Marcel looked on approvingly. She clambered down from the flat bed of the trailer and asked him something. He shook his head dismissively

231

and turned away. She grabbed his lapels and shouted. Ros heard, 'Now wait a minute –' but the rest was lost in echoes.

Marcel whirled around and knocked Claire's hands away, then shoved her hard in the chest and carried her back until she slammed against the side of her truck. '*Never* touch the suit!' he snarled, loud enough for Ros to hear.

'When are you going to let her go?' Claire sobbed.

'I don't know. Ask my brother.' He said it as a joke, but Ros thought his expression was more troubled than amused. Straightening his jacket he walked back to the trailer of his lorry and jumped back up onto the flat bed. He flicked a switch on the control console, then quickly jumped back down to the ground as the slab sides began to rise and the roof sections unfolded and reached for each other. Claire watched him for a moment, then stalked off back to her own truck. Ignoring her, Marcel climbed up into the cab of his lorry and put it into gear. The roof sections locked and the lorry shuddered as he fed power to the transmission. The lorry roared again – a beast with real teeth this time – and began to pick up speed towards the exit ramp.

Claire got back into her truck and slammed the door shut. With a squeal that cut across the growl of Patrick Marcel's engine, she accelerated across his path. For a horrible moment Ros thought she was deliberately going to crash into him, but she turned sharply and zoomed up the ramp ahead of him. Ros could just make out Patrick's head shaking in his cab, then he too had hit the ramp and was climbing slowly out into the real world, his engine making heavy weather of hauling the lorry's weight up the incline.

With sudden, blinding clarity, Ros noticed that the rear of the lorry had a man-sized door set into it, presumably for access when lowering all four sides would have been too time-consuming or too obvious. *And* it was secured by a simple locking pin.

Before her mind had made a conscious decision, Ros's body was sprinting across the concrete towards the lorry. It was halfway up the ramp when she reached it. She jumped, timing it perfectly so her right foot hit the access stirrup hanging from the tailgate at the same time her right hand caught on the access pin. She pulled herself to a safe position at the same time as the lorry straightened out and turned onto the road. Fortunately there was no padlock on the access pin, and it took her only a moment to slide it across. The door swung inwards, and she threw herself into the dark interior of the trailer.

And it was only then that she wondered what the *hell* she thought she was doing.

Beckett held his head in his hands as delicately as he would a container of nuclear waste. Given the sick throbbing inside, he had a feeling that the only cure might actually be to bury it under the seabed for several thousand years.

He tried to start with the basics and work up from there. He was sitting on a metal-framed bed. That much was unarguable. There was a thin mattress on the bed. So far so good. The bed was inside a cage. There was a girl inside the cage as well, staring at him as if he had somehow let her down. OK, widen the focus a bit, see what happens. The cage was in a room filled with monolithic, humming transputer units. Between the cage and the nearest transputer was a freestanding, horseshoe-shaped control console with buttons, knobs, an embedded trackball and an illuminated computer display. Sitting at the console was a man so big that Beckett had to blink a couple of times to check that his eyes weren't playing him up. The man was wearing a three-piece suit and a pair of half-moon spectacles. The seat was too small for him, leaving him poised over the console like a bank manager sitting on a crowded train. He had a crate at his feet. A crate about eight feet long and a few feet wide.

There, that wasn't too bad. Despite his head feeling as if the world's biggest tooth had been extracted from the middle of it, he seemed to have the basics of the situation down pat.

Oh yes, the girl's name was Katie. She was the daughter of Ed's friend Claire.

And the man was Jean-Daniel Marcel: French gangster and criminal mastermind.

Anything else?

Jean-Daniel was poring over a manual of some sort, and making minute adjustments to the controls. The computer display by his head showed a large-scale map of most of Europe. Two locations were represented by red dots.

'You recognise them?'

Beckett flinched slightly. Jean-Daniel's voice was disinterested, unaccented and cultured.

'London and Geneva,' Beckett murmured.

Jean-Daniel nodded. 'Computer Recall's biggest clients are in those cities. We worked hard to fix it that way. Can you imagine why?'

Beckett wasn't sure if Jean-Daniel was trying to make conversation, probing to see how much Beckett knew or boasting about his plans to conquer the world. Whichever it was, Beckett thought he might as well play along. It had to be better than sitting there feeling sorry for himself. 'I think I probably can,' he said. 'You sell services to big multinationals *and* to struggling little minnows. You buy up the minnows and use the inside information from the multinationals to help them grow.'

Jean-Daniel smiled slightly, more a twitch of the lips

than a real emotion, and inclined his head. 'Very good. Now take it one step further.'

What was this – a masterclass in villainy? Beckett tried to hold the thin thread of logic and follow it through the maze of pain in his head. What would he do, given that scenario? 'Then ... you knock out the big boys,' he said tentatively, 'and bring your own companies forward to step into their shoes.'

'And how?'

For a moment there was no pain in Beckett's head, just the blinding white light of dawning realisation. 'You kill everything on their computers! You use something like a pulse weapon from an arms dealer you already control. This building is screened against all electromagnetic waves – you've made sure of that – so –'

'So a pulse weapon wouldn't touch us.' Jean-Daniel nodded. 'Unless it went off on the inside of the building of course, and there's no chance of that.'

'So all your computers' – Beckett said, gazing at the rows of transputer units – 'are safe. Then when your big clients are helpless and need their backup material, you don't give it to them. That way, you make a bundle when the small companies you *do* control move into the economic niches vacated by the bankrupted big companies.'

'Big disaster. No recovery.' Without any change of expression, Jean-Daniel added, 'You know you're going to die?'

So much for making conversation. And so much for megalomaniacal boasting.

'I'd guessed,' Beckett replied, trying to maintain the same level of disinterest as Jean-Daniel.

The big man nodded. 'Just so we know where we stand.' Dismissing Beckett from his mind, he looked down at the manual resting on the console, then checked a digital reading on the map display.

Beckett glanced over at Katie. She gazed back, as expressionless as Jean-Daniel. 'Did you hear all that?' Beckett asked quietly.

She nodded.

'Don't worry,' he reassured her.

'I'm not,' she said levelly. '*You're* the one he doesn't like.'

Enough light filtered in through air vents and the open doorway for Ros to make out the sleek, sharklike forms of the missiles on their launch rails. She staggered over, pitching with the motion of the lorry, and quickly examined the setup. She had to find a way to disable them, and fast. She wasn't sure what the Marcel brothers were planning, but it had to be big and it had to be soon.

Her first thought was to pull out the bundle of cables joining the launcher stand to the control pedestal, but they were locked in place and sheathed in braided metal. Her next thought was somehow to disable them from the control pedestal, but it was dead and there wasn't any obvious on/off switch. She tried some of the less obvious ones, but they didn't work either. Her *next* thought was to sabotage the missiles physically, and she was busy prising an access plate open with a screwdriver from her coat pocket when the lorry shuddered and lurched to a halt with a great hum of electrostatic brakes.

Before she could even think of hiding, the sides of the lorry opened up like a time-lapse flower, revealing an increasingly large slice of blue sky and Patrick Marcel pointing a gun at her head.

The rear side of the lorry came to rest angled down against the ground. Newsom's Coachbuilders had very cleverly built a set of steps into its inside surface, and Patrick Marcel used them to climb up onto the flat bed of the lorry. He kept the gun aimed at Ros's head all the time, walking around the edge of the lorry until the missiles were behind him and Ros was in front of him, standing by the controls.

'I don't want to hit anything vital,' he said, smiling genially. 'Unless it's on you, of course.'

Beckett turned his attention from Katie back to Jean-Daniel. The man's fingers were moving with surprising delicacy across the controls, and the map on the display changed to a more detailed map showing roads and buildings. Beckett thought he recognised the area around the Computer Recall building. A pulsing red dot was stationary near the building.

Jean-Daniel reached out and pressed a switch. Beckett craned his neck. The label beneath it read *Erect aerial*. Jean-Daniel waited until a green light flashed on the console, then pressed another switch. The label beneath this one read *Transmit firing instructions*. Beckett didn't like the sound of that. He didn't like it at all.

Jean-Daniel turned, aware of Beckett's intense scrutiny. 'You can lose that hungry look,' he chided. 'I can launch the missiles anywhere out in the open. I've already sent them their targeting instructions, and all I have to do now is –'

He pressed a mushroom-shaped green button. Beckett didn't even need to look to know what it said on the label beneath it.

Fire.

'One minute and counting,' Jean-Daniel said helpfully.

« Fifteen »

'Hostage?' Ros suggested hopefully.

Patrick Marcel shook his head ruefully. 'We've got your friend as a hostage – the one who pretended to be in charge of Newsom's Coachbuilders.' He smiled at her surprise. 'Oh yes, we knew about that. Such a clumsy ploy, by the way.'

Something flashing on the control pedestal attracted Ros's attention. Her gaze slid sideways to check it out.

'I wouldn't worry about that if I were you,' Patrick warned good-naturedly. 'The controls are dead, and they'll remain so until my brother activates them with a signal from inside the building.'

But they weren't dead. Ros could distinctly see a red LED countdown on a display in the centre of the controls. *30 ... 29 ... 28 ...* Seconds slipping past, carried away as she and Patrick Marcel drifted downstream towards ... Towards what?

Her gaze flicked back towards Patrick Marcel, who reached behind him to pat the nearest missile on the flank. 'And when Jean-Daniel starts the launch sequence,' he continued, 'then *nothing* will be able to stop it.'

She glanced at the pedestal again. *19 ... 18 ... 17 ...*

Unstoppable? Well, if he said so. She glanced back at the missiles. It was all becoming so terribly clear.

'Well,' she murmured, 'they said you were the stupid one.'

Patrick's face creased into a suspicious frown. 'What was that?'

She couldn't seem to tear her eyes away from the exhausts at the rear ends of the missiles. The exhausts from which hot gases would be spewing in –

10 . . . 9 . . . 8 . . .

– in just a few short seconds.

'I said I wouldn't want to be you.'

'Oh no? Well, let me tell you something. This is only the beginning. I'm going to go a *long* way!'

Ros glanced at the display.

5 . . . 4 . . . 3 . . .

'Further than you think,' she said, and dived behind the pedestal. The impact of her shoulder against the metal of the lorry bed drove the air from her lungs. She scrabbled to pull her legs and arms in behind the protection of the metal unit, still trying to draw a breath.

'And what do you think *that* will –' Patrick Marcel started to say, but his words were lost in a sudden waterfall of noise: a raw scream of energy that penetrated Ros's skull even though she had her palms clapped tight across her ears. Smoke and heat washed around the pedestal like whitewater rapids tumbling around a rock in the middle of a river. The lorry trembled beneath the assault, then suddenly lurched as if something had crashed into it. A tremendous double *whooosh!* diminished to a tremulous whistle within a few seconds. The trembling faded, the heat and the smoke just dissipated like bad dreams. All that was left was the smell of burnt fuel, and the smell of burnt flesh.

Ros peered out from behind the pedestal. The

launcher was empty. Both rails had shed their loads and were still smoking. High up in the blue, blue sky two points of light were moving apart, trailing curved ribbons of vapour.

She climbed to her feet. The controls were dead again, but she couldn't tell whether that was because they had been switched off remotely or the launch backwash had disabled them. There was no sign of Patrick Marcel.

Ros walked to the edge of the lorry. Birds were starting to sing again. The lorry was parked in the middle of a large expanse of empty car park. The nearest buildings looked deserted – victims perhaps of the sort of cut-throat competition the Marcel brothers were taking advantage of.

Patrick Marcel's charred body lay halfway between the lorry and the nearest building. The intense heat had curled his body into a foetal position. His precious Rolex watch had melted down his arm.

Ros forced herself to look away. Jumping down from the lorry trailer, she walked around to the cab section and unhooked the various cables that joined them together. When she had separated them she climbed up into the transparent blister of the cab and slid behind the wheel. The controls were more like the flight deck of a plane than any lorry she was used to. Touch-sensitive buttons. Multifunction LCD screens. A head-up display projected directly onto the windscreen.

'Oh *yes*,' she breathed. 'This is *motoring*.'

Two dotted red lines were curving away from each other on the map, their projected ground traces passing over streets, railway lines and plazas.

'The missiles are in the air,' Jean-Daniel said, glancing at Beckett over his half-moon spectacles. He could have been reading out the stock exchange closing figures from the paper, for all the passion he put into his voice. Turning back to the console, he skimmed his fingers across a trackball set into the surface. The map on the display blurred and refocused to show a map of another city. 'Target one: Geneva. The business district. Elevation: one thousand metres.' He pursed his lips. 'I could put it through a window if I wanted to – the missile guidance package is that accurate – but with an airburst I can cover most of the city.'

Beckett felt as if something was expected of him. 'Very impressive,' he said.

Jean-Daniel manipulated the trackball again. The map blurred.

Something tugged at Beckett's jacket. He looked down, and saw Katie by his side. He opened his mouth to say something along the lines of 'Not now, Katie, this is important', but she held a finger up to her mouth and then pointed out of the cage, to one side of Jean-Daniel.

To where a metal trolley sat on castors near one of the parallel-processing nodes.

On the top shelf of the trolley was a jumble of cables. On the bottom shelf were a roll of electrician's tape, a set of screwdrivers . . . and a pair of wire-strippers. It was a few yards away – too far to reach – but it offered a chance. He smiled at Katie, and nodded. Without any change of expression, she turned and retreated to the little nest she had made at the end of the cage.

Beckett looked back at Jean-Daniel's impassive face. The two of them could have been father and daughter.

'Oh, isn't that sweet,' Jean-Daniel said in his unexpectedly cultivated voice. Beckett followed his gaze. The big man was looking at the picture displayed on one of the many monitor screens that ringed his map display. It seemed to be showing the output from a security camera outside the building, angled onto the projecting lobby and the datachute that Ed had put the camera case into earlier. On the screen, a dark-haired woman with a harried but determined expression was pulling at the doors to the lobby. She had a vicious-looking weapon slung over one shoulder as casually as a handbag.

Katie was suddenly at Beckett's side. She didn't say anything, but she looked up at him beseechingly.

'Mummy?' he asked.

She nodded.

Jean-Daniel rose from his seat and walked across to the cage. Beckett and Katie backed away in tandem, but all the man did was rattle the padlock holding the door shut. Satisfied that it was firm, he turned away.

'Hey,' Beckett called. When Jean-Daniel turned back, he jerked his thumb towards Katie. 'Let her go.'

Jean-Daniel shook his massive head. 'I don't think so.' He turned away again and walked over to a packing crate projecting from behind the control console. Bending, not without some effort, he opened the crate and pulled out a –

Beckett blinked. That *couldn't* be a bazooka, could it?

It could.

It could and it was.

With the bazooka dangling from one hand, Jean-Daniel strolled casually out of sight.

Ed had parked his bike some distance away and approached the Computer Recall building on foot, toting a heavy rucksack that he'd filled at the Weapon-Works premises on the way. Claire was pulling forlornly on the doors to the lobby that projected from the side of the building. Ed managed to get within a few feet of her before she heard him. She swung her gun up, but Ed knocked it away. 'Hey, Claire, come on!' he protested.

'No!' she cried. He grabbed hold of her, but she struggled to pull free. 'Ed – Katie's in there!'

'So's my friend Beckett. Claire, you're right where the cameras can see you. Come *on*!'

He pulled her round the corner. She struggled, but only half-heartedly, as if she couldn't think of anything else to do. A clear strip of land ran around the perimeter of the building, but it all looked far too exposed for Ed's liking. They could be picked off by anyone on the roof. He scooted across the open ground, dragging Claire with him, until they were both in the shelter of a leafy bush.

And not a moment too soon.

When Ed looked back at the building there was a figure standing on top of it, silhouetted against the sky like some stop-motion animated colossus in a film. The figure was almost as broad as it was tall – at least, that was the way it looked to Ed – and it had a long tube slung over its shoulder. The figure's head swung slowly to and fro with the metronomic regularity of a radar dish. Nothing else moved.

Jean-Daniel Marcel: it had to be. 'I swear I've seen something like him throwing bananas in a computer game,' Ed said.

Claire wasn't listening. 'They promised me,' she whispered. 'They *promised* me.'

'Well, now you know what their promises are worth.' Ed felt like a bastard, saying it, but sometimes the brutal truth worked better than sympathy.

Claire flinched as if slapped, then looked away. Ed looked back at the statue-like sentry, and scrabbled around the ground for a stone big enough to throw. His fist closed over one, and he waited until Jean-Daniel was looking away from him, along the length of the building, before standing up, stepping to one side and throwing the stone as hard as he could in the opposite direction. Before the stone had reached the apogee of its arc, Ed was safely hidden behind the bush again.

243

The stone hit a small tree with an audible thud. Jean-Daniel's head snapped around, the bazooka following a half-second behind. Jean-Daniel spotted the leaves shaking on the tree and his fingers were tapping information into the bazooka even as he was swinging it up to firing position. A plume of flame erupted behind him, and suddenly the tree wasn't a tree any longer, it was a smoking hole in the ground and a shower of splintered wood. Jean-Daniel lowered the bazooka slowly, his face unmoving. He waited for a moment, then smiled slightly – the first expression Ed had seen on his face – and turned away. A few steps took him out of sight, beyond the edge of the roof.

'He's good,' Ed said grudgingly. He took Claire's hand. 'Come on, I've got an idea.' Before she could object, he pulled her at a crouching run across the empty ground between the bush and the wall of the building. He slammed himself against the wall, flattening his body against the pastel-coloured plastic panels as hard as he could. Claire joined him, too out of breath to say anything. Ed counted to ten. When there was no explosion, he knew Jean-Daniel hadn't seen them.

He sidled up to the corner and edged around, looking out for any activity around the entrance lobby. There was nothing going on, just Claire's truck and his motorbike standing there. He sprinted along the edge of the building, still pulling Claire with him, and skidded to a halt by the data safe. He knew there had to be a camera around there somewhere but, if he was lucky, he could get into the building before Jean-Daniel got back to the monitor. Ed pressed the button on the intercom.

'Please state your business,' the computer-generated voice snapped.

Ed glanced at Claire. She looked back at him uncomprehendingly. He nodded towards the intercom, then back at her.

'Er . . . WeaponWorks,' she stammered eventually.

'Our telephone line's down, so I'm dropping in the backups by hand.'

'State your client ID number.'

'Six, five, five, two –' She hesitated, uncertain.

'Jeez, Claire, speed it up!'

'– nine, five!'

The slot in the wall hummed open. 'Please deposit your data in the safe,' said the voice.

Before it could close again, Ed climbed into the cylindrical metal chamber, pulling the bulky rucksack in behind him. He had to scrunch up as tightly as he could to get in, and his back was almost bent to breaking point. He tried to breathe, but he could pull in only half a breath before he had no space left to expand into.

He twisted his head and looked up at Claire. She reached out a hand to his cheek, but the chamber rotated, closing off his view. The last thing he saw was Claire snatching her hand away before it could be severed by the edge of the hatch.

'Thank you,' the artificial voice said, muffled by the metal. 'Now please leave the premises.'

A loop of cable had slipped from the trolley, and lay curled on the floor like a sleeping python. It must have been knocked off by somebody brushing past. The other end of the cable was plugged into the back of the monitor on the top shelf: if Beckett could reach it then he could pull the trolley over and retrieve the wire-strippers, but he couldn't even get his hand through the mesh of the wire cage.

But if *he* couldn't . . .

'Katie, you see that wire over there?'

She looked over to where he was pointing, then looked back at him and nodded once.

'I can't get my hand through to reach it. Your hand is smaller. Can you do it?'

She looked back again. Bit her lip. Looked at her hand.

'Look,' he said, 'it's not going to bite. Just give it a try, hmmm?'

Katie dropped to her knees and reached through the mesh. Her slender arm fitted through up to the shoulder. Beckett watched, hardly daring to breathe as her fingers waggled a few scant millimetres from the cable. 'Take your time,' he breathed.

She shifted position, putting her weight on the wire mesh until it gave slightly, giving her the extra distance she needed. Her fingers brushed against the cable. She scooped at it, her fingertips pulling at the insulation, dragging it back a bit at a time until she could close her hand around it and pull it back towards the cage.

'Well done,' Beckett said as she pulled the cable in through the mesh and handed it to him. He pulled on it, trying not to pull so hard that the cable would detach from the monitor. To his immense relief, the trolley shifted a few inches. Reeling the trolley in like a fish on a line, he pulled it towards the cage until it nudged the mesh; then he reached through and retrieved the wire-strippers.

Ten seconds later he had cut a hole in the mesh, and he and Katie were out of the cage. Katie headed for the door, but Beckett crossed straight to the control console, still displaying the map of Geneva. She looked back at him, annoyance on her face. 'Sorry, kid,' he said, 'but we have to save the world. It's an obligation of the job.' He glanced at the screen. 'Hmmm – target one: Geneva,' he mused. 'Let's say the lake. Elevation: minus one hundred metres. Let's hope none of the fish are wearing pacemakers.'

Katie was standing by his side with an expression that said, as clear as day, 'you're talking rubbish, aren't you?'

Beckett glanced at her, glanced away, then glanced back again. 'Look,' he said, feeling foolish at having to justify himself to a kid, 'the missiles are steered from here. That means we can change the targets and make the missiles alter course so they end up going off somewhere harmless – like the bottom of a lake.'

She raised a scornful eyebrow.

'I'll show you,' he said. He let his gaze roam over the console, taking in the position of the switches and the writing on the labels. His confidence wilted somewhat when he realised there was nothing he recognised. He hated doing this: it was like being put into an aircraft cockpit for the first time and being asked to take off with no training.

What was the button marked *THXP* for? What was the difference between *Add-1* and *Add-2*? Why was the dial on the left hand side of the console marked up to *10* while the one on the right was marked up to *11*? His hands hovered impotently above the surface while he tried to decypher the unfamiliar hieroglyphics.

Perhaps the trackball? He ran a finger gingerly over it. The map on the screen blurred dizzyingly and came to rest showing a mountain range.

'I just wish this was as easy as it looked,' he muttered, and nudged the ball again. The mountain range whizzed dizzyingly away, and suddenly they were looking at a blank screen. A malfunction? An area of ocean? He couldn't tell.

With a little huff of impatience, Katie slid between Beckett and the console. He stepped back.

'Katie, I don't –'

Her hands skipped over the controls, pressing buttons, nudging levers and steering the trackball with one confident finger. The screen blurred again, but this was a *purposeful* blur, an *intentional* blur, and it cleared to show the street plan of Geneva again. With three swift motions that Beckett tried to follow but couldn't,

Katie zoomed in on the lake and reset the target position and height. *New target locked* flashed across the screen.

Katie looked up at Beckett, and smiled.

'You've done this before,' he accused her. Turning back to the screen, he added, 'Target two, now –' But Katie's hands were already moving across the console.

Beckett was beginning to feel ever so slightly redundant.

Ros took the corner into the Computer Recall car park so fast that she almost tipped the lorry over. Wrestling with the computer-aided steering, which seemed to take a perverse delight in resisting her every manoeuvre, she skidded the empty trailer around and accelerated towards the pastel-coloured, pipe-encrusted building.

A figure was standing in front of the lobby, which looked like a late addition bolted onto the outside of the building.

Ros considered accelerating and running the figure down, until she recognised Claire Bishop. Even then, it was touch and go for a moment.

Claire ran to meet her as Ros pulled the lorry up with a hum of electrostatic brakes.

'I couldn't stop the launch,' Ros said before the woman could say anything. 'Have you seen Ed?'

'They're all inside,' Claire gasped. 'Ed, Beckett and Katie – but I don't know how they're going to get out. There's a madman with a bazooka wandering around, shooting things, and the building's an armoured shell!'

For a moment Ros wondered whether the shock of the past day had unhinged Claire's reasoning, but she seemed lucid enough. A man with a bazooka? After Easterhaus and his bombs, she guessed that anything was possible. 'OK,' she said, 'we can fix that – no problem.'

Claire climbed up into the passenger seat as Ros gunned the engine. The lorry rolled forwards, slowly at first but gathering momentum fast. Ros aimed it directly at the projecting lobby. The building loomed up before them with frightening speed, but Ros kept her foot firmly on the accelerator. Warning lights flashed all across the dashboard as the lorry's radar proximity-warning system realised a crash was imminent. Ros overrode all the safety cutouts with a sweep of her hand. She waited until she could see her reflection in the armoured perspex of the lobby, and the reflection of Claire's horrified face, before spinning the wheel around. The cab twisted to the right, but the mass of the trailer still carried it forwards. Gradually the trailer skidded around until the entire lorry was travelling sideways – but still towards the lobby.

It hit with a sound like that of the world breaking apart. The lobby had been built to withstand a lot of things, but its designers had never envisaged having to protect it against a lorry crashing into it. Glass broke and metal folded. The lorry just kept ploughing on – taking designer sofas and potted plants with it – until it slammed into the archway that led into the building proper. Ros and Claire were thrown from their seats, ending up in a tangle of limbs down by the pedals.

Silence, apart from the occasional tinkle of perspex falling out of a buckled frame.

'And that,' Ros said, hauling herself painfully upright, 'is how not to park a lorry.'

Beckett watched from behind one of the parallel-processing nodes as Jean-Daniel Marcel strode past. The ground shook as he moved. He was still carrying the bazooka, and Beckett noticed that it was smoking. He'd been busy.

Beckett counted to fifteen, then emerged from behind the unit. Katie peered out from the next one along the line. He nodded, and they met in the aisle between the units.

Jean-Daniel had disappeared, somewhere among the units. The place was like a maze. Every unit looked the same. Every aisle between rows of units looked the same. Within a few minutes of walking away from the control console, after resetting the target point for the second missile, Beckett had been lost. He didn't want to admit that to Katie, though.

Beckett looked in the direction that Jean-Daniel had come from. All he could see were parallel-processing units in endless repeating patterns, but he knew that there had to be an exit down there.

Somewhere.

Probably.

He took Katie's shoulder and was just about to move off when an enormous bellow shook the units. It sounded like a minotaur whose sacrifice has just legged it.

Katie held up her hand. She was holding the track-ball from the control console.

'Yes,' Beckett said to her unspoken question. 'I think he's noticed.'

She kept looking at him with her usual solemn expression.

'No, I don't think he's pleased.'

She didn't bat an eyelid.

'Yes, I *do* think we'd better make our escape.'

Beckett moved quickly down the aisle, his hand folded around Katie's. Any moment he expected to see the doors to the lift. Any moment.

Nothing. The aisle ended abruptly in a blank wall.

Beckett turned and scanned the aisles leading away from that point. They could retrace their steps, but that would put them right back in Jean-Daniel's lap. Best thing to do would be to follow the wall. Unless the lift was set in a central block, like the one in Easterhaus's skyscraper, then they would come to it. Eventually.

Right or left?

No way to tell. All he could do was pick a direction at random and make the best of it.

'Come on,' he said as cheerfully as he could, and they followed the aisle to the left, paralleling the wall.

Beckett kept his head twisted to the left, looking down every aisle that they passed for Jean-Daniel; so it was a shock when Katie pulled him back and he looked around to find that they had reached a corner. The wall went off to the left again, the aisle vanishing in a grey haze of perspective some way ahead.

He glanced down at Katie. Her mouth was compressed into a thin line. 'You think you could do better?' he asked.

This time she raised both eyebrows.

'Come on.'

They passed three aisles, Beckett checking each one as they walked by.

Jean-Daniel was standing in the fourth aisle.

« Sixteen »

Jean-Daniel was twenty feet away, side-on to them at the junction of two aisles, fitting between the units like a bowling ball in a pipe. His bazooka was held level with the ground. The only thing that moved was his head as he swung it slowly back and forth. He was looking in the opposite direction when Beckett saw him, but his head was swivelling towards them.

Beckett pressed Katie back with his forearm and stepped into the lee of one of the parallel-processing units. The intensity of Jean-Daniel's gaze seemed to illuminate the aisle like a lighthouse as he stared down it. For a long moment Beckett held his breath, just in case Jean-Daniel could hear it. His heart thudded, and he desperately concentrated on it, trying to quieten the pounding. He even did his best to still the clamour of his thoughts.

And then the preternatural scrutiny passed on, and Beckett knew that Jean-Daniel was looking away. He peered out from behind the unit, looking along the aisle to where the man had been standing, but he was gone.

'Quickly,' he hissed, and pulled Katie along as he raced down the aisle, still keeping the wall on his right.

He kept snapping his head left to check the aisles as they passed, then snapping it back to check ahead of them in case Jean-Daniel had magically appeared – but he was moving so fast that he kept missing aisles out.

Something was different down one of the aisles. He had gone past two more before his brain processed the information. Halting, he took a few steps backwards and edged around one of the units to check.

The aisle led away like an architect's perspective drawing, bounded on both sides by the units. But in the far, far distance, Beckett could make out the open doors to a lift. Light spilled out from the lift's interior: bright, welcoming, safe.

Beckett yanked Katie into the aisle and started sprinting down towards the lift doors. Parallel-processing units flickered past like the frames on a silent film. The doors seemed to retreat from them at the same speed as they were running, as if they were trapped in some eternal Keystone Kops chase sequence.

And that was when the lift doors started to close.

Gracefully.

Slowly.

But damningly.

Beckett sprinted ahead of Katie. If he could get to the doors and hold them open, it might give her enough time to run the remaining distance.

He seemed to be spending his whole life running.

What remained of it, anyway.

The doors were twenty metres away and one metre apart. His breath was jammed up in his throat. His teeth were drawn back in a snarl. He could feel the beat of his heart vibrating across his whole chest like the tolling of an iron bell.

The doors were ten metres away and fifty centimetres apart. His vision was hazing as his muscles sucked up all the available oxygen and his heart laboured to deliver some to his brain. He couldn't feel his arms or legs: he seemed to be a disembodied presence hurtling along the corridor, six feet above the floor.

The doors were five metres away and ten centimetres apart. With his last conscious thought, Beckett stopped running and twisted his body sideways, skidding across the carpet like a baseball player coming into the home plate a millisecond ahead of the ball. He extended his leg, aiming for the gap. If he could just get his foot through and into the lift, the automatic sensors would open the doors again.

No such luck.

The lift doors were a centimetre apart when his outstretched foot hit them. His leg folded up as his body crashed into the unyielding metal. The impact knocked the wind from his body and the sense from his mind. His last sight before his head hit the lift doors was that last millimetre of welcoming light thinning to nothingness.

The rebound sent him flying back down the corridor and into Katie. She twisted out of the way. He hit the floor and rolled.

When he got to his feet, Katie was staring back the way they had come, wide-eyed.

Beckett turned.

Jean-Daniel was striding towards them like the Angel of Death.

Beckett calmly reached out, put his hand on Katie's shoulder and pushed her gently behind him. He could feel her cower into his back.

Jean-Daniel stopped ten metres away. 'Very touching,' he said in the same tone of voice he might have used to discuss the price of root vegetables with his grocer, 'but futile.' Holding the bazooka in one hand, he pushed the keys on the tiny control panel with his sausage-like fingers. 'All I have to do is type in the range, the size and the type of target, and in return I can take both of you out with one shot.'

'That's probably the worst case of overkill I've ever seen,' Beckett said, defiant to the last. 'Why not just shoot us?'

'Perhaps more practical,' Jean-Daniel conceded, 'but infinitely less satisfying. As my late, lamented brother once said, I must have my little games.'

He smiled – briefly, coldly – and swung the bazooka up until it was centred on Beckett's forehead.

For one infinitely long moment, Beckett knew that he was dead, and he was surprised to realise that death didn't frighten him. At least he had scotched the Marcels' plans to wipe the computers of the world's two major centres of finance and take them over by stealth. It was his failure that really bothered him – his failure to save Katie.

He took a deep breath, and stared straight down the barrel of the bazooka at the snub nose of the shell.

Jean-Daniel cocked his head to one side and placed one eye against the telescopic sight. He screwed his other eye shut in a surreal wink, and Beckett saw his knuckles whiten as he took the slack up on the trigger.

Beckett's last thought was how stupid Jean-Daniel looked, using an aiming device at a range of twenty feet.

Beckett's last thought plus one was that the lift doors behind him were opening. He could hear them sliding. Who the hell had such bad timing as to come out of a lift just as a madman was about to fire a bazooka into it?

'Am I too late for the party?' said an Australian voice.

Beckett whirled around. Ed walked out of the lift to join them, grinning his usual inane grin. He had some kind of cylindrical backpack on, and was cradling a flexible tube that connected it to a strangely shaped weapon, which looked like a miniature version of Jean-Daniel's bazooka.

Jean-Daniel grimaced. Beckett could tell from his

face that Ed's arrival was just a minor inconvenience to him. The bazooka could take out all three of them.

The bazooka.

The electronically controlled bazooka.

With his head full of the noise of two facts accidentally colliding, Beckett said, 'Stop!' in such a commanding tone of voice that Jean-Daniel actually moved his head out from behind the aiming device and looked at him. 'There's something you ought to be asking me!'

'Like what?' Jean-Daniel's voice had that same tone that parents used to humour tiresome children.

Time to play the trump card and hope that his timing was correct.

'Like, exactly where did we retarget that second missile to?' Beckett said.

The door to the lorry's cab was buckled and wouldn't open. Ros had to kick it a few times before it gave, with a groan of rending metal.

That was one lorry that wouldn't be going anywhere in a hurry.

She took a few paces backwards so as to admire her handiwork. The lorry had completely demolished the projecting lobby of the Computer Recall building. The cab had come to rest jammed against the arch leading into the building proper. All they had to do was kick open the door on the other side and they could walk through the cab and into the building.

Ros wondered if Jean-Daniel had heard her coming.

Claire was sitting in the passenger seat, shaking the glass out of her hair. Ros had expected her to be rigid with shock by now, but she seemed as determined as ever. She glanced at Ros and opened her mouth to say something, but the words seemed to catch in her throat. She was gazing over Ros's shoulder, and her eyes were widening as if she couldn't believe what she was seeing. A sound began to intrude on Ros's mind:

a high pitched humming, like the world's biggest hornet.

She turned.

For a moment her mind just wouldn't process the information it was getting. All she could see was a black dot. It was growing in size as she watched, and was surrounded by a halo of smoke and flame.

Then she realised.

It was one of the missiles, heading straight for her head.

Ros turned. 'Claire, get out of the cab!' she yelled, and dived to the floor. Through the open driver's door she saw Claire fumbling with the lock, her face a mask of panic. The humming cut through Ros's mind like a buzzsaw, loud enough to block out all rational thought.

Claire flung herself against the jammed door. It held fast.

She flung herself at it again and it gave suddenly. She fell out of sight.

The missile zoomed over Ros's head, its backwash shrivelling the hairs on her neck, and passed straight through the cab of the lorry, side to side.

And vanished.

The explosion, when it came, was so quiet that Ros had to strain to make it out. What an anticlimax, she thought.

Jean-Daniel shook his massive head wearily. Beckett expected some last word, some final jest, but it didn't come. He just looked through the aiming device again and recentred the bazooka on Beckett's head.

Somewhere in the depths of the building there was a crash, as if someone had dropped something heavy. At the same moment, Beckett felt a shiver pass through his body. From the way Katie suddenly tensed against his back, she felt it too.

'What the –?' Ed said.

Every light in the building went out.

The lights on the parallel-processing units.

The lights in the suspended ceiling.

The lights in the lift.

The only illumination was the daylight filtering in through windows somewhere beyond the rows of computer equipment.

Beckett looked at his watch. It had stopped.

Not one to be distracted, Jean-Daniel pulled the trigger on the bazooka. Beckett wasn't surprised when nothing happened. Only a slight twitch of the cheek indicated that Jean-Daniel was.

'The bazooka has an electronic ignition system,' Beckett explained helpfully, trying to keep the relief from his voice. 'The electromagnetic-pulse warhead on the retargeted missile just killed it.'

Casting the bazooka aside, Jean-Daniel spread his arms wide and rushed towards them, roaring loud enough to shake the walls. He might not have been able to blow them up, but he could certainly crush them.

Ed stepped in front of Beckett. 'This doesn't have an electronic ignition,' he said. 'Just an old fashioned trigger.'

Feet braced, he pulled it.

The tube joining his backpack to the weapon jerked, and a thick rope of fluorescent pink goo erupted from the weapon. It shot towards Jean-Daniel faster than he was running. Expanding in mid-air like a conjuror's trick, it was the size of a mattress and had the consistency of candyfloss when it hit him. He ploughed through it, scything his arms wildly. For every bit that he dispersed, twice as much clung to his suit. Gradually he slowed as he tried to fight his way through the gunk. Ed had taken his finger off the trigger by now, but the material was still expanding.

Jean-Daniel was hardly visible behind it: all Beckett could see were his hands waving as he tried to swim through it.

And it was thicker than it had been. Thicker and darker, as if contact with the air was causing it to set. Jean-Daniel's movements were slowing, like those of a man fighting his way through wet cement.

Beckett laughed suddenly. He couldn't help himself. Partly it was the sudden realisation that he wasn't going to die after all. But mostly it was the sight of the apelike but oh-so-fastidious Jean-Daniel encased in great billowing clouds of solidifying pink goo.

'It's a glue-gun,' Ed said, looking back at Beckett. 'Picked it up from Claire's company premises. Thought it might come in useful.' He jerked a thumb over his shoulder at Jean-Daniel. 'The harder you fight it, the harder it sets.' He reached out to ruffle Katie's hair as she emerged from behind Beckett's back. 'Hiya, munchkin. Let's go find your mummy, hmmm?'

She nodded. A smile broke through the stormclouds of her face at the sight of the big, pink marshmallow that was standing where Jean-Daniel had been.

'There should be some stairs around here somewhere,' Beckett said. He walked towards Jean-Daniel. The other two followed. As he passed the stationary form, he paused and leaned closer. One rolling eye and part of a cheek were all that was visible.

'Stick around,' Beckett said, and walked on.

Ed made tea for them all – back at Gizmos. Ros had never known him do that before. Perhaps it was the presence of Claire and Katie that sent him into a domestic frenzy. While Ros and Claire chatted on the sofa, he brought in the full silver-service works on a tray – teapot, china cups and saucers, three-tiered cake stand with *petits fours*. The works.

Ros didn't dare ask where he'd got it all from, but she

was certain that Gizmos didn't own anything like it.

The offices looked like a bombsite, but for once Ros didn't feel like apologising. After all, a bomb of sorts *had* hit them. They could clear up later. Or they could just junk everything and set up somewhere else, with entirely new kit. The world was a bright, shiny toy. She was alive. They were all alive.

Noises interrupted her conversation: noises of giggling and muffled protests from the balcony area.

'I thought Beckett always said he didn't like children,' she called to Ed, who had just popped into the kitchen area to get the sugar.

Ed reappeared. 'Nah, he's just an old softie.'

'The ones who say they don't like children usually are,' Claire agreed with a smile.

A louder burst of giggles made Ros crane her neck to see what was going on. 'Well, they seem to be playing happily up there.'

It was difficult to tell from her position, but Katie appeared to have tied Beckett to one of the office chairs with a roll or two of insulation tape. She was walking around the chair, adding the final layers. As Ros watched, the roll ran out and Katie pressed the edges of the strand into place.

'Look, Katie,' Beckett said in a reasonable voice. 'If your mummy ever wants to get married again, she'll choose someone for herself.'

'Not good enough!' Katie sang, reaching for a new roll.

'I don't know her! Besides – that's not how grown-ups do things. Katie! Take this stuff off, *please*!' Desperation was showing through the shreds of his reasonable attitude.

'Do you think one of us ought to go and help him?' Claire asked. She was holding a *petit four* in one hand and her cup in the other. It didn't look to Ros as if she was volunteering.

260

'Seems such a shame,' Ros said. 'After all, they're having so much fun.'

'And a good babysitter's so hard to come by.' Ed sat down on the sofa beside Claire. 'I say we make the most of it.'

'Help!' a voice cried from above. 'Ed – Ros – someone come and help me! At least bring me a gun!'

Ed reached for the teapot. 'Another cup?' he asked.

« Epilogue »

The cell door slid shut behind the governor with a heavy clang, and he glanced nervously over his shoulder. The armed guard behind him was tensed and ready, her baton in her hand. She was trained in the martial arts and she was in the peak of physical condition. Even if the prisoner succeeded in getting past both her and the governor, the electronic key dangling from her belt was keyed to her fingerprint and hers alone. There was no way out for him.

The cell was sparsely furnished: just a bed, a bench and a latrine. No knick-knacks. No ornaments. The only distraction from the pristine decor was the governor's laptop computer sitting on the bench. The prisoner was already spread-eagled against the transparent wall of his cell, alerted to the governor's approach by the watching guards behind it. He was under continuous observation. It had been made clear to the governor in no uncertain terms that not only was he dangerous and fiendishly intelligent, but there was a high risk that someone would make an attempt to break him out.

He didn't look intelligent. He looked just like your average thug. He was bigger than the governor. Bigger than the governor and the guard put together. The governor could see, beneath the prison uniform, the outlines of his slablike muscles. His head was shaven: stubble covering it like iron filings.

Still, the governor thought, if he's *that* intelligent I may as well take advantage of him.

The prisoner slowly turned his head and stared at the governor with bovine incuriosity.

'Well?' the governor asked, nodding towards the laptop. 'Did you find out what's wrong with it?'

The prisoner gazed at the governor for a few moments, then said, 'It's a simple problem: a dry weld on the motherboard. If you give me the tools, I could fix it for you now, rather than you having to send it away for repair.'

The governor shook his head. 'No sharp objects, no soldering irons, nothing that could be used as a weapon. Those are the rules.' He felt a pang of guilt at the unfairness in his tone, and cast around for a sop with which he could mollify the man. 'Perhaps there is something else you want?'

The prisoner shrugged. 'Perhaps some books. Camus, Kierkegaard, Nietzsche and Sartre, if possible. It does get so lonely in here. And a small computer of my own might be nice. Nothing as complicated as yours, of course: just enough for me to get some . . . work done.'

The governor thought for a moment. He couldn't see any harm in those requests: they seemed innocuous enough. 'I'll give it some thought,' he said. 'Is there anything else?'

The prisoner smiled, slightly. 'Not for the moment,' he said.

BUGS – The TV Series

This book is based on two episodes of the TV series
BUGS: 'A Sporting Chance' written by Colin Brake,
and 'Pulse' written by Stephen Gallagher. These
episodes were first broadcast on BBC1 on 3 June and 10
June 1995. They were directed by Ken Grieve and Brian
Farnham respectively.

Producer – Brian Eastman
Co-Producer – Stuart Doughty
Production Designers – Rob Harris and Mark Raggett
Series Consultant – Brian Clemens
Executive Producer for the BBC – Caroline Oulton

BUGS is a Carnival Films production.

Read the full story in Virgin's non-stop action novels

Available from all good book shops!